MORNING CALM

JASON MORWICK

MORNING CALM

A NOVEL

NORTIA
PRESS

orange county, california
www.nortiapress.com

NORTIA
PRESS

www.nortiapress.com

2321 E 4th Street, C-219
Santa Ana, CA 92705
contact @ nortiapress.com

ISBN: 978-0984225248
Library of Congress Control Number: 2011929956

Manufactured in the United States of America

AUTHOR'S NOTE

All characters appearing in this work are fictitious. Any resemblance to real persons, living or dead, is purely coincidental. There are no military posts in the Republic of Korea known as Camp Kayes or Camp Guardian, and no army unit known as the 1-77th Infantry.

ACKNOWLEDGEMENTS

Writing is never a solitary activity. Many people have contributed to this project in a variety of ways to help bring this story to publication. I would like to thank my many friends who served and shared their experiences with me in Korea during the 1990s. To Bob ("The Bob"), Tony ("Hoj"), Roland, Rick, Mike, Steve ("Flounder"), Jason, Mark, Bill, Erich, Argot, Shannon, Kendall, Tim, Jake, Josh, Jon, Chris, Sean, Rob, Rich, Doc, and many others, thank you for the inspiration. It certainly was a different world back then. Also, thanks to my close friend Evan for his continuous support, optimism, and friendship during this endeavor. I also owe Evan for introducing me to Doug Savage. Doug has been an editor, coach, and mentor to me over the past several years, and without his guidance, this story would have never made it into print. Most of all, I thank Doug for his friendship and support.

I would like to thank Nathan Gonzalez at Nortia Press for taking a chance with this story. Countless authors endlessly search for an editor and publisher that will support and commit to a manuscript. Getting published is usually a lopsided fight against an author. I am deeply grateful to have found Nortia Press and have Nathan in my corner.

Lastly, I would like to thank my family. My parents were the first to read early drafts and provide input and support (only a mother's love could cause someone to read the vile subject matter and still remark, "I'm so proud of you!"). Most of all, thanks to my wife Christa, and my children, Ainslee and Maston. Not only do they provide endless support and encouragement, but they have to sacrifice time as a family while I continue to write. It is a sacrifice I am well aware of, and I am forever in their debt.

Jason Morwick
Orlando, Florida

1

ARMY LIFE

DEMILITARIZED ZONE, REPUBLIC OF KOREA. JUNE. MID-1990s.

Private Ko Songyung tossed in a drowsy, pre-sleep state on top of the wool blanket covering his bunk. Thick summer air clung to the interior of the open bay platoon barracks. His ears were numb to the persistent rattling of an oversized metal fan and the heavy breathing of the other soldiers sleeping nearby. He opened his eyelids slightly, unable to make out the outline of the closest bunk. The shades were drawn and no auxiliary lighting cast the slightest shadow.

Private Ko fell into a dreamless sleep, face-down. He awoke abruptly when hands clamped around his ankles. As he tried to roll over he felt a body heavy across his bare upper back, pinning him. Hands yanked his shorts down past his knees. Ko was still half asleep when the first man grabbed his buttocks and then entered him. The searing pain shot through Ko's entire body. He tried to scream but could only manage a coarse gasp. Within a minute, it was over. The man on top of him briefly moaned and pulled away. Ko felt the men pinning him loosen their grip and heard them shuffle across the cement floor as they slipped away into the darkened barracks.

Ko cried softly for a while until he was sure the men were gone. Then he staggered to the latrine and vomited.

Curled up on the cool tile floor, Ko continued to weep softly. Private Ko Songyung had only been in the army for a few months, the worst experience of his life. He blamed the Americans for all of it. The Americans had sent him up here. The Americans created the Demilitarized Zone. Ko wished his country had no DMZ and he imagined the day when he would no longer wear a uniform.

As the tears dried on his cheeks his thoughts drifted from earlier civilian life to the mountainous North Korean landscape he stared at daily from his post overlooking the DMZ. He wondered if it would have been better to be born on the other side of the border.

■ ■ ■

A half mile south of the DMZ, Lieutenant Colonel Harold Gibson stood in the command tent at the center of the battalion training area. He listened intently as each of his company commanders reported the events of the day. His tall, bony structure was slightly hunched forward. The captains stood rigidly at attention, captivated by their battalion commander.

"Thank you, commanders," Gibson said in a low voice with a touch of a southern drawl. "Tomorrow is our last day before we head back to the rear. Keep the soldiers focused on the qualification ranges. Good job so far."

The four captains were dismissed and began to file out of the tent. Slowly rubbing his receding gray hair, Gibson sat in front of a large map posted on a makeshift bulletin board.

"Sir, may I have a word with you. In private?"

Gibson looked up at his battalion executive officer, Major Jeremy Streeter, standing in front of him. Streeter was wearing his Kevlar helmet and all his field gear. He was sweating profusely.

"Sir, we have a problem," Streeter said as the two men stepped out of the back of the tent.

"Someone hurt?"

"Negative, Sir. We've lost some electronics; a sensitive item."

"What did we lose, how did we lose it, and what are we doing about it right now?" Gibson asked calmly.

"Sir," Streeter inhaled deeply, "it's an ANCD."

Gibson's lean face, always confidently composed, tightened. His jaw line throbbed.

"So, somehow we managed to lose an automated network control device," Gibson said coldly. "Somewhere out in the brush is a black box the size of half a carton of cigarettes which could decrypt all our secure communications for the North Koreans. If they find it before we do, we might as well publish our field orders in the goddamned *Pyongyang Times*."

"Yes, Sir. All the way up to Division, I suppose."

Gibson rubbed his forehead as if seized by real pain and was silent for several seconds.

"How in the hell did we lose an ANCD?" Gibson finally asked. "That shouldn't have left Camp Kayes. The soldiers should synchronize the radios and then put it back in the arms room. Goddamn, this is bad."

"Absolutely, Sir," Streeter told his commander. "We've already checked the soldiers' gear and the vehicles. We'll cancel the training planned for tomorrow and everyone will get in line and we'll start combing the training areas for it."

Gibson was silent for a long time.

"Okay, make it happen. Get me all the facts. Then I'll notify the brigade commander."

■ ■ ■

The battalion spent the next day scouring the area looking for the black box. Side by side, soldiers trampled through the underbrush looking for the ANCD. Major Streeter spent most of the day in the command tent listening to updates from each company as it failed to find the black box.

The sunlight slowly faded behind the mountains as Streeter paced outside the command tent. He could feel his uniform sticking to his skin from the humidity of the early summer air. He eyed Gibson's tall silhouette as the battalion commander stood, watching the soldiers march in after a day of futile searching. Streeter knew that Gibson was still fuming.

"Sir, I hesitate to say this, but we may have to face the fact that the box is probably irrecoverable," Streeter said. He spoke slowly and deliberately. "All of the training areas were checked and no one has any clue when it was lost. That box could've fallen out of a Humvee anywhere between here and Dongducheon."

Gibson stared silently at Streeter.

"I don't know if it is worth torturing the entire battalion for an accident that could have happened to anyone," Streeter continued. "It doesn't excuse the fact that it shouldn't have been brought to the field in the first place, but this was a careless act from a single soldier or small number of soldiers, not the entire unit."

"Cut to the chase. What are you getting at?" Gibson asked.

"Sir, are we trying to recover the box or is this punishment for losing it?"

"That damn box is the mother-load of information for an enemy cryptologist. You know that. Password information. Code-names for radio conversations. Encryption details. Might as well televise our battle plans, too. We just gave the enemy the ability to gouge the communication network on the ground in Korea. No, Major, we need to do everything we can to find it."

"Yes, Sir. I understand."

"This is a great unit," Gibson said quietly as he turned his back to Streeter to watch the soldiers. "Losing a sensitive item is a discredit to all of us. I don't want one screw-up to ruin everything we've worked so hard to create. I want to find that box and we're going to continue looking."

"Yes, Sir."

"Where's the S-2 when I need him?" Gibson asked, referring to the battalion intelligence officer.

"Still on mid-tour leave, Sir. So yesterday, I reached out to some contacts I know up at Division and they referred me to Lieutenant Foster over in the intelligence detachment."

"And what can he do for us?" Gibson asked, still watching the soldiers.

"*She* can help you, Sir," a woman's voice behind Gibson said.

Gibson turned to face a young, blonde lieutenant standing at attention.

"My apologies, Lieutenant. We don't get many female visitors here."

"No worries, Sir."

"I've seen you before. Where?"

"Probably the dining facility, Sir. I know a lot of the lieutenants in your battalion."

"Okay. Well, I assume you know our situation."

"Major Streeter gave me the details over the phone, but I thought it best to make a trip up here to get the facts. I'll start working with the encryption folks when I return to Kayes. They'll distribute new electronic signal operating instructions with new cryptographic keys to all units as soon as all the data has been changed," Foster explained.

Streeter stared at the woman as she locked eyes with Gibson. She was tall, slightly muscular without appearing too masculine. Streeter remembered seeing her in a bikini at the post recreation center pool, almost flaunting a six-pack of abdominal muscles. Streeter tried to keep his attention on her wide, bright green eyes, but found his own eyes wandering to her chest. Even the unflattering battle dress uniform couldn't hide her figure.

"All units? Across Camp Kayes, I assume?" Gibson asked.

"Perhaps broader, Sir," Foster said slowly. "This will have to be Division's call."

"Jesus H. Christ," Gibson muttered. "Thank you, Lieutenant. I appreciate your candor."

When she was out of sight, Gibson turned back to Streeter.

"Every unit in this damn country will be inconvenienced by this. What a monumental fuckup."

Gibson turned quickly and walked away without another word. When Gibson was out of sight, Streeter shrugged and headed back to the tent.

■ ■ ■

Streeter was surprised when Gibson called off the search the following morning. Streeter walked over to the command tent early and found his commander cradling a small Styrofoam cup of oil-thick coffee.

"What are the orders for today, Sir?"

"Work with operations to arrange for trucks to pick the men up and bring them back to Kayes."

"We calling this off, Sir?"

"Yes. I have no expectation that we'll ever find this thing." Gibson stretched and sighed heavily. "You know Colonel Robertson?"

"Over in the tank battalion?"

"That's him. He's an old friend. He arrived in country a few months before I did and took command immediately. His first time to the field, the unit loses three pairs of night vision goggles. Three sets. Do you believe that? All in one night."

"Wow, Sir. Now that's bad."

"Right. He made the unit stay in the field for two whole months."

"They find the goggles, Sir?"

"Not one. Two extra months in the field and nothing to show for it. He was pissed. He was so pissed he would have kept his men out longer if the brigade commander didn't rope him back in."

"Sir, that's a lot of time walking through the brush."

"I thought if something like that ever happened to me I would be more rational." Gibson paused and took a sip of coffee. "Now karma has bitten me in the ass. As angry as I am, I'm not going to take it out on everyone."

"Sir, for what it's worth, I think this is the right call."

"I want to find out what happened, get to the bottom of it, and then take the appropriate action."

"Sir, I agree."

Gibson marched out of the command tent with Streeter in tow.

"I'll have to brief the brigade commander personally as soon as I can get back. I want a Report of Survey kicked off the moment we hit the pavement in the battalion area."

"Yes, Sir," Streeter replied. "I'll pick the survey officer myself."

"You have someone in mind?"

"Sir, I was thinking of Lieutenant Thomlin."

"The platoon leader over in Alpha Company?" Gibson stopped for a moment. "You sure he's the right man for the task?"

"Sir, I think he's a good choice. He's been in country longer than any of the other lieutenants. Plus, I know he'll get it done fast. I assume it will look better if we can come to a quick resolution and be able to explain this to the brigade commander sooner rather than later."

"True, but remember, he's got 60 days to complete the investigation. It would be a good thing to get this done and over with quickly, but more important, it needs to be done right."

"Roger that, Sir. This should be pretty cut and dry. I'll make sure Thomlin works fast, and I'll personally provide oversight."

Gibson shook his head quickly and climbed into the seat of his Humvee. "Okay. Your call. You picked him."

2

FIRST CALL

DONGDUCHEON, REPUBLIC OF KOREA. JULY. 0445 HRS.

The Korean girl beside First Lieutenant Greg Thomlin gently nudged his elbow, waking him for the first time. Thomlin felt queasy as he forced his eyelids open. He knew better than to drink as much as he did on a weeknight. Had it not been for his most recent misfortune, he would not have drunk himself to near blindness.

P'igonhae? Are you tired?" she asked softly. Thomlin grunted a reply as he attempted to prop himself on his elbows and shake the sleep off. His head started to throb from all the soju he drank the night before, and as he swung his feet to the floor the alcohol hit him with full force. The room spun wildly, churning his stomach as he desperately tried to keep up. Thomlin focused on the spiraling floor as the girl began to move her fingertips slowly up and down his spine. Normally this would have a soothing effect, but the soju vice grip on Thomlin's head prevented him from having any thoughts of pleasure.

In faint, predawn light Thomlin could make out the girl's features. She was sitting up behind him with the bed covers curled up over her breasts. Her long, silky dark hair draping almost down to her waist partially covered her face. His head cleared enough to recognize the thin face with a small rounded nose. The thin lips slightly pressed together along with the large brown eyes were expressionless as she inspected his body. Her beautiful almond colored skin contrasted with the pale skin of the man beside her. Thomlin tried to recall the girl's name. He thought her name was Hae Sook or Mae Sook or something like that.

Thomlin stumbled navigating through the one-room apartment as he began to search for his clothes. The place was typical of most Korean apartments—bedroom, living room, and dining room confined into one tight area. A compact kitchenette separated the room from the front door and a bathroom with its shower—an oversized bucket and garden hose.

"Damn it," Thomlin cursed out loud as his shin discovered the small angular coffee table buried under stacks of magazines. He stumbled along the floor trying to find his belongings while attempting to ignore the thick odor of kimchi and other foreign smells that filled the air. Thomlin silently asked himself why he had never grown accustomed to the smell. The apartment walls were covered with traditional oriental paintings and foreign posters creating a collage of Korean and American pop culture.

"How many other women your age have the same pictures on the wall?" Thomlin wondered out loud. The girl stared at him, not understanding the question.

"You go now?" she whispered. It was more of a statement than a question. Thomlin nodded and finished putting on his clothes.

With one last kiss goodbye she slipped a piece of paper in his hand with a phone number scrawled across it.

As he stepped outside the light morning rain fell across his face and he quietly cursed himself. Another beautiful morning in Korea, he thought. It rains every damn day in this country. It was not a hard rain, just the constant drizzle and mist of monsoon season that never seemed to break. Thomlin stood motionless on the steps leading down from the apartment watching the rain until he heard the clicking of high heels on the steps.

Thomlin looked down and noticed a beautiful Korean woman coming toward him. The woman's dark hair hung straight down just inches past her shoulders. She looked up noticing Thomlin, revealing large dark eyes with eyebrows that naturally formed a point. Her slender nose was typical for Korean women, but she had full lips and high cheekbones that made her stand out from the usual oval faces. The small slip of paper gently dropped from his hands.

Thomlin could not help but stare before she leveled her gaze on him. He was directly in her path. She tilted her head slightly as if to welcome some comment.

"*Ahnyong haseyo*," Thomlin greeted.

She gave a wry smile but didn't respond.

"You speaky English?"

Her smile became broader but she still didn't speak. Thomlin put his hand on the railing and leaned closer.

"I'm an American, you asshole," she said.

"Oh. Sorry." Thomlin's head hurt more than ever. He couldn't think of anything to say.

"Would you please move?" she asked as she pushed by.

"Look, I'm sorry."

"Save it."

"Are you a friend of Hae Sook? We were just hanging out last night," Thomlin said, noticing the woman going into the apartment.

"Her name is Byung Soon."

"Shit. Right. That's what I meant. If you tell me your name, I promise not to forget it."

"No thanks. I wouldn't want you to pull a brain muscle."

Before Thomlin could think of a reply, the woman was in the apartment and slammed the door. He shook his head and walked down toward the street. At this hour in the morning the streets were barren and there were no lights to guide the way, save for the few headlights that shimmered in the distance. Thomlin glanced at his watch as he moved quickly along the uneven sidewalk. He knew he had exactly 45 minutes to cruise through the main gate of Camp Kayes, walk two miles to his unit, the 1-77th Infantry, change into his gray physical training uniform, and stand tall for reveille. Only the swishing of tires through the street puddles stirred him from his thoughts.

Like trying to recall a faded dream, Thomlin struggled to remember heading downtown the previous evening. He knew there was something important in the cloud of images that drifted through his mind. There was one single thought he tried to pin down, but the harder he reached for it the further away it slipped. He turned his attention to walking back to the military post. Then, it flashed to him.

"The Report of Survey," he whispered aloud.

The Army had a unique procedure for property losses. When small-dollar-value items were lost, such as a canteen or other piece of a soldier's standard issue field gear, a soldier signed a statement of loss causing the amount to be automatically deducted from the soldier's paycheck or the soldier purchased the item directly and replaced it. Bigger-ticket items, especially sensitive items, were more challenging. In situations such as this, Reports of Surveys were conducted to determine who was at fault and who should pay for the property.

Typically, the Report of Survey trickled down through the adminosphere—the unseen realm where higher command floated—and was assigned to a lieutenant in the unit where the loss occurred. Lieutenants, the lowest rank in the hierarchy of officers, were always good targets to carry out the many mundane administrative tasks that required an officer's involvement. The assigned lieutenant would complete an internal investigation, interview all involved, gather information, and then make a recommendation. The recommendation would offer an explanation for what happened and who was liable. If no one was at fault, then Uncle Sam would eat the cost and it was business as usual. Not surprisingly, the United States Government did not want to absorb unforeseen costs and normally preferred to find someone to share the burden.

"The goddamn Report of Survey," Thomlin said again. No lieutenant welcomed the additional work of a Report of Survey. Lieutenants were chosen at random by the battalion adjutant and Thomlin cursed his luck for landing this one.

"Hey, you," a voice called. "That's right, I'm talkin' to you."

Thomlin noticed a young solider stumbling along the opposite side of the street. The solider was taller than Thomlin but skeleton thin. He stomped across the street toward Thomlin with clenched fists and his lats flared.

"C'mon, there's no time for this crap," Thomlin grumbled as he tried to turn away, but the solider quickened his pace and now stood directly in front of him.

"I saw you come out of Unji's place. That's my woman you're screwing around with, you know that?"

Thomlin sighed. He could smell the alcohol on the soldier's

breath and noticed him swaying slightly as he stood, mean-mugging Thomlin.

"Look, dude, I don't want to get into this with you. First of all, her name is Myong Sook, not Unji. You would know that if you were her boyfriend. Second, there are plenty of women around. I'm sure you'll find one sooner or later."

"You asshole," the soldier screamed. He swung a wild right hand at Thomlin's face. The soldier was operating at drunken speed and Thomlin easily ducked the blow. Thomlin grabbed the soldier's t-shirt collar with both hands and drove his knee into the soldier's groin as hard as he could. As the soldier crumpled, Thomlin threw another knee into the soldier's forehead.

"Next time, go easy on the soju," Thomlin advised.

"Nice going, wild man," a voice from behind said.

Thomlin spun and saw a lieutenant from an adjacent unit wearing a rumpled button-down shirt. Thomlin recognized him but couldn't recall his name. He was just another frequent traveler on the Walk of Shame.

"Hey," was all Thomlin could say.

"I saw him attack you, in case, you know, you need a witness or something."

"Well, you could have jumped in if you were watching the whole thing."

"I was about to. I would have kicked his ass but I saw you had it under control."

The pair continued toward the main gate. Thomlin hardly noticed others, still wearing clothes from the night before, shuffling along the same route. The military police at the Camp Kayes gate eyed Thomlin and the other lieutenant as they approached. They mimed pulling out their invisible military identification cards, the MP yawned and waved them through. Thomlin smirked slightly as he thought about the level of security on his military post. He breathed a heavy sigh of relief as the soju head harness began to loosen while he walked.

"Damn, it's humid."

"Always is this time of year," Thomlin responded.

"I guess. If it was any more humid, we could swim back to the barracks. I'm already soaked."

"Yeah, it doesn't matter if the sun is up or not."

"How are things down in the 77th?"

"Okay, I guess. You know: same shit, different day. How about over where you are?"

"Cool. I got three more months before I head home. I'm count-ing the days. Hey, I heard you guys lost a plugger when you went to the field," the lieutenant said, referring to a handheld GPS.

"No," Thomlin said, "we did better than that. We lost an ANCD."

"Holy shit," the lieutenant said. "Your battalion commander must have gone ape-shit. Was your whole battalion on lock-down?"

"No, but to be honest this whole thing is still cramping my social life."

"I bet," the other lieutenant laughed. "You know, over in my battalion we screw with the Report of Survey officer as much as possible when he's doing his investigation. Just for fun, you know? But this, this isn't something we would joke about."

"Trust me, I know."

"Feel bad for the poor bastard that has to be the survey officer on that one."

"Yeah. Unlucky bastard."

The lieutenant said goodbye to Thomlin and turned into his battalion area. Thomlin picked up the pace and slowly jogged the remaining half-mile home. With about ten minutes to spare Thomlin reached his room in the Quonset hut that housed the other lieutenants in the company and changed for morning formation.

He fumbled his way into his physical training gear and quickly ran a razor over his bony, angular face. The extra large gray t-shirt draped over his lean torso. His body was muscular and almost absent of any body fat from the constant running and road marching. He filled his hands with cool water and splashed it over his scalp. His light brown hair was nearly shaved to the skin on the sides of his head, leaving only an inch-thick layer on top. Thomlin rinsed his mouth and moved to the road where a company of soldiers was forming up.

The large figure standing in front of one end of the formation was the platoon sergeant, Sergeant First Class Ty Wilson, who stared at Thomlin as he neared the platoon. Thomlin could already see the pencil thin eyebrows close together in an indistinguishable line, causing numerous wrinkles on Wilson's shaven head. At six-two, 220 pounds of chiseled, black muscle, the 38-year-old noncommissioned officer could scare the life out of any new second lieutenant.

The Army had relied on both commissioned and noncommissioned officers since its inception. The practice had origins dating back to the days of the Roman legions, when appointed senators commanded armies and experienced legionaries were given responsibility over smaller units. In the modern army, college-educated officers were appointed, or commissioned, upon graduation while noncommissioned officers were promoted through the enlisted ranks. Noncommissioned officers, the backbone of an army, enforced discipline and trained soldiers but the officers were ultimately responsible for everything the unit did or failed to do.

Thomlin ranked Wilson, yet every infantry platoon in the Army possessed a vital balance between the platoon leader and the platoon sergeant. Thomlin wielded the legal authority of his rank while Wilson came with real field experience. It was a marriage of power. If the marriage went sour, the platoon would become as dysfunctional as a family with an abusive father and alcoholic mother. Luckily for the men of second platoon, Alpha Company, the relationship between Thomlin and Wilson was solid, even with the occasional spat.

"Morning, Sir," Wilson said as he saluted.

Centuries of tradition and the delineation of roles within the military called for certain protocols and courtesy. Officers were saluted and referred to as Sir or Ma'am and noncommissioned officers were called Sergeant. The many rules and code of conduct that governed the interactions between officers, noncommissioned officers, and enlisted soldiers were considered vital to maintain good order of the unit.

"What the hell, Lieutenant? You reek of alcohol. I'm gonna strangle you," Wilson whispered a few inches from Thomlin's ear.

"Good morning, Sergeant," Thomlin bellowed loud enough for the entire platoon to hear. "I'm fine, thanks. How are you this morning?"

Thomlin leaned forward and said so only Wilson could hear, "Can you really smell it or is this some form of clairvoyance you picked up in the hundred years you've been in the Army? I know, you probably developed it when you put Nostradamus through Basic Training."

"No, Sir," Wilson hissed. "It was probably a sixth sense I picked up when I was in Granada. Or maybe it was Panama. Then again, it could've been in the Gulf. With all the combat, Sir, I sometimes lose track."

"I understand. The post traumatic stress can cause memory loss. I hear it also causes erectile dysfunction."

Wilson's Adam's apple was moving up and down at an incredible speed. Thomlin whispered, "Are you actually growling at me?"

"Sir, I'd like to cause some traumatic stress right now…".

"Good talk, Sergeant," Thomlin shouted again for everyone to hear, cutting Wilson off. "We'll catch up later."

Before Wilson could say anything more, Thomlin moved to the rear of the platoon and waited for the flag to go up. He stared at the backs of the soldiers in the formation before hearing the boom of a cannon and the sound of bugles over the battalion PA system. Thomlin curled his fingers by the seam of his shorts and stood rigidly at attention as he listened to reveille.

Immediately after honoring the colors, Wilson put the platoon through an hour's worth of push-ups, sit-ups, and a brief run that would make a gazelle pant. Thomlin felt grateful that his 24-year-old body was young enough to allow him to poison himself on a nightly basis and still survive the morning workout without major difficulty.

When physical training was finally complete, Wilson handed the platoon over to the squad leaders and said to Thomlin with a smile, "Sir, may I please have a word with you for a moment?"

Wilson followed Thomlin into the company barracks. As the door swung shut Wilson violently yanked Thomlin by the ear lobe and pulled him into the company laundry room.

"Sergeant, I think you might have something wrong with you. I'm seeing those little veins on your forehead again. Oh, look, the bulging veins on your forearm looks like a road atlas. That's really neat."

"I'm gonna fucking kill you, you know that?"

"Sergeant, are you upset this morning?"

"Just what in the fuck do you fucking think you're doing?"

"Relax big sarge," Thomlin said.

"Shut the hell up. If I was younger, and if I didn't care about losing my rank, I would tear your fucking head off for pulling this stunt over and over. How in the hell can you stumble in here reeking of that rice paddy shit you think is so good? If you were one of the soldiers I would take your fucking, weasel-like neck…".

"Just how many f-letter words and combinations of profanity can you wield into a single sentence? I'm losing count."

"You're not getting it, are you el-tee?"

"I'm just saying that I think your obscene vernacular is worth an award. Four years of college and I'm still impressed with the language of noncommissioned officers."

"I'll remember to thank the person that helped me get my GED. Don't change the subject. I'm still ready to put my size thirteen boot into your ass."

"Hold up, Sergeant," Thomlin interrupted, stressing the word sergeant. "You know, I really do love it when you switch back into drill sergeant mode. You were a drill at Fort Benning, right? God, I can only imagine you in dress uniform with the large rounded hat pulled low over the front of your melon. I bet you were the Army's ideal welcoming committee for new recruits."

"Sir, I'd like to take you back to Benning right now. Specifically, the wood line behind the barracks."

"Listen, was I late this morning? No. Am I ever late? No. Do I ever have a problem with a morning run? Never. Hell, you know I could smoke half the soldiers in the platoon on a run, sober or not. Don't worry yourself with how I spend my off time."

Wilson took a step back, clenched his fists, and stared coldly at Thomlin.

"Relax," Thomlin said. "Don't do anything that'll guarantee some personal space at Fort Leavenworth."

"I'm weighing my options, Sir."

"One more thing, Sergeant," Thomlin said. "What was the weasel comment about?"

Wilson let out a breath and shook his head. He muttered under his breath as he walked out of the room, "Goddamn lieutenants."

3

CHOW TIME

Private Ko glanced around the dining facility. At the far end of the room, noncommissioned officers relaxed by sipping tea and trading stories. Ko and younger soldiers sat at the opposite end, cupping bowls of rice and kimchi. They shoveled food into their mouths with metal chopsticks. They spoke little and did not make eye contact.

Weeks had passed since he was attacked and the men had not returned. Still, Ko had trouble sleeping. As the sun set each evening, the knot tighten in his stomach. His body went rigid as he waited. He had no idea what he would do if attacked again.

"Don't worry, you'll have your turn someday," an older soldier consoled Ko one morning in the open shower room. Other soldiers nearby were giggling. Ko left the shower room without turning off the water. In the nearest bathroom stall he doubled over and vomited.

"I hate them," he gasped and threw up again.

At breakfast, Ko noticed some of the younger soldiers had swollen faces. He never spoke of his own attack and he was too afraid to ask the other soldiers how they received their bruises. He wondered if young North Korean soldiers were also brutalized. As the weeks drifted by, Ko increasingly thought about life in North Korea. He desperately wanted to know more about his Korean countrymen on the other side of the border. He longed to communicate with them.

■ ■ ■

Thomlin loaded his tray with eggs, bacon, and grits before heading to a small, cornered-off room in the battalion dining facility. Thomlin pulled a chair next to his best friend and company executive officer, First Lieutenant Lane Nelson. Nelson slowly sipped his coffee while listening to the other lieutenants.

"I was only in the club for a few minutes before these two Korean chicks asked me to come home with them," one of the lieutenants explained.

"Are you sure it wasn't three or four?" another asked. Laughter erupted from the group.

"Seriously. No shit. I was afraid the Korean cops would be called from all the screaming in their little apartment."

"Why? Were they that hysterical when they saw you naked?"

"Listen, I wore those poor women out. One of them told me she wasn't going to be able to walk straight for a week."

"That's as believable as Thomlin getting promoted someday," First Lieutenant Nicole Foster laughed, revealing a set of perfect, veneer-like teeth. The small crowd pounded the table as they laughed. Foster glared down the long slender table toward Thomlin.

"Nicole, I didn't notice you," Thomlin said without looking up from his food.

"Well, this is the closest dining facility. Did you forget how close my military intelligence unit is to your battalion?"

"Well, that makes sense. You come here because it's so close. And our officer billets must have the closest bed you can find."

More laughter boomed through the narrow room. Foster raised her hands to her head in mock disbelief. Her bleached blond hair pulled completely back exposed dark streaks from her black roots.

"Now, now, Greg, don't get upset. We're all friends here," she said.

Before Thomlin could respond, his attention shifted to a young enlisted soldier standing in the doorway. He was a statue holding a tray full of steaming food.

"Can I help you?" Thomlin asked as others began to notice the soldier. The soldier remained motionless.

"Excuse me, gentlemen, and lady," a noncommissioned officer said from behind the soldier. The sergeant put a hand on the soldier's arm and steered him back into the main section of the dining facility. "My apologies. The young man obviously didn't realize the O-club was holding breakfast in here this morning. Or every morning for that matter."

Thomlin smirked and waved at the pair as they left. Foster resumed the conversation.

"By the way, Greg, I heard your commander complaining that you were dragging your ass on the Report of Survey. Have you started it yet or are you still searching for that little black box in every bedroom in Dongducheon? I think anyone else would've been done with it already."

"Why do you care? It's really not your concern," Thomlin shot back.

"How long have you had it for? Three weeks? A month?"

"My plan is to take the maximum amount of time allowed to fully investigate the situation. No shortcuts. Even if it means crimping my extracurricular activities."

Laughter rippled across the table.

"Wow, Greg, you say that so earnestly. You're almost believable. What's your motto? If you wait until the last minute, it only takes a minute? Never do today what you can put off until tomorrow?"

"Again, I don't see how this is any concern of yours."

"You know, your battalion commander called me to come to the field and help out when the box was lost. I could help you with the survey if you want."

"Really."

"Sure. I just want you to grovel; I mean, ask nicely."

"I would rather have the Report of Survey pinned to my liver."

"Good luck with that," Foster laughed and stood to leave. "See you boys later."

Nelson turned to Thomlin once Foster was out of earshot. "You look like you had an interesting night."

"Oh, the usual. The never-ending pursuit of alcohol and women. If our commander-in-chief can bang Gennifer Flowers, I should be able to have a little fun too."

"Easy, bro. Don't say that too loudly. By the way, since Foster already brought up the subject, how's the survey coming?"

"Haven't started it yet."

"Jesus, man, what's so hard about it? I know it was a sensitive item, but a report is a report. Just knock the damn thing out."

"Yeah, I know." Thomlin thought for a moment. "You know, losing the black box wouldn't be an easy thing to do."

"What do you mean?"

"Weapons are locked away in the company arms room, but the black box is locked in a safe in the back and the safe is chained to the floor. The items aren't usually taken to the field. The radios get synced and then it's locked back up again."

"Yes, but this time it was brought to the field. And it was lost. That's the reason they're not supposed to go to the field in the first place. Someone screwed up."

"You got that right. Someone screwed up big."

Before Nelson could even nod, Kevin Ward, a fellow platoon leader from Alpha Company, slid alongside the two lieutenants.

"Hey, man, I just got back the results of my HIV test yesterday," he announced with a smile.

"If we were in the movies, I would expect the jukebox record to skip and motion to stop right now," Nelson said.

"Should I pound the table for a drum roll?" Thomlin asked.

"Hey, don't give me that. I'm clean, guys. Have either of you been tested in the last decade? I know that neither of you put a helmet on that three inch trooper before you send him through the front lines."

The comment raised a few chuckles from the lieutenants still at the table. Thomlin quickly changed the subject by grabbing the morning copy of the *Stars and Stripes* lying in the middle of the table. A story about North Korea's nuclear program was on the front page.

"Would you look at this shit," Thomlin said as both Nelson and Ward leaned over. "Looks like a TWA flight was shot down over New York City."

"Yeah, right," Nelson said as he snatched the newspaper from

Thomlin. "More likely it fell out of the sky. Besides, you're missing the important news. Sheryl Crow is now banned from Wal-Mart. Good luck finding her CD at the post exchange."

■ ■ ■

Lee Min Yong sat at the kitchen table in his dark and quiet Uijeongbu apartment, puffing his cigarette. He listened to the busy morning traffic and voices just outside the window. The thick morning humidity seeped in but Lee hardly noticed. He was dressed for work in a short sleeve button-down shirt and khakis, all neatly pressed but several years out of style.

"Good morning, Father," his daughter greeted him in English as she came through the doorway. She wore a brightly colored sweat suit with a trendy logo emblazoned across the front.

"My daughter," Lee exhaled, "the child I hardly see. Are we back to speaking English?"

"I have to speak Korean all day. My tongue is sore and my head hurts."

"All those years your mother and I tried but we were no match for your friends or television."

"Oh, please don't start. You know as well as I do that back in the States English had to be my first language. By the way, where is Mother?"

"Out," Lee sighed. "The only two women in my life are constantly missing. Your mother shops, and you, well, who knows where you run off to. Before she went out, Mother made you *kimchi bokkeumbap*. She knows how much you like it."

Lee's daughter sat down across from him with a large bowl of fried kimchi mixed with shrimp, vegetables, and steamed rice. She picked at the fried egg lying on top of the meal with a pair of chopsticks.

"Care for some?" she asked.

"No. I am not a college student, nor am I unemployed. I can afford a better meal."

She shook her head at the joke and said, "By the way, I was out with some friends last night."

"I know," Lee smiled, "I heard you come in this morning. Let me guess, you were in Itaewon. You must have taken the first train back this morning to get in so early."

"Actually, I was in Dongducheon. And yes, Father, I got on the train when they started running this morning. I have to work today, you know."

"Is that what we call teaching a few wealthy children how to speak English?"

"Not all my clients are wealthy, Father. I taught a girl yesterday up in Dongducheon who would never be considered upper class. I'll teach whoever wants to learn."

"How noble. I do hope they pay you something. Someday you might have to move out and live on your own."

"Of course. I don't work for free," she laughed. "By the way, I'm going up to Dongducheon again tonight to visit a friend. This one is not for work. Before you ask, I'll be late."

"Again? There's nothing up there."

"That's not true, Father."

"It is true, unless you are going to see an American soldier."

"I'm just visiting a friend, Father."

"Oh, Yumi," Lee groaned, "please don't get too hung up on some GI."

"I really don't understand you at times. You grew up in the war. You always say that the Americans saved you. That's how you ended up in the States."

"Yes, that's true."

"We owe much to the Americans," she mimicked him, "but *I* am an American."

"I know," Lee said sadly. He watched her long, thin fingers stir a cup of tea. With her long hair, dark eyes, and full body she reminded Lee of her mother in her youth. "It's your only imperfection. I wish you were more Korean."

A silence fell between them for several minutes.

"Do you remember it well?"

"Remember what?"

"You know, the war."

"Not much. I was only seven at the time."

"So what do you remember?"

"Nothing really," Lee said quietly.

"Nothing at all?"

"It was a very long time ago."

"But I'm sure you must remember something."

"I remember holding my mother's hand."

"That's it?"

"Holding my mother's hand and walking and running. Lots of walking and running," Lee said after a moment. "We fled our home in panic and went as far south as possible."

"Then the Americans came?"

"Yes. There were some Americans already there but I remember when the American reinforcements arrived. They looked like soldiers I saw in the movies once. They seemed invincible."

"I bet you were happy then."

"Oh, yes. It was amazing. These young men came from half a world away to help us. People cried at the sight of seeing them, they were so happy. My father and I volunteered to help them. We did whatever task they needed. In exchange, they provided food and clothing for my parents, my sister and me. It was hard labor at times, but my father did whatever was needed to provide for the family."

"And they took you back to the States?"

"No, Yumi, that was many years after the war."

"You see, this is why I don't understand you. You can talk about how American soldiers helped during the war and how you were able to immigrate to the U.S. but you still have this bias against Americans."

"That's not true, Yumi. I have always appreciated the Americans. I had fantastic dreams when I left here and went to the States. But when I got there I saw that we were outsiders. Outside Fort Lewis we would have Koreatown and our own areas. We could even run our own businesses, but we were never really accepted. Even on Camp Red Cloud it's no different. The soldiers come and go every 12 months. Some never even leave the post or make it past the main street outside the front gate. They'll never understand Koreans."

"I still don't understand you."

"Perhaps if I had taken this reassignment when you were younger, before you went to college, then you might have seen it differently."

"What would have been different then?"

"If you came here when you were younger you might have been more open minded."

"Are you joking? Are you saying that I'm not open minded?"

"You said it yourself. You're an American. You see everything as they do. If you grew up here things would seem a lot different."

Lee stomped his cigarette out in a ceramic ashtray and exhaled loudly.

"If you are looking to meet someone nice, I could arrange

something, you know," Lee offered.

"Oh, my God. You mean, like, one of those matchmakers? Or is that only after you and the other family agree that we are a suitable match? What about falling in love with someone?"

"Yumi, that's just the Western view of things. It's not the traditional way. Love is not always necessary between a new husband and wife. That comes later."

"Ah," Yumi sighed. Her eyes narrowed. "Let me see. I should be matched, then become subservient and live to support my man. Don't speak first or contradict my husband, don't show my teeth, don't stand when a man enters the room and don't receive more education than my husband. Isn't that how it goes? Gimmie a break. Sorry, Father, but I have a little more ambition than only to be someone's wife or mother."

"Things aren't quite that traditional nowadays," Lee responded.

"Well, remind me to send Confucius a thank you note for formally putting us women in the backseat."

"I guess I will spare you the traditional view of sex," Lee laughed.

Lee's daughter rolled her eyes as she got up from the table. Before leaving the kitchen, she leaned over and kissed her father on the head, smoothing over his long gray hair with her palm.

"Thank you for the offer, but I'll take my chances finding my own boyfriends. I'll be home late. Don't wait up for me."

■ ■ ■

At 0847 hours Thomlin was late for his company commander's quarter-to-nine meeting. Thomlin was the last to arrive; the others had already assembled in their usual seats across from the commander. Captain Joe Watts sat behind an oversized oak desk in a high leather chair. Nothing below the name tag of his uniform was visible above the desk. He over emphasized checking his wristwatch as Thomlin came in.

Thomlin noticed Nelson sitting to his right, scribbling away on a note pad. Nelson was accustomed to this routine and preoccupied himself while Kevin Ward filled his bottom lip with tobacco and waited for the fireworks to ensue.

"Would you care to have a seat, Lieutenant Thomlin?" Watts asked pleasantly.

"No, Sir, it makes the morning ass chewing easier if I stand," Thomlin said. He chose his tone carefully to hide the sarcasm.

"Well, next time wear rubber shorts if you decide to be late to my morning meeting. It's not like this is a surprise. We only do this every single day." Captain Watts beamed at Thomlin with a large grin on his face. Thomlin started to feel nervous.

"I have a mission for you this morning," Watts said.

"Okay, Sir," Thomlin responded automatically. To Thomlin, Captain Watts always seemed like he was shouting his words.

"This morning you are going down to the turtle farm to pick up a cherry lieutenant who just arrived. You will take him by the hand and see that he gets in-processed to the battalion."

"Roger that, Sir." Great, Thomlin responded internally.

"Then, you will bring him to me. After that, you will be responsible for training him before he takes a platoon in my company. Maybe he can learn from all your screw-ups and become a halfway decent platoon leader."

"Yes, Sir." Asshole, Thomlin thought.

"Think you can handle all that?" Watts asked with an overly concerned look on his face.

"Hooah, Sir." Thomlin turned for an early escape and headed for the door.

"Hold up," Watts barked. "Where the hell is the Report of Survey you're working on?"

"Work in progress, Sir. Deadline is not for another month."

"Lieutenant Thomlin," Captain Watts said slowly, "perhaps you don't understand the gravity of the situation here. We're not talking about Private Snuffy's missing poncho liner. We're talking about a damn ANCD."

"Yes, Sir. I understand. I know we're talking about a few thousand dollars worth of equipment."

"You see, this is exactly what I mean," Watts snapped. He was stirring in his chair and started to wiggle across the top of the desk. "The black box may only cost a few thousand bucks to manufacture but that's not its value. You see where I'm going? Do you know what the ANCD does?"

"Yes, Sir."

"Do you know how valuable the information stored on that little black box is?"

"I can guess, Sir."

"Then you can probably guess how important this is and why I need you to act with a little more sense of urgency than if you just returned from the field and realized your canteen was no longer hooked to your belt."

"Roger, Sir."

"You know, *Stars and Stripes* is covered with North Korea's nuke program."

"C'mon, Sir. They're decades away from developing anything close to that kind of capability. And it's even doubtful that those idiots could ever assemble one. Even if they could someday make a nuke, that has nothing to do with the ANCD."

"You just don't get it, do you?"

"Sir, right now there's some asshole in Atlanta trying to blow people up at the Olympics. Up until a few months ago we had that crazy-ass guy in Montana sending people letter bombs. And last year, McVeigh blew up that building in Oklahoma. There's more danger from one of our own back in the States than there is here."

"Look, you may think the North Koreans are in the stone age but they're progressing every day. We're superior to them, not just because we're a bunch of badass infantrymen, but because of our technology. Every piece of technology, whether it's a damn GPS or pair of night vision goggles, is an opportunity for them to catch up. Do you get it? Now, when are you planning to have the Report of Survey done?"

"Sir," Thomlin said calmly, "I'll have it done before the deadline, at least by a few days."

"Completely unacceptable," Watts frowned and leaned far back in the leather chair. "I want it done within two weeks."

"Hooah, Sir," Thomlin responded again. Before Watts could think of anything else to say Thomlin was already out the door.

4

TURTLE

The Turtle Farm was a small, fenced off area in the center of Camp Kayes where all incoming and outgoing personnel completed their initial or final paperwork. It always reminded Thomlin of some movie set, POW compound from World War II. The small Quonset hut where incoming personnel initiated their paperwork stood only a few dozen feet from the Quonset hut where all outgoing personnel completed their final paperwork. It took a full 365 days to move an individual's paperwork from one hut to the other. With the slow pace of a turtle, soldiers finally moved from the in-processing to the out-processing Quonset hut before they could jump onto the Freedom Bird bound for home.

Everything revolved around time in Korea. Soldiers began counting their days left in country the day after they arrived.

New soldiers were called turtles because they had just begun their slow journey from the in-processing hut. Anyone with over six to eight months in Korea was considered an old timer and this gave that person the prestigious right to talk trash to anyone else who hadn't been in for an equal or greater amount of time. Thomlin smiled and remembered the conversation he had with a more senior lieutenant after he arrived in country.

"How long have you been in Korea?" Thomlin was asked.

"Three hundred and twenty-two days."

"Oh, yeah? Well, I've been here for 348 days, you damn turtle."

Whether it was a month or a day, time equaled stature among soldiers.

■ ■ ■

The driver of the Humvee barely rested his foot on the gas pedal as the vehicle moved toward the turtle farm. The snail-pace speed limit on Kayes was infuriating to Thomlin, who did not care to be the company welcome mat. The driver had his entire head bobbing out the window, humming to himself as he eyed the people on the sidewalk. At the speed they were traveling the driver didn't need to pay attention to the road, so Thomlin slouched in the passenger seat and said nothing. Early morning drizzle became a steady rain.

"Hey, was that a guy in a wheelchair that just passed us?" Thomlin asked.

"What's that, Sir?" the driver responded.

"Nothing. Just try to make it there before lunch, okay?"

As the vehicle rolled into the parking lot, Thomlin pointed to the driver. "That must be the new guy."

Under the small insignia for the 1-77th was a second lieutenant with several duffel bags. The look on his face was like someone just grabbed him from behind.

"It's always easy to spot the new guy," the driver laughed. "Sir, did you look that wide-eyed and scared when you first arrived?"

"Never. I admit I might have felt slightly out of place when I first got off the plane, but I was never clueless. Everyone goes through a little culture shock."

"Sure, Sir."

"Okay, smartass. I'm serious. At least I knew a little bit of what I was doing."

"He looks like he just got off the bird a couple of hours ago, Sir."

Thomlin knew the new lieutenant had been in country for four days. Initially, soldiers were ferried off the planes at Gimpo International Airport in Seoul to nearby Camp Yongsan. At Yongsan, the new guy spent two days getting in-briefed and filling out paperwork before being sent north to Kayes. At the turtle farm he spent another two days doing the same paperwork he did in Seoul. As the vehicle rolled to a stop, Thomlin hopped out of the vehicle and extended his hand.

"Welcome to the 1-77th. I'm Greg Thomlin."

"Brent Dougall," the new lieutenant offered, shaking off the daydream he was in. He was an inch shorter than Thomlin, blond and blue-eyed. His eyebrows were arched up in a constant look of surprise and Thomlin guessed that Dougall was only a year or two younger than himself, though Dougall had a much more adolescent look about him. Dougall began to gently place one of his bags in the back of the Humvee, as Thomlin slammed the last two right on top.

"Nice tan," Thomlin smiled. "You enjoy some good leave time before coming over here?"

"Yeah. The beach," Dougall managed to say. Dougall started

to say something more but Thomlin had already turned and motioned for Dougall to get in the vehicle.

Thomlin and Dougall rolled out of the turtle farm for the eternity-long ride back to battalion with Dougall sitting directly behind Thomlin. In the side view mirror Thomlin watched Dougall crane his neck back and forth taking in all the details of the post.

"I like the welcome sign above the in-processing center," Dougall said, pointing to the large wooden sign spanning the road. WELCOME TO THE SECOND INFANTRY DIVISION—HOME OF THE MOST POWERFUL DIVISION IN THE WORLD.

"If this is the most powerful division, I don't wanna know where the weakest is," Thomlin chuckled. "Probably in a stateside suburb getting their asses kicked by a bunch a slingshot wielding Cub Scouts."

"What do you mean by that?"

"You'll see soon enough. Most of the units on Kayes are critically under strength or receive hand-me-down equipment from the States. Barracks that would be condemned by normal standards are okay for soldiers to live in here. There's not a whole lot of continuity in any of the units because everyone rotates so quickly. As soon as someone learns his job, that person rotates home. Commanders struggle just to build their units to a level where they can accomplish basic tasks to military standards."

"Really? But, isn't this the most forwardly-deployed unit in the world?"

"Well, all of us here," Thomlin said, referring to the roughly 35,000 soldiers stationed in the Republic of Korea, "are more of a deterrent than an actual fighting force. That sign should read: Welcome to the Second Infantry Division—Home of the Biggest Speed Bump in the World."

Dougall quickly changed subjects. "Does it always smell this bad? I mean, the whole country doesn't smell like this, does it?"

The initial shock of the foreign smell of this land assaulted the olfactory nerves. It was not the rotten stench of old garbage. Pollutants and manure from nearby farmland created a horribly strange smell to anyone arriving in less metropolitan areas outside Seoul.

"You'll get used to it," Thomlin shouted to the backseat. "It's mostly from all the rice paddies and local pollution. The Koreans supposedly use human feces to fertilize the land. And yes, the whole country smells this damn bad."

"What's the unit like? What's the battalion commander like? How often do you go to the field? What are the chances that I'll get a platoon right away?"

Thomlin expected the litany of new-guy questions and gave canned answers. He then braced himself for the expected barrage of personal questions.

"How long you been here? Why did you extend? You have a serious Korean girlfriend? You piss off the chief of staff?"

Thomlin again replied with readymade answers while the stunned-mullet look never left Dougall's face.

A silence fell between the two lieutenants and Thomlin resisted the urge to make idle conversation. Out of the corner of his eye, Thomlin could see Dougall's lips part slightly as Dougall strained to think of something to fill the lull.

"I read in the paper that, uh, the North Koreans are starting some rough talk. They, I mean the North, say that they are going to turn the South into a sea of fire and rid the peninsula of the evil American puppeteers."

"Well, to be honest, I really don't think about it that much," Thomlin sighed. "Korea has always been a pretty turbulent place."

Thomlin knew Korean history but spared Dougall a lecture.

The Japanese dominated the land from the late nineteenth century to World War II, the Cold War superpowers created the division between North and South and then, of course, the two sides collided during the Korean War in the 1950s. Even after the war, the two Koreas had only a signed armistice, a temporary ceasefire, rather than come to closure with any sort of real peace agreement.

"The two sides have been preparing for war for over half a century. This is just business as usual," Thomlin said casually.

The vehicle glided into the battalion area. At battalion headquarters Thomlin spotted Foster standing with her arms folded in front of the personnel building. Thomlin stepped out of the vehicle and began helping Dougall with his bags. Foster remained motionless.

"Hey, don't worry about it, Nic. We got the bags," Thomlin said casually. Foster ignored the comment.

"Who's the FNG?"

The acronym was short for Fucking New Guy. Thomlin cringed. Dougall would be no stranger to soldier slang. Dougall didn't respond. The absence of any sort of acknowledgement caused Foster to repeat the question in a louder voice.

"Hey, Nicole, way to make a first impression." Thomlin blew past Foster and into the building without ever introducing Dougall. Dougall was on the heels of Thomlin and cruised past Foster as well. Thomlin knew that Dougall meant nothing to her. Dougall was new to the unit and new to the Army and could offer nothing.

"People around here always so friendly?" Dougall asked once they were inside.

"Don't worry about her. There's one in every crowd. You still haven't met Captain Watts."

Before Dougall could ask another question, a short, plump, freckled soldier handed him some papers to fill out. Dougall's eyes were fixed on two cards. One resembled a credit card and the other was a plain white card with black lettering.

"That's your Ration Control Plate," Thomlin explained as Dougall thumbed the fancier card. "It controls the amount of certain items you can buy from the Post Exchange. It's to prevent you from selling stuff on the black market. More important, it controls how much booze you can buy. You only get three bottles of booze per month or a case of beer per day. Don't ever think of going over it or it'll be your ass."

"The Koreans don't drink?" Dougall asked.

"Far from it," Thomlin chuckled. "There's plenty of beer and soju to go around but they don't have a lot of the liquor common in the States. It's a big underground business. Just do yourself a favor and never bring any alcohol off post.

"Now, the other card is worth your life. Literally. It's your Status of Forces Agreement card. It represents the agreement made between the South Korean government and the United States Army. Basically, it's your get-out-of-jail-free card. If you ever get picked up by the Korean police for anything, just show them the card. Don't look at me like you'll never ever have a problem with the police. Trust me, you may need it someday. For now, keep both cards very safe."

Dougall complied by pulling out his wallet and then quickly turned his attention to the stack of forms the young soldier brought for him. Thomlin caught himself before emphasizing the importance of the cards by telling an old war story. He decided to save it for later. Better not to overwhelm the new guy on the first day.

After several minutes of watching Dougall fill out forms, the pair was back outside in the rain, heading toward battalion headquarters. The battalion commander was standing in the hall talking to a few captains. Thomlin immediately noticed the stress lines that creased down from Gibson's eyes, making him look a decade older than he actually was. Thomlin studied the commander for a moment while locked in the position of attention. He wondered if Dougall immediately perceived Gibson as he did. Not an imposing figure, Gibson radiated an aura or presence that blessed men born to lead other men.

Gibson's uniform told the story of a warrior. The Combat Infantryman's Badge rested above the tower of other badges on his chest. A special parachute badge awarded during his days as a noncommissioned officer in the Special Forces underneath the Combat Infantryman's Badge, over the Pathfinder and Air Assault badges. The 82nd Airborne patch on his right shoulder signified his last tour of combat with that unit in the Persian Gulf. Dougall and Thomlin stood with their bodies rigid, waiting for their turn to speak.

Within a few minutes, Gibson dismissed the captains by turning his attention toward the lieutenants. He extended a hand to Dougall, then slapped him on the shoulder.

"Welcome, Lieutenant Dougall. You're very fortunate. You came to the 1-77th, one of the best units in Korea. It's a good first assignment to have as a new lieutenant. Between the officers and NCOs, we'll set you up for success," Gibson said in a calm, fatherly manner. The colonel's gaze never left the unit's newest addition. Gibson studied the face of the new soldier, searching for strengths and weaknesses.

Finally, Gibson shifted his x-ray vision from Dougall to Thomlin, who felt the blood rush to his face and beads of sweat form under his hairline. Suddenly, it felt like someone had turned off the air conditioning.

"Mr. Thomlin," Gibson started. His words were slow and deliberate. "How is the Report of Survey coming along?"

"Just fine, Sir," Thomlin responded.

Gibson nodded slowly, never taking his eyes off Thomlin, and never blinking. This guy must be half reptile, Thomlin thought.

"That's good," Gibson continued after a brief silence that bordered on complete awkwardness. "Time is of the essence with these things, as I am sure you know."

Gibson leaned forward and Thomlin felt Gibson's hand clamped on his shoulder. Thomlin swallowed hard. He was beginning to feel the sweat trickle down the small of his back. Thomlin was now completely unaware of anyone else in the area except Gibson.

"Some things are best done quickly. Get to the bottom of the problem, assign parties responsible, if necessary, and be done with it. I've seen some lieutenants try to make something more complicated than it actually is, when the reality is, it's not that complicated. Just get it done."

"Yes, Sir," Thomlin responded robotically.

"Swing by the adjutant's desk before you head out and have him set some time aside for Lieutenant Dougall and I to meet so we can sit down and talk in more detail," Gibson offered as he turned toward his office. Thomlin realized it was time to introduce Dougall to Captain Watts.

■ ■ ■

Thomlin and Dougall entered the company area, quickly passing Foster, who was correcting a young enlisted soldier for not saluting her from across the parking lot. Thomlin took Dougall to the CO's office and began to give the introductions when Watts cut him off.

"Damn it, Lieutenant Thomlin, didn't they teach you military courtesy when you went through ROTC?" Watts barked at Thomlin without ever looking up from his large desk. "Why don't you walk out and have Lieutenant Dougall report to his commander like it is common in every other unit in the Army?"

Thomlin and Dougall marched back out, turned around, and Dougall banged on the door three times.

"Good luck," Thomlin whispered to Dougall as he entered. The door shut quickly behind Dougall. Thomlin imagined Dougall's eyes getting even bigger as Captain Watts began his little act, breathing fire and brimstone into the new lieutenant.

Dougall left the company commander's office 30 minutes later for the last time after exiting and re-entering the office a half dozen times until he got his reporting procedures up to the Watts Standard. Thomlin could follow the thin lines of sweat that traveled down from Dougall's scalp. Dougall's lips were twisted together and waves of wrinkles creased his forehead as if someone kicked him in the groin a few times. The look of wonder had vanished and despair replaced it.

"Are you hyperventilating?" Thomlin asked casually.

"That wasn't the company commander," Dougall gasped. "I know that's not my new boss."

"It's really not as bad as you think. Just take everything with a grain of salt around here. Watts doesn't mean half the shit he says, just wants to keep you on your toes."

"Yeah, okay. You're lying to me, aren't you?"

"Mostly. Don't go off and take a bath with a few razor blades just yet, okay? Think of this part as your initiation into the company. Time flies around here. Before you know it, your tour will be up and it'll be time to go home."

"Yeah, right," Dougall replied in disbelief. Thomlin made no further effort to console him.

Dougall followed Thomlin upstairs as they headed to the platoon area. Thomlin had arranged to have all the squad leaders in the platoon sergeant's room to meet their new platoon leader. As the two entered the room Thomlin could hear the sergeants joking and laughing with one another. As formality dictated, the platoon sergeant called the room to attention and everyone rose to their feet. Thomlin nonchalantly waved them to sit down as he began to introduce Dougall.

"Good morning, Third Platoon. I want to introduce you to your new platoon leader," Thomlin said. "I'm not going to waste my breath with the introductions because I know the secret pipeline of info among you has already provided you with more details than I can give."

Six sets of eyes drew a bead on Dougall as the sergeants eyed him from head to toe. The noncoms in the room already knew everything there was to know about Dougall, yet they scrutinized him as if to verify what had already been mentioned by the grapevine.

Immediately, they eyeballed the glowing gold bar on Dougall's collar. Out of the corner of his eye, Thomlin caught two squad leaders flashing a slight frown. They had just inherited another cherry lieutenant. Thomlin smiled a little as he noticed that, within seconds, everyone was focusing attention on Dougall's left shoulder.

"Psst," Thomlin whispered loud enough for everyone to here, "he does have a Ranger tab."

The men chuckled. Thomlin caught them giving a quick check to ensure that Dougall had a small, half crescent Ranger tab above the large Indian head patch of the Second Infantry Division. The award certified that the new platoon leader had made it through one of the most demanding courses the Army had to offer. Although this didn't mean the noncoms and soldiers would quickly accept Dougall as their leader, it did suggest that they wouldn't whisper behind his back or treat him like the local village idiot trying to learn quantum mechanics.

"Sir, welcome. We're glad to have you. After you get settled I'll be glad to sit down with you and get you squared away," the platoon sergeant reassured his new platoon leader.

"Sir," one of the younger squad leaders said, "we're ready for the speech."

"And what speech is that, Sergeant?" Dougall asked.

"The same speech every new officer makes," another young sergeant laughed. "You know, the one about the North Koreans are coming and the platoon will personally lead the offensive to drive them to the Yalu. You know, something like that. Like MacArthur."

"Not every officer makes that speech," Thomlin quickly pointed out.

"Excuse me, Sir, almost every incoming officer." The squad leaders laughed.

"I think I'll spare everyone the speech and just focus on getting up to speed," Dougall said.

"Sir," the platoon sergeant said, shaking Dougall's hand, "you're going to work out just fine."

Thomlin excused himself and led Dougall from the barracks. The pair next headed for the battalion headquarters to grab a vehicle and a driver. On the way over the lieutenants passed a few Koreans in Battle Dress Uniform. Thomlin turned to Dougall and asked, "You know about KATUSAs right?"

"Yeah, a little bit. I heard a lot of stories in the States. What's the real deal?"

"KATUSA stands for Korean Augmentee to the United States Army," Thomlin explained. "It was a program instituted by MacArthur in 1950. After units began arriving from the States way under strength U.S. commanders were in a panic. Some brass think-tanks came up with an unofficial solution to incorporate some Korean combat vets from decimated South Korean units into the U.S. Army. In exchange for clothing and food, some Korean civilians volunteered to be used for labor while others volunteered for a chance to help fight the effort against the evil communist aggressors. Remember, by this time Seoul was a giant ashtray and most of the countryside was not exactly hospitable either. Korean policemen and other soldiers, who were left with no towns or cities to protect asked to join as well."

"You study a lot of history?"

"I saw a documentary down at Yongsan once. Anyway, the Army was soon using raw civilians in its ranks, training them for only a few days before putting them on the front lines with American units."

"You mean these guys only a have a weekend's worth of training before they show up?"

"Well, nowadays, it's more like several weeks versus a few days. Korea relies on conscription, the good old draft. It's not like our all-volunteer force. All men in Korea have to spend at least two years in service for their country once they are of age. Ideally, the smartest Koreans or the ones who speak the best English are supposed to serve in American units. The benefit for us is that Koreans can possibly identify enemy soldiers and equipment, advise commanders on the customs and culture of the land, and help soldiers adapt to life in Korea. In reality, KATUSAs are the rich kids or the kids with families with the right connections. Service in the U.S. Army is considered easier than serving in a ROK Army. They normally get hazed or beaten under those guys."

"Rock army?" Dougall asked.

"Sorry," Thomlin responded, forgetting that some of the in-country acronyms were lost on the new lieutenant, "ROK—Republic of Korea."

Dougall nodded and Thomlin continued, "Personally, I think the real reason the Army still uses the KATUSAs is because they mean less manpower for us, and more savings for the defense budget."

"How many are there?"

"Usually, every infantry platoon has two or three KATUSAs. They're not supposed to be just translators. They serve in positions that are also held by American soldiers. But their promotions are based on time rather than performance. For example, by the end of his two years of service, a KATUSA will automatically rise to the rank of sergeant and serve as a team leader in charge of three soldiers. For this fact alone, a lot of enlisted American soldiers resent their presence. You'll see this come to a head when a KATUSA sergeant either doesn't want the position of responsibility or doesn't have the leadership skills to accomplish the mission."

"You mean to tell me that some of them don't speak English so good?"

Thomlin chuckled. "You'll be surprised when you get a brand new KATUSA to the platoon. It's really a crapshoot. A lot of them show up and can only say, 'Yes, Sergeant.' Others, like my KATUSA named Corporal Pak, were English majors in college. Sometimes this gets pretty comical. 'Hey, private, do you understand me?' 'Yes, Sergeant.' 'No, I'm an officer, call me Sir.' 'Yes, Sergeant.' 'Would you like it if I made you run through the snow naked with your head on fire?' 'Yes, Sergeant.' You'll see what I mean?

"By the time their two years is done, most of the KATUSAs can speak English pretty well. However, this language barrier becomes a real problem if they're in charge and don't grasp English enough to command soldiers in a simulated combat exercise."

Thomlin surprised himself by giving a semi-intelligent response. Dougall thought about this for a minute. "Would you trust them to go to war with you as an actual team leader?"

"I've thought long and hard about this question too. Some of my soldiers think that KATUSAs would actually betray U.S. forces and fight for the other side, while others think the KATUSAs would become instant pacifists in a time of war, praying for the unity of their land no matter who was in power." Thomlin shrugged and he smiled when he added, "By order of the Commanding General, the KATUSAs will fulfill their role in the Army regardless of whether it is in a peacetime scenario or in combat."

Thomlin lost his tight smile. "If war does actually break out, I'm taking their rank away and reducing them to the role of translator."

"I heard they're pretty lazy."

"They're not any different than American soldiers. They sometimes pretend like they don't understand what you're saying, you know, playing dumb. But that's where the ROK Sergeant Major comes in. Every U.S. Army battalion like ours has a Korean, career noncommissioned officer attached. The ROK Sergeant Major's job is to ensure that the KATUSAs are doing their job. He also handles any disciplinary problems. If a KATUSA is playing dumb or is a problem child, then platoon leaders or platoon sergeants threaten to bring in the Sergeant Major."

"What will he do? Beat them?" Brent asked.

"I once had a KATUSA with a bad attitude since the moment he arrived to the platoon. No matter how many times he was counseled or threatened, he wouldn't change his ways. Finally, I brought him to the ROK Sergeant Major. The young soldier simply didn't care. He would shrug his shoulders and roll his eyes like it was no big deal. The ROK Sergeant Major assured me he would take care of the situation. That day the soldier disappeared. He went to what is called 'ROK Re-train.' The retraining consisted of two weeks of beatings and inhuman amounts of physical exercise, while only being fed a daily bowl of rice and water. The soldier eventually returned to the platoon."

"And I suppose that training bridged the language gap?"

"Well, unfortunately it didn't. We eventually had to transfer him to a ROK unit. But it did have a big impact on the other KATUSAs across the company. All of them seemed to have a new outlook on life and no one posed another problem to the unit. The mere suggestion that the ROK Sergeant Major was paying a visit would cause some of the KATUSAs to turn pale and begin convulsions."

By the time Thomlin finished the story they were standing outside the battalion headquarters and Thomlin waited for Dougall to digest all the foreign information before looking for a vehicle.

Within minutes, Thomlin found himself once again sitting in a vehicle moving at the speed of pond water. As ordered by Captain Watts, Thomlin took Dougall down to the Central Issue Facility so Dougall could receive all of his field gear. There was a line of about 70 or 80 soldiers, from privates to majors, all waiting to do the same. Thomlin bid Dougall good luck as he entered the line while Thomlin leaned back in the Humvee to catch up on some sleep. About 30 minutes later the driver woke Thomlin and pointed out Dougall. Dougall emerged from what looked like a metal garage converted into office space with two Army green duffel bags packed with equipment. Dougall gave the thumbs up sign and then gestured for Thomlin to wait another minute as he returned to the building with a handful of paperwork. Thomlin suddenly noticed the duffel bags Dougall left on the pavement in front of the building were gone.

"Oh, crap," Thomlin huffed. Thomlin pointed out his observation to the driver.

"Well, Sir, the bags might have sprouted legs and walked away," the driver laughed.

Dougall arrived at the scene and began to scour the ground as if he lost a contact lens. Although Thomlin was approximately 100 yards away, he could see the blood rushing to Brent Dougall's cheeks, distinguishing himself from the other soldiers like some sort of dyslexic chameleon.

Dougall found a sergeant with a clipboard and an oversized brass belt buckle, obviously signifying someone in charge of this equipment quagmire.

"Sergeant, I, ah, lost my equipment. I mean, someone must have accidentally taken my gear while I was inside," Dougall explained.

Thomlin slumped down into the seat of the Humvee, mentally predicting the event that was about to unfold.

"Alright, everyone," the sergeant bellowed in a deep Southern drawl across the parking lot, "Listen up. Stop what you're doing right now and get on your gear. Hey, you! I said get on your damn gear now. This here lieutenant is missing his stuff."

Unsure of himself, Dougall's eyes darted back and forth looking for the blazing neon "JACKASS" sign hovering somewhere over his head. All activity within a fifteen-mile radius ceased and at least a million eyes were bearing down on Dougall. Thomlin envisioned a slight gust of wind blowing tumbleweeds through the foreground. Thomlin now finally understood how enlisted soldiers came up with stories about officers.

"Sir, I think one of the soldiers has, ah, mistakenly grabbed your gear," the sergeant in charge calmly explained to the young lieutenant.

With eyes downcast, Dougall re-entered the line to draw his equipment again. Forty-five minutes later Thomlin was stirred again. This time it was Dougall who woke Thomlin as he crawled into the back of the vehicle. Dougall said nothing, and Thomlin could see the lines drawn across his face. Dougall's first day in the unit had not been what he anticipated.

"How could someone else end up with my duffle bags full of equipment? There's no way someone could mistakenly end up with twice the amount of stuff and not notice it," Dougall complained.

"TA-50 Alley," Thomlin said without thinking.

"What's that?"

"TA-50 alley. That's the nickname for a small row of shops in Dongducheon where some Koreans sell TA-50," Thomlin explained using the Army nomenclature for standard issue field gear. "It's off limits but anyone who's been around for more than a week knows where to find it. It comes in handy when soldiers lose a few minor items and need to replace it cheaply. But the Koreans don't make the TA-50, they buy it off of soldiers. Someone obviously saw an opportunity to score some extra bucks by swiping two full duffle bags of unsupervised equipment."

"Sir, you think that's where the black box ended up?" the driver asked.

Thomlin turned to face the driver.

"That's an odd question since the black box was lost in the field. What do you mean?"

"Nothing, Sir. I just thought that, um, someone might have sold it down TA-50 alley, that's all."

Thomlin stared hard for several seconds.

"Out with it," Thomlin ordered. "What's the rumor on the

street?"

"Sir, I don't know." The driver started to squirm in his seat. "I just overheard some guys in headquarters bullshitting about the black box. One of them made a joke that it hadn't really been lost. I thought they meant that someone had stolen it. I swear, Sir, that's the only thing I've heard."

Thomlin scrutinized the driver for a few seconds before turning and gesturing to go back to the battalion area. He made no attempt at conversation on the ride back.

Once back in Alpha Company, Thomlin forgot the driver's comments. He focused on lightening the mood by swinging Dougall by Lane Nelson's office. As they walked in, Nelson was preoccupied with a game of computer solitaire. His entire body seemed fixated with the game, leaving only his forefinger moving, quickly clicking the mouse.

"How'd it go? You get everything okay?" he asked without looking up.

"Don't ask," Thomlin said with a grin.

Lane gave a small smile, knowing that Thomlin would recount the entire story in intricate detail, along with a few exaggerations, later over a couple of beers.

"I hope everyday can go this smoothly," Dougall said dryly as he flopped into a chair. "I don't know if I can ever match up to the Watts standard, but do you guys have any first day advice?"

Brent Dougall's sarcasm gave Thomlin a good laugh. Maybe he would be one of the guys after all.

"Sure I can," Nelson said with a straight face. "Rule Number One: admit nothing, deny everything and as soon as accusations are made, make counter accusations. Rule Number Two: don't sweat the small stuff, chief. And Rule Number Three: never make any promises and be careful who you trust. By the way, we have a Hail and Farewell tonight. You will be getting hailed so make sure you have a speech ready. You know, where you're from, how much you like being here, and all that shit."

Dougall arched his eyebrows and gave his famous look, "Speech?"

5

HAIL AND FAREWELL

A festival of drinking for the unit's officers, the Hail and Farewell, was designed to foster unit cohesion and esprit de corps among the members of the unit. New personnel were given a warm welcome and instilled with an initial sense of pride for being part of an outstanding organization. Outgoing members were bid a fond farewell and were forever engraved with touching memories of their brotherly team they had grown to cherish over the past twelve months. To ensure the success of such a monumental event it was imperative that those who worked behind the scenes thoroughly planned every intricate detail and war-gamed all contingencies. If a situation arose or if something was amiss, those responsible would immediately rectify the problem or risk utter disaster, failing their mission.

Thomlin approached the bar at the Camp Kayes Officer's Club as Lieutenant Kevin Ward pounded the counter top with his fist.

"Why the hell isn't the bar open yet? Open bar was to begin exactly at 7:30 and my watch says 7:32. Where the hell's the goddamn beer?"

Others in the crowd began to lose their identities as a mob of sober officers started to form. The Korean barmaid, not understanding the English but clearly recognizing the impatient expressions, glanced around the bar for help. All 40 or so officers of the 77th began to throw themselves toward the bar like teenagers at center stage of a rock concert. The girl was clearly in mortal danger.

"Goddamn," Ward cursed. "Where's battalion staff when you need them? They're supposed to take care of this."

"Okay, turtle," Nelson said. "Get your wallet ready. If we don't get some free beer soon, you'll have to get first round."

The crowd became louder. A tray of glasses was knocked over and the men cheered at the sound of the shattered glass.

■ ■ ■

Specialist Kenneth Wickersham frantically searched the whirling room. The prostitute behind him coolly sat on the mattress and lit up a cigarette. She eyed Wickersham with a mixture of annoyance and distaste. He started to rummage through the woman's belongings in a desperate hunt for his lost package. He was convinced that his backpack containing a small black box was still somewhere in the disarray that made up the woman's small, one-room living quarters.

"You go now," the woman said firmly. She was 42 years old, slightly plump, and barely stood over five feet. Wickersham stopped to face her. He looked at her coldly and noticed the wrinkles underneath the makeup as she casually brought the cigarette to her lips. She had thick black hair that Wickersham suspected was a wig.

"You go," she repeated. She was staring off into space, only stealing a glance at Wickersham to say the few English words she knew. Wickersham began to feel nauseous. Only a short time before, he had managed to stumble upstairs and had his way with her. Twice. The woman lay on her back and moaned in what Wickersham took as the throes of ecstasy, never noticing the woman's distant look in her eyes. Wickersham stood motionless fixing his gaze on the woman's small breasts that rested above the sheets. He remained locked until a voice from the doorway startled him.

"It's a little early to get drunk and get some short time, don't you think?" the figure in the doorway asked.

It was a voice of authority and Wickersham did not need to face the man to know who it was. Wickersham stood motionless and was mute.

"Where's the box?" the voice asked. Wickersham suddenly realized he had lost his backpack containing the ANCD. He could feel the pit of his stomach and the lump forming in his throat. He lost it.

"I don't know," Wickersham managed to get out. There was water rising in his eyes.

"You better find it. I don't care what you have to do. Find the damn black box. Now."

The person in the doorway was gone and Wickersham was trembling. He didn't know what to do. The alcohol clouding his thoughts confused him even further. The woman didn't even seem to notice the figure that almost entered the room and was now demanding payment from Wickersham. Wickersham suddenly became enraged with the woman; as if it were her fault he could not find his backpack. The woman angrily yelled at Wickersham in Korean for money. Wickersham snapped. He closed the distance between him and the woman with a surprisingly swift movement for his altered state and began to physically vent his frustration.

■ ■ ■

A captain from the battalion headquarters finally arrived at the O-club and beer was given to the masses. Following Ward's lead, Thomlin fought his way to the front and snagged a six-pack of Budweiser. Others did the same before heading to the main dining room that was sectioned off for their benefit. The dining tables were arranged in a large horseshoe for all lieutenants and captains. At the opening of the shoe was a smaller, separate table seating Gibson and his staff. The battalion executive officer, Major Jeremy Streeter, sat on Gibson's right side while the battalion operations officer, Major Mike Pierce, sat to the battalion commander's left. The battalion chaplain, Captain Park Hyun-sun, was also seated at the table next to the battalion operations officer.

"That's Major Streeter," Thomlin pointed out to Dougall. "He's probably the best battalion executive officer this unit has ever had."

"Why's that?" Dougall asked.

"The guy is completely professional and unflappable under stress. Everyone admires his cool demeanor. He's personable enough to be approached by any soldier and he's the only field grade officer I know that takes the time to mentor and coach the junior officers in the battalion."

Dougall nodded as Thomlin continued with a smile, "We all love him for another reason as well. When we have events like tonight's Hail and Farewell, Streeter will party as hard as any of the younger officers. He sometimes leads the way in conducting aircraft carrier landings in the officer barracks."

"Aircraft carrier landings?"

"Yeah. We'll attach garden hoses to the sinks in the barracks and water down the hallway. Then we'll take turns diving face first across the slick surface while everyone else in the hallway pelts the human fighter jets with ice and other stuff to simulate stormy conditions. The landings may last until the early morning hours when someone will inevitably split their head open on a doorframe or concrete wall. It's a blast. Streeter loves to do the first landing. The guy doesn't try to put himself on a pedestal or pretend to be higher caliber than anyone else."

Thomlin wondered what Streeter had been like as a company commander. He pictured Streeter standing in front of an infantry company, commanding the complete attention of the soldiers by his personality alone.

"But how come he doesn't have a Ranger tab?" Dougall asked.

Thomlin also thought it was odd that Streeter's uniform was mysteriously missing the tab on his shoulder but said, "Don't know. Honestly, no one seems to care. Streeter is one of the few officers able to get respect without it."

Thomlin sighed and took his place with the other officers in his company. This ritual forced him to sit close to Captain Watts, but Thomlin made every effort to distance himself from the man as much as possible. Nelson, Ward, and Thomlin downed a few bottles quickly while they tried to prep Dougall for the big show. Several cute Korean women with large fake smiles served food rapidly. The laughter and conversation in the room rose to a mild roar as Thomlin smiled. He reflected that the entire ritual of this night probably dated back to the days of the Roman Legion.

As dessert was dropped on the table, a hush covered the room and the chaplain rose to his feet to give a brief invocation. Chaplain Park spoke in a monotone, forcing the words as if he had only recently mastered the language. "Lord, please bless these officers with courage and wisdom as we welcome the newest members of the 1-77th, the best infantry unit in the world. Bless those that are returning home and grant them safe journey. Most of all, please show mercy on those who may receive the Big Boot award. All this we pray in Your name, amen."

A loud "Amen!" followed as Dougall leaned close to Thomlin and asked about the Big Boot award.

"It's for whoever has screwed the pooch the most," Thomlin explained. Thomlin pointed to a large combat boot mounted on an oak plaque sitting on the colonel's table. "The boot is so you can boot yourself in the ass as you try to think of a way out."

"Bring out the grog," the colonel bellowed.

The lights dimmed and a large iron pot, similar to the one the witches of *Macbeth* might have used, was brought before the colonel to begin the ceremony. There were several lieutenants lined up beside the pot with bowls or cups in their hands. One by one they approached the pot and recited the significance of each element they poured into the cauldron.

"From the battalion's campaign in the Pacific during World War II, I offer palm leaves," one lieutenant said in a serious tone as he dropped leaves into the pot.

"For the battalion's efforts in the Korean War, I offer water from the Chosin Reservoir," another said as he poured a brown tinted liquid into the cauldron.

"For the battalion's efforts in Vietnam, I offer rice paddy water," a third recited as he dumped what appeared to be mud into the grog.

"From our last field exercise, I offer dirt from our landing zone," another lieutenant added referring to the unit's air mobile mission.

"Lastly, I provide pavement from the Walk of Shame and lots of soju," a lieutenant shouted as the men in the room beat the table tops and hollered.

With the presentation complete, it was time to call the newest members of the unit forward to ingest the grog. Once they physically had the battalion's historical elements coursing through their veins, they would become full-fledged members of the unit. What the new members did not realize was that they were actually drinking a combination of soju and Kool-Aid located in a small container behind the pot. Dougall stood at the front of the line, ready to be initiated.

"I will now welcome our youngest member," Gibson said as he moved to center stage. "As you all know, the biography I am about to read is 100 percent accurate. Second Lieutenant Brent Dougall is from California. He attended school at the University of California Institute for Young Men with Alternative Lifestyles."

Laughter was spreading through the room as Dougall started to look a little flush, still not realizing what was being said.

"At this prestigious college he majored in the anatomy of young Greek boys. His hobbies included naked leap-frog, bug collecting, and soliciting dates from the local Women's Penitentiary. He was unsuccessful during his past nine attempts at finding a future mate through the intercontinental mail-order bride program, and he now hopes to engage in a meaningful relationship with a kind, sensitive young man or large gerbil."

The officers in the room were now in an uproar.

"From this moment on, Lieutenant Dougall will be known as," Gibson paused dramatically, "Blondie."

People pounded the tabletops as they repeated his new name

in unison. Dougall reacted to the alias with a large grimace. The colonel handed Dougall an oversized beer mug filled to the brim with the grog and instructed him to down the sludge as quickly as possible, ending with the mug upside down over his head.

"Go, go, go!" The crowd chanted.

Liquor poured down the side of Dougall's mouth, staining the front of his shirt. He completed the task and quickly turned the mug upside down allowing a trickle of juice to slide out.

"Re-train!" screamed the officers.

"Sorry, lieutenant," Gibson said. "That is simply unacceptable. Do it again."

Dougall repeated the process three more times until he finally completed the mission successfully. Although Thomlin was 40 feet away, he could almost hear Dougall's insides fluttering in protest. The battalion commander shook Dougall's hand, slapped him on his back, gave him a battalion coin and then stepped back.

"Speech, speech, speech," the crowd chanted.

Dougall made an attempt to clear his throat, trying to shake off the effects of the grog that was already attacking his cerebrum. He opened his mouth to speak. His tongue reached the roof of his mouth as his lips formed a small oval shape. Only one syllable was allowed to escape into the air.

"Shut-up! Sit down!" the entire room violently shouted. A defeated Dougall with eyes fixed on the rug took his seat.

"Welcome aboard," Ward said, clicking the neck of his beer bottle against Dougall's Budweiser. Dougall responded with a smile.

"Consider tonight one long rite of passage among many that will make up your journey through the Army," Ward smiled. "Just think, before long you'll be sitting here in this same o-club, laughing and shouting at the new personnel."

"Now that you are an official member of the battalion, it is my duty to brief you on the Lieutenant Protection Agency," Nelson said with a smile.

Dougall was silently dry heaving under the table, still trying to recover from the grog. He lifted his head just long enough to nod, signaling that he was still conscious.

"We all look out for each other. As a general rule, during the Hail and Farewells a lieutenant will never nominate a fellow lieutenant for the Big Boot award unless the poor bastard has screwed up so badly that we can't cover his ass. We stick together and usually try to pin the nomination on some unsuspecting captain. The captains in battalion operations are a good choice. This also carries over to other more serious matters. Help other lieutenants out, even if they're not in your company, even if they don't even come right out and ask for your help. We're all in this together, one for all, all for one, that sort of thing."

The ceremony drew closer to a conclusion with nominations for the infamous Big Boot award, an excellent demonstration of how the Lieutenant Protection Agency worked. The adjutant announced the nominees and reviewed the rules.

"Let's get ready to rumble. Leave your ego at the door. If you're easily offended, you better wait outside, because this is a no-holds-barred competition to rip on whoever has screwed up the most. The only rule is that at least ten percent of the information presented must be true. The winner will be decided by the amount of applause or noise generated from the crowd. Without further ado, let's bring on the first nominee."

As several officers left their chairs and started to assemble for a live reenactment of someone else's misfortune, Ward leaned over and whispered, "Someone should nominate Headquarters Company for losing the goddamn black box."

"That's not funny," Thomlin said. "No one has the balls to

bring up that incident. Gibson would likely execute someone on the spot."

"What happened?" Dougall asked Thomlin.

"The last time we went out to the field over a month ago, it was primarily for weapons qualification. It was ten days of hitting all the firing ranges so everyone could qualify on their individual weapons. Three times a day we did a sensitive items check, checked all the weapons, night vision goggles, GPS systems, whatever. We radioed all this in as usual. The night before we were supposed to head back to Kayes, headquarters comes up short. They're missing the black box. Everyone said a collective 'oh, shit' because we knew what was about to happen. Within hours, the entire battalion was scouring the ranges and Tent City before we're all ordered to start going through the field. I mean, it was every soldier in the battalion in one long line, arms width apart, moving through rice paddies and the brush to look for this damn thing."

"Wow," was all Dougall could say.

"Yeah, well, we never found it. Lucky for me, I was assigned with the Report of Survey," Thomlin said and turned his attention back to the Big Boot nominations.

Skits were executed with elaborate detail, homemade video movies were shown and obscene poems were recited in an effort to present the best nomination. As Nelson promised, no lieutenants were nominated. A captain on battalion staff who burned down half his room in an attempt to cook while drunk graciously accepted the award. A nominee had a chance to get out of receiving the Big Boot award if he could come up with a comical rebuttal, comical enough to sway the crowd in his favor and blame someone else for his mistake in the process. This time, there was nothing that could be said to spare the captain's ego. The young captain took the award and would eventually hang it in his office with a mixture of pride and embarrassment until the next Hail and Farewell. After the completion of the presentation, the ceremony ended with the chaplain giving the evocation and a reminder from the battalion commander to be safe.

6

DOWNRANGE

Phase 2 of the party began. It was now time for the officers to go downrange, to go to the ville, to go outside the front gates of Camp Kayes and invade the bars of local Dongducheon. In the acronym filled vocabulary of American soldiers, Dongducheon was simply known as TDC for those challenged by Korean pronunciations. Soldiers didn't seem to notice that the official English translation of the city did not begin with the letter "T." The trip downrange was the most anticipated part of the drinking festival. It was the one night of the month all the officers of the 1-77th, including the commander, would go out and relieve stress or drown their thoughts for at least a night. Camaraderie and unit cohesion among the members of the battalion was at its highest during this point. The soldiers of the battalion also realized what was going on and would steer clear and not try to start any trouble with the officers on this night.

The men piled out of the officers club and raced for the bus stop.

"There're only three ways to make it to the gate. Find a taxi, walk, or risk getting on the bus," Thomlin explained to Dougall.

"How far away is the gate?"

"Too far to walk in the summer heat. It's about a mile and a half. The bus runs every fifteen minutes, but this time of night, the buses will be packed to max capacity."

The lieutenants watched two buses stream by without slowing. The buses were crammed with so many bodies the lieutenants could see the outlines of clothing logos pressed against the windows. Dougall could hear loud drunken screams echoing as it passed.

"Jesus. Can we just catch a cab?"

"Good luck finding one. I've seen fist fights break out over an open cab. The bus is the necessary pain to get to the gate."

A bus finally stopped, but there was standing room only. They all made an effort to muscle their way on, jamming people to the back. The last three men were forced to stand on the stairs, barely allowing enough room for the door to close. The noise created from the drunken laughter and conversation was almost deafening.

Dougall noticed that in the front two seats of the bus were two sergeants in uniform. He turned to Thomlin to ask, "Why are they in uniform?"

"Bus monitors," Thomlin tried to explain over the drunken chatter. "They're supposed to maintain good order and discipline within the vehicle."

The expression on the faces of the two uniformed soldiers

clearly showed how unhappy they were with their hard luck at being selected for the duty. The two sergeants rigidly sat with their head and eyes facing to the front.

"I've been onboard on more than one occasion when a brawl broke out. The only thing those guys can do is tell the bus driver to turn around and beat it back to the military police station."

After what felt like several hours, the lieutenants reached the main gate and fell off the bus. Most everyone poured through the military police checkpoint at the gate. A small group trickled in another direction, including the officers, toward a large building near the gate called the Main Post Club. The Main Post Club was an all ranks club, a replacement for many officer and enlisted clubs that failed to draw in enough revenue or crowds by only depending on a selective population of the post. Every night of the week the Main Post Club had its own theme, and tonight was Hee-Haw time, Country Western music for the entire evening. All the cowboys or wannabe ranch hands were jamming the place with the colorful Garth Brooks style button down shirts, hub cap size belt buckles and ten-gallon hats. On a large raised dance floor couples were two stepping to Shania Twain, occasionally interrupted by a line dance to the "Macarena."

"This is usually a good place to start off the night's activities," Thomlin explained. "We can swig down a few more cheap American beers before heading downrange."

Thomlin spotted a majority of his soldiers hanging about, drinking without causing any ruckus. A few officers from the battalion moseyed up to the bar and made the club their last stop for the night. Ward said something in Nelson's ear and gave the hand signal to move out.

The group quickly left the club and headed in the direction of a few enlisted soldiers emblazoned with large black and white MP armbands. They were casually hanging out in front of the gate watching the crowd head out. Kevin Ward stumbled as he entered the doorway to the checkpoint. Thomlin imagined that the max fill line imprinted somewhere on Ward's liver was passed more than an hour ago.

"How are you two fine young soldiers tonight?" Ward asked, making his first mistake. Ward's slurred speech sounded as if he asked them how they like their meat. He fumbled with his identification card and tried to strike up a conversation with the military police soldier in order to compensate for his lack of dexterity. Ward's loud voice echoed through the small corridor like the PA system at a baseball stadium. He managed to twist the English language into a long string of grunts and guttural noises blending all thoughts into one long word.

"I'm sorry, Sir, what did you say?" the uniformed soldiers quickly exchanged glances and broad smiles with one another, giving Ward every opportunity to make a complete ass out of himself. Ward made a second effort to complete an entire sentence but only managed a few grunts and slurred syllables.

"Well, you men hold down the fort while we check out the local scenery," Ward finally shouted, attempting to play it cool.

"Sir, I don't think it would be a wise decision if you left post tonight," said an eighteen-year-old soldier in a parental tone.

"No, no, I… fine," Ward protested with a couple disjointed gestures and broken syllables. The MP gently placed a hand on Ward's arm. Ward looked like an animal caught in a bear trap, internally debating whether or not he should gnaw off the limb. For a brief moment Ward looked down at his arm and Thomlin actually thought Ward was going to sink his teeth into his own bicep, though the lieutenant soon succumbed to the police.

"The rules of the ville are simple," Thomlin whispered to Dougall. "Don't start trouble, the police are always right, Korean nationals are always right regardless of how wild their accusations, and if trouble arises run as far and fast as you possibly can."

Dougall nodded and watched as Ward was escorted to a telephone counter where the police called a taxi to bring Ward back to the barracks. The rest of the lieutenants bid him a goodnight as they walked out the door onto the sidewalk of MSR 3, the main road that cut through Dongducheon. As soon as they were in the clear, the group burst out laughing.

"Don't let me forget to remind Ward of this little incident for the next eight months or so," Thomlin laughed.

"The winner of the next Big Boot award is…" Nelson chided, "Kevin Ward, for getting too drunk to successfully navigate a ten foot hallway."

The lieutenants lined up at the cross walk, waiting for a break in traffic.

"Are you ready for a human game of Frogger?" Thomlin asked.

Korean taxi drivers and truck drivers gunned their small Hyundais and Daewoos between the intersections. The traffic light dangling above the road blinked from green to yellow to red without affecting the little fiberglass rockets that plowed through the intersection. Horns blared as cars narrowly missed repeated collisions.

"How do they not hit each other?" Dougall asked.

"No clue," Thomlin replied. "I still haven't figured that out."

There was a short lull in traffic so the group made an Olympian effort to get to the far side. From the other side of the intersection they walked only a few hundred yards more.

"Well," Thomlin announced, "this is downrange."

"This is it? It looks like it's only a few city blocks," Dougall said.

"You're absolutely correct. Were you expecting something different?"

"It looks like some B-rate movie of Saigon in the sixties."

The narrow streets connected with numerous alleys formed a figure eight littered with nothing but bars and nightclubs. The pavement was worn with cracks, potholes and small piles of trash. Although it was late in the evening, little Korean kids scurried about, playing soccer through the streets. There were no streetlights, only the glow from the bright neon nightclub signs that produced more than enough light. The stench from trash and local rice paddies hung in the air and would probably bother a more sober mind without numbed senses.

"What's down there?" Dougall asked, pointing to a large crowd of people loitering around the intersection of the figure eight.

"Later. We have to make our first stop at the second home to the officers of the 77th," Thomlin replied. Thomlin's crew steered clear of the crowd and headed down the backside of the loop to a small bar called Kim's.

As they burst through the door a half dozen Korean bar girls turned on their barstools to shout a greeting. In the States, Kim's would be considered a dive, inhabited only by bikers and unrecovering alcoholics, but here the place was a personal haven and a successful business for the owner. Christmas tree lights hung on the ceiling cast a surreal red-green glow on the people sitting at the bar, amplifying the expressions on their faces as if they were the living caricatures off a sketchpad. Pictures of some American rock groups popular in the late 1970s adorned the walls, along with a large sea turtle shell that served as the bar's centerpiece.

"I take it that Greenpeace has never visited this place?' Dougall asked.

"I don't think Koreans ever bothered to check their decorative styles with them," Thomlin laughed.

The owner, Miss Kim, was an attractive middle-aged Korean woman standing behind the bar wearing a plain, long gray dress.

She smiled at most of the customers and occasionally made conversation with some of them by appearing friendly and casual, but her eyes gave her away. Thomlin had been around long enough to know that her role here was to keep a watchful eye on the girls working the outside of the bar. Between the smiles she sometimes snapped orders in Korean or cast a disapproving look toward some of the girls.

"Beware of the bar girls," Thomlin warned.

"Why's that?" Dougall looked almost scared.

"They have only one mission," Thomlin grinned. "To suck as much money from you as possible. For a small fee, around ten bucks, a girl will sit down next to you for a short period, usually until you no longer pay for anymore drinks, and act overly interested in whatever you tell her. The drinks the girls deliver to themselves are nothing more than colored soda water, but the drinks are supposed to look like some exotic mixed drink."

Thomlin knew that as more drinks were delivered, the bar girls acted more intoxicated. They were highly skilled in the art of flirting and sexual suggestion, however, no sexual acts were ever offered and any advances made by the customers were quickly brushed off. In the hierarchy of downrange, these women rested on a tier above women working the streets. Each of the girls dressed in tight shorts or miniskirts with a half-shirt or tank top.

As Dougall ogled the women Thomlin continued, "As long as you know what they're here for, you'll be okay. Take a look around. All of them are beautiful, some of the best Dongducheon has to offer."

"They all seem to know you," Dougall laughed.

"Of course," Thomlin winked, "I'm one of their best customers. But they don't bother with any sexual innuendos. I stopped paying for drinks a long time ago."

The only Korean man in the bar sat in a small disc jockey booth. He spun old records on two turntables.

"They've never heard of compact discs?" Dougall asked.

"Are you kidding? I'm still amazed Kim's is not still using eight-tracks."

None of the music the DJ played was close to being considered recent. Every other song vaguely resembled Don McLean's "American Pie."

Thomlin saddled up on a bar stool as Miss Kim came over to shake his hand. He introduced Dougall to Miss Kim as she took his hand.

"Are you married? You lieutenant, right? When did you get here? Where are you from in the States?" Miss Kim smiled as she quickly fired off questions.

She nodded her head with each response and then rang a large iron bell over the bar. With Dougall's hand still in hers, she turned her head and said a few words in Korean to the girls sitting around the bar. Thomlin could almost hear the ka-ching of the mental cash register in the minds of some of the girls as they glanced at Dougall. Miss Kim made Dougall go to the centerpiece and rub the turtle shell for good luck. By the time he returned to his seat there was a shot of soju and a Budweiser waiting for him. A short, young looking Korean girl with long, flowing hair was also waiting for him at the next bar stool. Thomlin took a long look at the girl and remembered her with much shorter hair only a week ago.

Nelson raised his own shot of soju to toast Dougall, "Well, bud, welcome to the Land of the Morning Calm and bad hangovers."

Dougall made a contorted expression after taking a swig of formaldehyde tasting beer. Thomlin forgot to warn his new friend that Koreans recycled their glass bottles differently than in the United States. The glass was not melted down; instead it was merely sterilized, refilled, and bottled again. Thomlin laughed and pulled a thin package off the bar top.

"Here, try this," Thomlin suggested as he unwrapped what appeared to be dark green sheets of paper. "Dried seaweed. Good drinking food."

Dougall snapped a piece of the brittle substance and ran his fingers over the rough texture before putting it in his mouth.

"All I taste is salt."

"Exactly."

"Don't eat that junk," Nelson said before turning to one of the bargirls. "*Yaki mandu, chooseyo.*"

The girl quickly returned with a plate full of small, crescent shaped pieces of dough.

"Eat this," Nelson smiled. "It's the only food around here worth eating. It's like dumplings. It's got minced meat, vegetables, and who knows what else inside, but it's good."

"Yeah, that's probably the only local food soldiers know around here," Thomlin laughed.

Thomlin downed another shot of soju before Miss Kim lingered in front of him, casually resting an elbow on the bar. Her eyes drew to a narrow slit as she surveyed her girls, obviously displeased and making mental notes of one of the bar girls who had indulged in too much alcohol. Thomlin distracted Miss Kim, asking, "What's the intel for this week?"

After a second or two she pulled close to Thomlin and responded with a smile, "Wednesday you have alert. It only last few hours, then you go to field."

Thomlin thanked her and turned to Nelson, "Looks like we're heading to the field Wednesday morning."

When Thomlin first heard Miss Kim's predictions almost two years ago, he was shocked with disbelief. How could a Korean national know information about activities on Camp Kayes before his battalion commander? Thomlin initially dismissed her warnings as mere rumors, but as time went on, Miss Kim's information proved accurate.

She placed a hand on Thomlin's shoulder and asked, "Please, you come help me carry some beer."

Thomlin followed Miss Kim through a narrow door into the back area of the establishment. Few were invited back to help stock the bar. Thomlin reached into a long open refrigerated tub and grabbed a milk crate full of beer.

"Thomlin," Miss Kim asked softly as Thomlin lifted the crate, "You do me small favor?"

"Anything for you, my friend."

"I not had Jack Daniels in long time."

Thomlin blushed slightly at the request. "Miss Kim, you have many friends that could get you that."

Miss Kim smiled and momentarily reminded Thomlin of some of the younger girls sitting around the bar. She gently placed her hand on Thomlin's chest.

"I know, but it tastes better from you."

Thomlin gave a boyish smile, "As always, I'll see what I can do."

Thomlin delivered the crate to the bartender and joined his group for another beer. After a final chorus of "American Pie" Thomlin decided that it was time to move on. He signaled Nelson and rescued Dougall before he bought the bar girl sitting on his lap another rum and coke without the rum. As they left the bar Thomlin spotted Captain Watts and the first sergeant, both in uniform, standing across the street. Watts was grinning like the Cheshire cat, as if he'd been waiting for Thomlin the entire time.

Every weekend an officer and a noncommissioned officer from the battalion pulled Courtesy Patrol to augment the military police. With so many soliders downrange getting rowdy and causing trouble it was impossible for the relatively small military police staff to be everywhere at once. Watts took particular joy in pulling this undesirable duty because it granted him a license to bust soldiers and search for an excuse to rid himself of lieutenants he did not like.

Watts was rocking back and forth in his boots as he yelled, "Having fun, lieutenants?"

Thomlin realized that the alcohol was already assaulting his brain stem and was smart enough to keep his mouth shut and not come back with a wise-ass remark. Nelson was smart too and simply responded with, "Hooah, Sir."

The grin never left Watts' face. He turned his attention to Dougall.

"Lieutenant Dougall, you should really watch yourself around these two. Both of them are bad influences. I wouldn't want to hold you responsible for some troublesome scheme they might devise."

Dougall stared at Watts without knowing what to say. Good man, don't say a damn thing, Thomlin thought. Watts paused briefly and then turned his gaze back to Thomlin. This time he spoke in a low voice without the smile.

"Thomlin, don't even think about doing something stupid on my watch. It would be a real shame for me to have to bust you and drag your ass back to the battalion area. Then, of course, I would probably have to relieve you."

"Hooah, Sir."

A smirk crossed Watts' face as the lieutenants turned away and headed for the main intersection. Watts didn't bother to follow them, though Thomlin was fearful that Watts would tail them at a distance out of sight, waiting for an opportunity to arise and then fall upon them. They managed to move only a few hundred yards along the narrow road before an old Korean woman accosted them. She was only four and a half feet tall with a crooked back bent at 45 degrees. Thomlin imagined the woman had to be at least six or seven hundred years old. She had more wrinkles and creases on her face than a catcher's mitt.

"Hey, GI, you want young girl?" she asked, but it sounded more like a statement. "Forty dollar short time, 80 dollar long time."

Nelson stopped and drew close to the woman, "*Ajoomma*, how much for me and you? I really like you. I pay a lot."

The old woman jerked away, offended.

The woman began to slap Nelson's shoulder as they picked up the pace and moved away. This time the men only made it about 50 yards before the woman's identical twin sister began asking the same questions. They decided to spare her their sarcastic remarks and ignored her as they passed.

After being approached for the third time, Dougall asked, "What's the difference between short and long time?"

"Short time means however long it takes you to get your rocks off and long time means all night, as many times as you can get it up," Nelson gladly explained.

"If she's some big pimp, where are all her girls?" Dougall asked.

"All of the girls are in nearby rooms down these small alleys and not all of them are young. Some of them have more mileage than Amtrak."

"Let me guess," Dougall grinned, "I spend 40 bucks for some cheap thrills and then a week later I'm at the clinic with an STD."

"No way, man. These girls actually have less VD than the American girls you'll find on Kayes. Each one of these girls is required to get regularly tested. It's kind of like the prostitute code around here. Ajoomma is a business woman, a real *chigeop yeosung*. She knows that if any one of her girls gets a case of the itch and passes it along to a soldier then word will get around and everyone will stay away from her. You think I'm bullshitting you? Ask the battalion doc if you don't believe me," Nelson said referring to the physician's assistant who lived in the battalion's area. "I once heard about some enlisted soldier contracting AIDS a few years back. The little old ajoommas cleaned house, got rid of every girl in town and brought new ones in from Seoul."

"Brought new ones from Seoul? What are you saying? There's a prostitute farm down there?"

This time Thomlin tried to shed a little light on this topic for Dougall. "No, no my naïve friend. These girls are more like indentured servants. I don't believe the rumors that their families actually sell them into this sort of business, but I do believe they are all extremely poor. As far as I can tell, they come from dirt-poor families, even by Korean standards, or they are badly in debt. They are coaxed to come up here to work for a few years as a waitress or some other mundane job until they arrive and find out what their role really is. Some probably end up staying because after they've been here a few years this is the only profession they know. Maybe they'll move up a level and become a bargirl or grow too old and become one of the ajoomas. The vicious cycle continues."

"Don't you feel bad for them?"

"Sure I do," Nelson smirked. "That's why I make large donations to their business on a bi-monthly basis."

The remark received a few chuckles from Thomlin, and a slight gasp from Dougall. Dougall appeared to be at a loss for words when they came up to a large crowd covering the intersection. There were so many Americans packing the small streets that moving through the intersection was like weaving through a crowded bar. The blaring music from the competing clubs poured into the streets and reminded Thomlin of a stereo competition in the hall of a college dormitory. The noise of a few hundred drunken voices combined with the music was almost unbearable for sober eardrums.

As they made their way through the intersection they passed a small metal shack inhabited by both the MPs and the Korean police.

"That's the penalty box," Thomlin warned Dougall. "Any American offender of the downrange rules is brought to the penalty box before they are turned over to the main police station inside Camp Kayes. If you're lucky, you're only held inside for a few minutes, read the riot act from the cops and then released on your own to return to post."

Although Thomlin didn't bother to explain to Dougall, Nelson and he had both checked this block on their list of rites of passage more than once. However, they had always been bright enough to follow the rules of the Box. Act sober, keep your mouth shut, be respectful, play stupid or pass the blame to someone else. As the three lieutenants weaved through the crowd, Thomlin made a silent promise to himself not to demonstrate any of these rules to Dougall on this night.

As they walked toward a more heavily populated area, Thomlin steeled himself as he noticed Foster walking in their direction. She was almost unrecognizable with her hair down, a tank top, and low hanging jeans. Foster had obviously spotted them and approached with a smile.

"Showing the new guy around?" she asked.

"Just showing him the sights," Nelson replied.

"Well, you both know what he has to do," Foster said with a slight laugh.

Thomlin knew what was coming and bit his lip. Dougall suspiciously looked to each of them. Foster looked directly at Dougall and said with a tone that was almost an order, "You have to see the midget of TDC."

"Another initiation?" Dougall asked.

"She's right," Nelson said trying to look serious, "you have to see the midget."

"She's the most renowned working girl in all Korea," Thomlin said. "She's a legend."

"She's been around for decades," Nelson added.

"And what if I don't want to meet her?" Dougall asked.

"This isn't a choice. We give her the new guys like an offering to an oracle," Foster laughed.

Foster gently slid her arm around Dougall's waist and pulled him in the direction of a nondescript looking bar. There was no sign out front or neon lights to make the establishment stick out among the other clubs. It was almost unnoticeable except for the large pair of old wooden doors with large brass knockers.

As they stepped through the doors they pushed through the wall of cigarette smoke and made their way to the bar. The bar was nearly empty except for a few soldiers seated at tables speaking with Korean women and a pair of soldiers playing pool on a table near the back. Lighting in the bar was almost nonexistent and music popular in the 1980s echoed through the air. Bar stools and worn tables were scattered on what was once a tile dance floor. An old Korean woman greeted the group from behind the bar and lined up several beers as they approached.

Foster grabbed a beer and motioned toward the end of the bar, "There she is."

Sitting on a stool at the far end of the bar was a short Korean woman barely over four feet tall. The woman was wearing a light-colored blouse unbuttoned halfway down her chest, a short leather miniskirt, and fishnet stockings. While taking a long drag from her cigarette between the small gap in her front teeth, she cocked one leg up on a nearby stool in an unladylike pose that displayed her garter belt. From the distance it was impossible to tell her age or examine her facial features. She ran her hand through her short wavy hair as she eyed the group.

"What's this about?" Dougall asked with a slight quiver.

"That's the most famous woman in the entire land. Every incoming el-tee to the 77th has to spend short-time with her to earn the right to become one of us," Nelson explained with a straight face.

Foster, Nelson, and Thomlin immediately began pulling money from their wallets and handing it to the bartender. Without asking, the bartender scooped the $20 bills and carried the wad to the short woman at the end of the bar.

"No, I don't think so," Dougall shook his head.

"Look, cherry, you have to do this," Foster said. She was in Dougall's face and spoke with a voice that bordered on anger. "She'll take you to her room in the back and you can let her do her thing. All the other real men do it."

"No way," Dougall said taking a step back.

Foster slid to Dougall's back and whispered in his ear, "If you don't do this, I'll start a rumor on the entire post that you don't prefer the opposite gender. Now, relax. All your brothers have done this. It's no big deal. Just get in there."

Dougall turned to Thomlin and Nelson for help.

"Sorry, dude, but she's got a point," Nelson sighed as Thomlin shrugged his shoulders. "You have to fuck the midget."

The woman counted her money before slipping it into her shirt pocket and hopping off the stool. She tossed her cigarette into an ashtray and sauntered up to Dougall, carefully looking him up and down.

"You new guy?" she asked putting her hands on her hips. "Okay, let's go."

The woman turned and headed toward a hallway behind the pool table. Foster violently shoved Dougall in the woman's direction. An ashen Dougall turned to Thomlin in a last minute plea but Thomlin made a hand gesture to move him forward. When Dougall and the woman were finally out of sight the group doubled over in laughter.

"Nicole," Thomlin said, "you are one cruel bitch."

"C'mon, Greg, don't act like you don't enjoy this routine," she joked back.

"You really do enjoy this, don't you?"

Foster turned and whispered to Thomlin, "You men are so easy to influence."

Within a minute and a half Dougall appeared from the hallway almost running toward the lieutenants. His polo shirt was half untucked and beads of sweat swam down the side of his face. He could barely catch his breath as he reached the bar.

"I can't do it," he stammered. "I'm sorry, but I just can't do this."

"Oh, my God," Foster said disapprovingly, "that was a test of your manhood. What do you have to say for yourself?"

"I was raised Mormon, you jerk."

The others blew up in wild laughter. Even the bartender chuckled openly. Dougall first appeared confused then slowly turned angry.

"You mean, this was a joke? Have any of you actually been in there?" Dougall demanded.

"Hell, no," Nelson screamed between fits of hysterical laughter. "What kind of freaks do you think we are?"

"I'll give you credit, though," Thomlin added, "you made it farther than any of us ever did."

"So, no one has spent short-time with her?"

"Only the artillery guys," Thomlin said. "For some reason the artillery guys love the midget."

Still laughing, Nelson put his arm around Dougall and the group walked out of the bar. Foster quietly departed to meet up with a group of other men standing outside. Nelson, Thomlin, and Dougall continued walking toward the heart of downrange where a large crowd of soldiers covered the street.

7

WALK OF SHAME

Private Ko quickly scrubbed the sinks in the latrine and finished his remaining tasks before preparing for lights out. He hung all of his items for the next day neatly, in precise order in his wall locker. The hum of the floor buffer buzzed in his ears and Ko barely noticed another young soldier approach.

"Is it true?" the soldier asked as Ko closed up the locker.

"Is what true?"

"They say you were assigned to an American unit. Were you?"

"Do you believe that?" Ko asked. He stared at the other soldier. The soldier had been in the unit for only a few weeks.

"No," the soldier smiled. "You're too tall."

"That's right. I knew since I was younger that I would end up here."

"If you were a little taller you might have been selected for one of the honor guard positions at Panmunjom."

The eldest of three siblings, Ko Songyung was tall by Korean standards. His father was no taller than five and a half feet, yet his oldest son was almost six feet tall. The South Korean Army posted only their tallest soldiers along the DMZ. It was a psychological ploy to intimidate the North Korean Peoples Army. North Korea's tallest soldiers stared back.

"You didn't answer the question. Were you?"

"Yes, I was," Ko responded after a moment. "My initial orders sent me there, but then I came here."

"Why? It would be easier to serve with the Americans."

"No. They expect too much. They are too hard on the Koreans in their units. Harder on us than their own soldiers. If you don't speak English well, or if they don't like you, they send you away for weeks as punishment."

Ko thought about the weeks of grueling exercises and hard labor that came with what the Americans called retraining. He clenched his teeth at the thought of being slapped in the face by the Korean sergeants in charge.

"So they sent you here?"

"It's better to be here," Ko said. "I feel bad for the ones assigned to the Americans. They do everything the Americans ordered because they are helpless to do otherwise."

The other soldier was silent for a moment before nodding and walking back to his bunk.

They sent me here, Ko thought. Because of them, I have to endure this.

■ ■ ■

Most of the activity downrange was around one of the nightclubs, Crossroads, the most popular in Dongducheon. Nelson, the largest of the group, barged his way to the front entrance.

The club was even more jammed than the street out front. Speakers lining the back wall were maximizing the sounds of the latest track from Roo'ra, a K-pop band. The words that weren't drowned by the bass sounded like gibberish, but that didn't stop most of the Americans on the dance floor from trying to lip synch the chorus. The song that screamed through the club had been played and re-played so many times that Thomlin initially thought it was the South Korean national anthem when he first arrived.

Amazingly, the bass from the speakers actually made Thomlin's internal organs vibrate in unison with the song. Thomlin had a feeling that if he made it to old age he would pay for this short excursion into the club. Nelson turned his head to Thomlin and mouthed something he couldn't comprehend. Strobe lights were flashing at a machine gun pace, turning every action into a disjointed movement like something from the early attempts at motion pictures. Other colored lights whipped around the place making it nearly impossible to make sense of anything. The DJ switched tracks to a deafening version of La Bouche's "Be My Lover." Nelson was shouting at the top of his lungs but it didn't matter. He turned his head and began skirting the dance floor with Thomlin and Dougall close behind.

After a ten minute struggle, they finally made a rush to the bar. Nelson was waving money in the air and shouting for the attention of the bartender. The bartender pulled close to Nelson and Thomlin watched Nelson mouth the word "Tequila" several times and finally the bartender nodded in comprehension. Three shot glasses materialized moments later. Thomlin quickly attempted to swallow the worst tasting tequila he had ever thrown down his throat and noticed two Korean women eyeing them.

Thomlin remembered a conversation with the first Korean woman he went out with when he arrived in country.

"You can tell the difference between officers and soldiers," she told him, "just by looking at them."

"How's that?" Thomlin asked

"The way they dress," she explained referring to how most enlisted soldiers dressed down, wore sagging jeans, faddish t-shirts not tucked into their pants, baseball hats hung low, all trying to look tough. Officers dressed more like they belonged in some college bar or frat house rather than down in the ville.

Thomlin shot a glance back to the two girls who were still locked on to them. He decided it was time to make contact so he waved them over. They looked apprehensive but moved in their direction.

"Hi, I'm Abe Lincoln, this is Billy Shakespeare, and this is Ron Reagan," Nelson said.

Both of them smiled and nodded at the introductions. Nelson pulled near and asked them if they wanted a drink while Dougall stood in the background. As Nelson pulled money from his wallet Thomlin scanned the surrounding bar.

Thomlin turned to his right and noticed the most beautiful Korean woman he had seen since he had been stranded in his foreign home. She was standing only a few feet from him wearing a short, sleeveless black dress. Her silky black hair hung straight down just inches past her exposed shoulders. Unlike most of the women in the room, this woman possessed a full figure and the dress exposed perfectly sculptured tan legs. Thomlin could not help but to stare for a moment or two before she leveled her gaze on him, noticing his appraisal. She tilted her head slightly as if to welcome some comment. Thomlin decided that he must meet her. In the absence of orders, always attack, he thought.

"Dougall, you're going to pinch hit for me," Thomlin said as he grabbed Dougall by the shoulders and pushed him toward the Korean girls standing in front of them. Thomlin turned and headed for his new interest.

"Hi. My name Greg. You likey me buy you drinky?"

"You are absolutely amazing, you know that?" the woman said.

Thomlin's mind cleared for a moment and he recognized the young woman. The tips of his ears were sizzling and his throat felt like he was trying to swallow a pad of steel wool.

"You're Mae Sook's friend."

"I already told you. Her name is Byung Soon, you jackass."

"I'm sorry, you know, I didn't mean to, ah, you know, come off that way," Thomlin faltered. He silently cursed himself for the lame attempt at a recovery.

"Hey, don't bother, okay? This is typical from you soldiers," she said while casually looking around the club.

"Well, you know, I'm not just a soldier, I'm an officer." Thomlin couldn't stop himself. As the words left his lips he wanted to physically catch them in the air before they were heard. "Set U Free" by Planet Soul began to thump through the club. Thomlin was starting to sweat.

"And what is that supposed to mean to me?" she asked with the same bored expression, but with a little more edge in her voice.

"What I meant to say was that I'm not your average GI. I've been here for a while, longer than most of the people around here, and I usually don't play the part of the ugly American."

She shot him a look of utter disbelief.

"I, um, know how you must feel, you know, with all these guys constantly trying to hit on you, treating you like you're, uh, not an American," Thomlin rambled on. He knew he had dug himself into a moon-sized crater. The comment almost made her laugh with disbelief at how stupid he sounded.

"You know how I feel? How in the hell can you know how I feel? Do dozens of American men come up to you on a nightly basis and talk to you in broken English, like you're an idiot or a small child?"

She was no longer checking out the scenery, her dark brown eyes were completely focused on Thomlin. Her lips were slightly puckered and even Thomlin realized that she was now extremely upset. If it was possible, there was even more blood flowing to Thomlin's swelling face and head. He found it hard to meet her gaze. He knew that the proper thing to do was to just walk away with his tail between his legs, mutter an apology, and head for the door. However, something inside him froze his body and prevented him from moving.

"Like I said, don't bother. Just do me the favor and leave me alone."

Out of the corner of his eye Thomlin could see Nelson laughing hysterically. Knowing that he would not live this one down once the men left the club, Thomlin decided to take the offensive.

"If you don't want to be hassled, then why do you come alone to a place mostly populated by American soldiers who, chances are, will try to take you home?"

This last comment set her back a little. At the very least, she no longer looked mad. She now appeared slightly confused. Her eyebrows arched before scrunching together as she tried to figure his intentions. Thomlin showed a brief grin and gave her a look that signaled he was waiting for a response.

"What's your point? If you're still trying to come on to me, you're doing a pretty lousy job."

"It just seems to me that you have to be looking to meet someone here tonight. You came here alone so you can't pretend like you're having a girls' night out or something, Maybe I'm not the type of guy you're looking for. I admit I was trying a bad line on you, but now I'm just interested to find out why you're here if it's not to hook up." By now Thomlin was actually speaking the truth. He no longer cared if she wanted to be with him, he was just trying to salvage what was left of his pride.

"I'm sorry, but I don't think I have to explain myself to you."

"That's true, but that response just proves that I'm right."

"It just so happens that I came to see an old friend."

Thomlin gave a condescending look, "Sure. Since your mythical friend isn't around, why don't we buy each other a drink and continue this conversation?"

"You know, you really are an ass."

This didn't faze Thomlin nearly as bad as the first time she said it. He started to parry this with a quick retort but noticed some movement out of the corner of his eye. Two guys who looked no older than nineteen were starting to muscle their way to the small group. Thomlin tossed a warning expression to Dougall who looked confused.

"Shit," Thomlin cursed and momentarily forgot about the woman in front of him. In a fraction of a second Thomlin grasped the entire scenario. The two women at the bar Nelson and Dougall were hitting on were already claimed by two other soldiers. Thomlin knew it didn't take a tabloid psychic to predict the outcome.

"Hey, fight heading our way," Thomlin shouted over the thumping music. Thomlin instinctively knew the two approaching men would try to start some drunken bar brawl in which the three lieutenants would all get snagged by the cops, put in the Penalty Box, receive reprimands, be restricted to Camp Kayes indefinitely, and Watts would have a cerebral orgasm at the outcome. As this revelation washed over Thomlin, Lady Luck threw herself to their rescue. When the larger of the two ensuing young men was only five feet away he accidentally knocked a beer bottle out of someone's hand. Instead of going straight to the floor and shattering, the bottle was projected upward and spilled all over a poor six-foot-five bystander.

Thankfully for Thomlin, the man wearing the beer was a good six inches taller and 20 pounds heavier than the oncoming jealous boyfriend. The larger man definitely wanted an apology. Too consumed with rage to pay any attention, the jealous boyfriend continued his frontal attack on the three lieutenants. The smaller of the oncoming duo was at least smart or sober enough to recognize the new threat and withdrew a few feet behind. The jealous boyfriend closed on Nelson fast when the Goliath in the new Budweiser suit clamped his hands down on the back of the neck of the approaching man, spinning him around until they were both face to face. Spit and obscenities came from the larger man, when suddenly, a beer bottle crashed into his temple. The smaller soldier had not backed down as Thomlin suspected, but merely outflanked his larger opponent.

Thomlin almost managed a smile as he turned to Dougall and Nelson and said, "Let's make like a prom dress."

Thomlin turned to see the Korean-American woman duck behind the bar. He felt the urge to stare at the woman a little longer before Nelson pulled him away.

"Forget the damn girl," Nelson shouted as he pushed Thomlin forward.

The three men darted for the front door, slipping their way through the dance floor as all hell broke loose. Like the bell at the beginning of a boxing match, the broken bottle immediately signaled everyone with penned up frustrations to relieve their tensions on the face of the nearest person. The DJ never missed a beat as the tracks changed to Real McCoy's "Another Night." Thomlin, Nelson, and Dougall all made it to the doors as military police flooded through the bar with raised batons.

Luck again smiled on the trio as Thomlin looked up to see the battalion executive officer, Major Streeter. Streeter was talking to another officer when the lieutenants got his attention to give him a get-out-while-you-can look. Watts was nowhere to be found. The three stepped it out toward the main gate of Kayes as fast they could while trying to appear as inconspicuous as possible. They made a conscious effort not to run, like they were fleeing the scene of a crime. Thomlin breathed a sigh of relief and silently thanked God for Major Streeter. The lieutenants cut through an alleyway back toward the main gate.

As the lieutenants crossed through the military checkpoint flashing their identification cards, Thomlin made a quick glance over his shoulder and noticed Watts standing off in the distance. It was too dark to make out the expression on his face, but Thomlin could feel what was going through his mind. Watts was privately cursing himself for missing a golden opportunity. Whether he saw them leave the bar or not, he knew that Thomlin was somehow involved in the incident. There was an audible sigh of relief from the three lieutenants as they walked within the limits of Camp Kayes, their sanctuary.

They walked another 50 yards to the bus stop. A massive crowd of soldiers awaited the arrival of the next and final bus for the night. As the bus approached, people began to violently jockey for position closest to the door.

"Hey, let's form a line," a lone sober voice in the crowd screamed helplessly. Bursts of slurred obscenities followed.

As the bus door opened the crowd transformed into a riot.

"Body bridge," voices in the back of the mass shouted as they pushed forward. The weight of the rushing mob propelled the people in front of the door onto the stairs as the soldiers behind them used the downed personnel as a human stepping platform.

"My legs, my legs," screamed a crumpled soldier. "I can't feel my legs."

"Stay down, doormat," another soldier screamed as he climbed over the bodies to get into the bus.

More obscenities were heard from the fallen soldiers as their only defense against the oncoming stampede. Anyone caught on the sides of the open door was crushed against the side of the bus. Thomlin noticed a few military police soldiers standing aloof on the rim of the mob, helpless against the sea of enraged drunks. Dougall briefly spotted several punches being thrown and hands attempting to grapple other soldiers.

Thomlin turned to his two companions and said, "Well, boys, I guess it's another Walk of Shame for us tonight."

"I really didn't expect anything else," Nelson grinned and those were the last words spoken for a while as they started their journey in silence. They staggered past the post exchange, the commissary, a few barracks, the Turtle Farm and another crowd of people hopelessly waiting to get on the last bus. They made it over a half-mile in the thick, damp air before Dougall finally broke the somber mood.

"Is this what I can expect every weekend?" he asked.

"No, you can expect this most every night you're in garrison," Nelson laughed and then corrected himself. "Actually, it's not quite this bad on the weekdays, mostly just the weekends. In the winter it gets so cold that people don't want to do the Walk, so they'll stick to the camp. But believe me, there are lots of die-hard soldiers like us on Camp Kayes who won't care about the weather."

"Do you ever wonder about being caught off guard? I mean,

what about an alert or a real life go-to-war scenario?" Dougall asked.

This time Thomlin answered the question that had been on Dougall's mind all night, or probably since he touched down in Seoul. "Let me tell you a story about a buddy of mine over at the mechanized battalion down the street from us. He was convinced last winter that the North Koreans were going to attack on Christmas Eve, which would be a logical assumption considering a lot of soldiers are on leave and everyone else is celebrating. He had his platoon locked down in the motor pool going through pre-combat inspections and rehearsals over and over again. Every single soldier, for Christ sake! Merry Christmas, sarge. Here's your Christmas present. Oh look, it's a fresh oil change for your Bradley fighting vehicle. Aren't you happy?

"Did the North decide to invade? No way. Where was I that same night? I'll tell you where I was. I was downrange getting more liquored up than humanly possible. Every morning you'll see something about North Korea on the front page of *Stars and Stripes*. Get used to it. Every incoming commander, from company commander to brigade commander, likes to believe that they are going to fight the great battle of the century during their year of command. You hear it every time they give their change of command speeches. 'The North Koreans are coming, men, I know this for a fact, and we happy few will stop them here,' and so on. I honestly believe that it's not going to happen. The North Koreans are starving themselves to death and cannot maintain a war for any significant period of time. Besides, even if they do attack and catch us running around with our pants around our ankles we'll most likely get wiped out within the first 48 hours. It'll be the reinforcements from the States that win the war."

At last this seemed to quell any further questions from Brent Dougall. The men walked the last half-mile in complete silence until they reached their hooch.

■ ■ ■

Major Jeremy Streeter pushed open the door to Kim's as the white interior lights turned on.

"Last call," someone yelled. A few soldiers noticed the uniformed major and began to stagger toward the exit.

Streeter walked slowly around the bar without making eye contact with any of the bargirls. He slumped down into a wooden booth near the DJ. He could hear the old bench creak under him as he shifted his weight.

"Good to see you. It been a while," Miss Kim smiled gently as she took a seat across from Streeter.

"I've been busy. Lots of work. Even tonight, I had to work."

Miss Kim motioned to one of the girls at the bar. "I get you drink."

"Sorry," Streeter replied. "I'm on duty. No drink for me."

Miss Kim nodded as a young girl brought a bottle and two shot glasses to the table. Miss Kim poured soju into the glasses and said softly, "Always working. I understand. You important man."

Streeter laughed. "Me? Who am I? I'm no one special."

"You major. That make you important man."

"Unfortunately, I didn't make major fast enough."

"What you mean? You still major. Why it matter how fast you be major?"

"Well, it used to give me a knot in my stomach to salute the guys I knew as lieutenants. They got choice assignments and I always managed to get the jobs no one else wanted, in places no one wanted to go. You have no idea," Streeter said. He was rambling and caught himself. He glanced at the woman sitting across from him. She was leaning forward, cupping her glass as she looked empathetically at Streeter.

"Still, you major and that make you important man here. Your colonel need you," she said.

Streeter rolled his shoulders back and looked at the ceiling. "Yeah, I guess so. The old man is probably the best commander I ever had. He's done all the things I ever wanted to do. He trusts me and I would do almost anything to protect him."

"Of course he trusts you. You are his major."

Streeter glanced around the bar. The soldiers had all returned to post. The bargirls worked quickly wiping down the bar and sweeping the floor. When he turned back to Miss Kim, she was holding a shot glass for him.

"You worry too much, Jeremy. Have drink with me. Just one."

Streeter took one more look around the bar. "Hell, okay. One won't kill anyone."

■ ■ ■

Dougall arrived at his quarters in the old Quonset hut and slowly prepared himself for sleep. For the first time since he joined the battalion he reflected for a moment and assessed his mentor, Thomlin. Thomlin was definitely likeable. Never one to take things too seriously, Thomlin had a sense of humor that would make life in Korea enjoyable. Dougall could picture Thomlin in college, probably in a fraternity, or at least someone with a close group of friends. One of the guys, others would say. As an officer, Dougall guessed Thomlin would be rated as middle of the pack, never making serious mistakes to cause a negative performance appraisal, but never outshining many of the other lieutenants. It was likely that Thomlin didn't care. Dougall thought Thomlin would be happy as long as anything didn't interfere with his social schedule.

What a strange place, Dougall thought. It was definitely not what he imagined back at the Officer Basic Course. Before flying overseas he read everything he could about the country. He was fascinated with the country's rich history. He was amazed that Koreans could trace their ancestry back 6,000 years to the Neolithic sites that had been discovered in the Han River basin near Seoul. Evidence of early urban civilization coincided with the founding of other ancient cities in the Tigris-Euphrates River Valley of Mesopotamia.

Dougall studied everything from a military perspective, from the invasion of the Chinese over 2,000 years ago, to the Mongols, followed by the Japanese, and later the Manchus. He knew that Korea only had a few brief centuries around 600 AD to experience complete self-rule when the country was divided between three kingdoms. Dougall even bought language tapes to prepare him for meeting native Koreans and he studied the religions of Confucianism and Buddhism. Now he wondered how that effort had anything to do with what he saw earlier that evening.

He expected constant vigilance and preparations for combat but now realized his assignment would involve the potential monotony of garrison life and the avoidance of career-ending mistakes. He already began to wonder where he would go after leaving Korea.

Kneeling down, staring at the green wool blanket on his bunk, he hoped Thomlin and the others were leading him in the right direction. He completed his nightly ritual with a quick prayer and slipped underneath the blanket. Like the other members of his party, he fell asleep alone.

8

MOVEMENT

As to be expected, Miss Kim's information was accurate. Thomlin woke to the sound of a fist slamming on his door.

"Red Thunder! Red Thunder!" a voice shouted from the opposite side. Red Thunder was the code word for an alert. Incoming personnel were taught never to say the word "alert" over the phone for the fear of informants that might be listening. It was a small security measure, but it was something that the command enforced vehemently. The security measure was reinforced to such an extent that no one even bothered to talk about alerts; they simply used the code word. Thomlin could hear the phrase shouted by different lieutenants over and over again in the hallway as people started shuffling about to grab their gear and head for their companies.

Thomlin gathered his duffel bag and field gear and headed to the first floor of the company barracks where Nelson was already standing there with a mug of coffee. Behind him, the arms room door was open with a line of people waiting to receive their respective weapons. Thomlin nodded good morning and moved upstairs to his platoon area. As to be expected, Wilson already had the platoon moving in an organized frenzy. Most of the soldiers had their rucksacks, Kevlar helmets, and other equipment, placed right outside their doors.

After throwing his gear in his office, Thomlin went back downstairs to receive the warning order, the 'heads-up' of what's happening. Captain Watts was over at battalion receiving the mission brief, so Thomlin wandered into Nelson's office to get the word. Dougall, with a neatly pressed uniform, was standing with AJ Fox, a tall lanky black man from Texas. Fox, an artillery officer, was the company Fire Support Officer. In combat, Fox would be the company's vital link to the big guns that would support the company's maneuvers. In garrison, he usually became the butt of jokes from infantry lieutenants like Nelson and Thomlin.

When Thomlin entered, Nelson kicked back behind his desk, yawning.

"Hey guys," Nelson said as Thomlin entered and sat down, "it looks like the usual. We'll move out this morning to Tent City, shoot the usual ranges for the first week and spend the next week and a half in and out of the field. Any questions? No? Good, because I don't have the answers."

■ ■ ■

Captain Watts stood with the other company commanders in the battalion commander's office waiting for Lieutenant Colonel Gibson. The men jumped to their feet as Gibson entered, followed by his executive officer. Gibson gave orders and checked the company status from each of his captains. The mission and movement to the field were routine but Gibson's low voice was tense. Within minutes, the final order of movement was given and Gibson dismissed the commanders.

"Joe," Gibson informally requested, "can you hold up for a minute?"

It wasn't unusual for the battalion commander to refer to his company commanders and staff officers by first name in private.

"How's your lieutenant doing with the Report of Survey?" Gibson asked casually once the other captains had left the room.

"Work in progress, Sir. He'll be done prior to the deadline."

"I'll just be glad when this damn thing is over with." Gibson took a seat behind his desk and leaned back.

"I understand, Sir," Watts responded.

Gibson swiveled his chair and stared at the plaques and pictures that adorned the wall. The photos and framed unit flags were not in chronological sequence. The order was only important in Gibson's mind. He had served all over the world in many units and he was proud of his career. It was not personal pride in his own accomplishments but the satisfaction of serving with units that performed well and earned respect.

"Did I ever tell you that I jumped at the chance to come here, to command in Korea?" Gibson said without turning away from the wall. "It's sometimes more difficult to command in a peacetime army. There's so much scrutiny on things, little things. In war, no one would really give a damn, but in peacetime, some things tend to take a life of their own."

"Yes, Sir."

"Before I came here, and before you took company command, the reputation of the 77th was not that stellar. The only thing I really wanted was for all of us to make a difference. To leave this unit better than we arrived."

"Yes, Sir," Watts responded quietly, confused.

"You think Lieutenant Thomlin will get this done quickly and properly?" Gibson turned back to face Watts.

"Yes, Sir. I'll see that he gets this done."

"Look, Joe, I don't want to rush things at the expense of not doing anything to standard. But all of us have worked hard—you, the other commanders, the staff—to bust ass and make the 77th stand out among all the other infantry units here on Kayes. I hate the thought of one fuck-up tarnishing the reputation of the battalion."

"Yes, Sir. I agree."

Gibson knew that any hope of getting a brigade command would rest on his evaluation as a battalion commander. He shook his head and tried to push the thought from his mind. He didn't want his own personal motivation to interfere with the situation.

"Whatever the outcome, whichever way this thing ends up falling, just do it right," Gibson said quietly. He was frustrated and wanted to push but knew it could not be done overnight.

"Sir," Watts replied, "I realize the importance of coming to closure with this. In my assessment, it is more important that we do this correctly than just slamming it through quickly. Give my lieutenant the time allotted and I will assure you that it will be done properly, even if I have to get involved."

Gibson let out a breath before nodding his head in agreement. Watts was dismissed and quickly exited. Gibson waited for the door to close.

"I hate having this damn black mark on the battalion's record."

"Yes, Sir," Streeter said.

Gibson was quiet for a moment and then said, "At least this is all a learning experience for you. For when you take command someday."

Streeter tried to lighten the mood, "Let's face it, Sir, that'll probably never happen. Too much time spent in staff positions and not enough time standing in front of soldiers. I'll be happy if and when they hand me the next rank."

Gibson studied Streeter carefully and didn't reply.

"Don't worry, Sir. These past nine months in the battalion have been some of the most enjoyable in my career. I'll make sure we clean this up."

Gibson leaned back in his chair, clasping his hands across his chest.

"Jeremy, you've been a great executive officer. There's no one else I would want as my right arm. I've always appreciated your counsel, you know that?"

"Thank you, Sir," Streeter replied trying to appear humble.

When Streeter left the room, Gibson turned his attention back to the wall. Gibson wondered where the plaque would be placed which he would ultimately receive when his command was done in four months.

■ ■ ■

The Alpha Company lieutenants sitting in Nelson's office were silent until Ward rushed in with the latest gossip.

"Hey, did you hear about the spec four over in Headquarters Company?"

The other three men gave Ward a confused look. It was obvious that Ward had tapped the soldiers' pipeline of information before any of them.

"One of the soldiers over there stumbled through the gate at two o'clock this morning with no pass, drunk, and covered in blood. The MPs nabbed him, but the guy said he couldn't remember a damn thing. Must have been one hell of a rough night."

"Where's this guy now?" Nelson asked.

"The MPs brought him back to the unit. They only have a holding tank down there at the station and no real place to keep soldiers longer than a few hours. I guess Captain Hadley went and claimed him. Now this guy gets to hang out in the rear while the rest of us go to the field."

"I bet Hadley's having a fit right about now," Thomlin joked as he thought for a moment about the Headquarters Company commander, Captain John Hadley. "He's probably one of the few officers that absolutely lives by the rules without any deviation. He's the most anal-retentive commander I've ever seen."

"That's probably why he's so successful as the headquarters commander," Nelson said.

Headquarters Company was the largest company in the battalion from a personnel standpoint. HHC, as it was known, included all the support elements of the unit, from the mechanics in the motor pool, to the medical platoon, to the cooks in the dining facility. It was a tough job, typically given to senior captains that had already proven themselves by commanding other line companies.

"HHC is Hadley's very first company command, but he does the job better than anyone can remember," Thomlin informed Dougall.

"I don't remember him from the Hail and Farewell."

"You wouldn't. Hadley doesn't look like much. He's the real thin captain with a face that looks like a hawk. He's always darting around like he's looking for something out of place. I can just imagine the look on his face when he got the phone call to go down to the police station and pick up one of his soldiers,"

Thomlin laughed.

"So, he's like Captain Watts?"

"No. He doesn't even raise his voice. When he's really pissed, there's a slow whispering sound that comes from his throat. Like air seeping from a tire."

"And you know this how?"

"I've been on the receiving end more than once. A couple of us, led by Nelson, got a little drunk once in front of the Quonset huts. We woke Hadley from his ritual eight-hour nightly sleep and he got a little upset."

"As I remember, he was more than just a little upset," Nelson laughed.

"Yeah," Thomlin said, "and as I remember, I was the only one getting my ass chewed in the middle of the night."

Nelson and Ward chuckled. The conversation in Nelson's office quickly died down with the absence of any additional rumors. Thomlin left with Dougall close behind as both men went to their respective platoon areas for last minute preparations for the field. When Watts returned, he called the lieutenants back to his office, quickly relayed the information about the upcoming field exercise, and released them. Watts was unusually civil. There was no dramatic fanfare or sarcastic remarks toward Thomlin, only an order to get their platoons ready quickly and get on the road. Within 30 minutes, the soldiers of Alpha Company were aboard vehicles heading north.

■ ■ ■

Dougall and Thomlin sat in the back of the Humvee, both staring at the Korean landscape. Ward was riding shotgun with the butt of his M16 hanging out the window. As they approached a stop sign and started to slow the vehicle, Ward arched his body out the window. An old Korean man riding a bicycle was almost parallel with the vehicle. The bicycle style might have been popular in the States in the 1940s but seemed to be en vogue here. Ward nudged the man on the shoulder with his rifle, hard enough for the man to lose control of the archaic two-wheeler and fall onto the sidewalk. The driver screeched in pleasure as he spit the Copenhagen out his mouth in wild laughter.

"Yeah! One down, Sir."

Thomlin shook his head in disgust while Dougall carried a look of anger, pain, and shock rolled into one on his face, almost as if someone had just kicked him in the groin. And people wonder why Koreans think we're such assholes, Thomlin thought.

"That was completely unnecessary," Thomlin told Ward.

"C'mon, Thomlin, it's not like I hurt the guy," Ward joked. The vehicle traveled further down the road, with Ward making several more attempts to derail unsuspecting bikers.

There were no highways. It was a maze of poorly paved city streets woven through the city. The countryside was no better. Roads clung to the limited level ground between the countless mountains. What would take only fifteen minutes by helicopter or 30 minutes on a normal highway took over an hour and a half on the current road network. Many of the old timers, noncommissioned officers who were in Korea before the Olympics were held in Seoul back in 1988, could remember the time when most of the roads were still unpaved. On straight sections of road, large Hyundai trucks known as terminators and other rice rockets raced by and still managed to put the fear of God in Thomlin. The local populace certainly did not obey whatever mythical speed limits actually existed.

"Sir, we're coming up on Terminator Alley," the driver shouted as the vehicle approached an intersection with trucks moving through at warp speed. The trucks did not seem to notice or care about the small traffic light dangling over the center. The driver slammed the accelerator to the floor as they dodged and weaved through the intersection unscathed.

"Why are we going faster?" Dougall exclaimed as he moved closer to the middle of the truck and frantically searched for a safety belt.

"Everything is backwards here," Thomlin calmly explained. "The rule is to move, and move fast, or else become part of the pavement."

They cut through a small city called Pobwon-ni, a town slightly smaller than Dongducheon. The busy streets were lined with shops, plastered with Korean hieroglyphics. Unlike Dongducheon, there were no English translations on the shop windows. The sidewalks were teeming with Koreans moving about with no Caucasians in sight. Between the small Korean cars parked almost on top of each other on each side of the street and the ones flying toward them there was barely enough room to squeeze through. The roads were never built for vehicles as wide as the American Hummer. The roads narrowed to one lane as they began to leave the city. Twenty-foot cement walls line both sides of a short, one-lane section of the road ahead. On top of the walls large cement blocks rested on stubby brick legs.

"What's that?" Dougall asked, breaking a long silence.

"It's a rock drop," Thomlin answered. Certain things had become so commonplace to Thomlin that he forgot what it was like to see everything from a new perspective. Seeing that Dougall still didn't understand, Thomlin continued, "These things are found all over the place here in the northern part of the country. If there ever is a war, demo would be placed under the blocks and blown so that the blocks would fall, covering the road. This would at least slow the movement of North Koreans as they headed south. Up near Munsan you'll see a large brick or cement structure that looks like a bridge but it's really another elaborate rock drop."

"The Koreans assume that the North will actually stick to the roads?" Dougall asked.

"Of course not," Thomlin said. "In some of the streambeds they have smaller cement blocks or posts known as dragon teeth that are also designed to prevent the passage of tracked vehicles. Supposedly, most of the actual bridges that are built over roadways have spots built in them for placement of demolitions so they can be turned into makeshift rock drops if it becomes necessary. If you think about it, almost everything has a dual purpose here. This is a country that has been preparing itself for an inevitable war for over 40 years. Maybe it explains why they refuse to build a decent highway system."

"Inevitable war? I thought you said it was never going to happen."

"Not in my lifetime, brother. This year the monsoons will ruin the crops up north. In winter they'll suffer from starvation and the cold. Next summer they'll have a drought that will ruin all the crops again. Those people can barely fend for themselves, let alone afford to fight a protracted war. I certainly don't believe it will ever happen, but the South Korean military doesn't like taking chances."

Finally clear of Pobwon-ni, Dougall turned his sights on the local farms and rice paddies while Ward looked for something new to amuse him. There were no more cyclists in sight so he pulled his weapon out of the window. Suddenly the driver spotted a young Korean schoolgirl dressed in white standing at a bus stop approximately 100 yards ahead and closing. On the road before her was a large puddle left over from the daily monsoon rains. Thomlin immediately sensed what was going to take place. Ward snapped a grin at the driver who sneered back at him in an unspoken signal of agreement.

"Don't even think about it, man," Thomlin said from the back seat, but he knew it was useless. At the last second the truck lurched toward the bus stop, tires blasting into the water, spraying the girl with muddy shrapnel. The shock wave almost propelled the girl into the back of the bus stop. Against his will, Thomlin turned his head and saw the expression of terror on her face.

"Now, that was really unnecessary. You realize that?" Thomlin snapped.

The driver either didn't understand Thomlin or didn't care. Ward and the driver cackled as they sped down the road.

"Years from now that girl will probably be a student at the University in Seoul and protest against the American presence in Korea outside the gates of Kayes."

"Oh, well," Ward said. "She will anyway. This is what I call preemptive payback."

"Still, completely un-cool."

Dougall stared at Thomlin with a look that seemed to question whether Thomlin was going to do something more. Thomlin shrugged and turned to face the back of Ward's head.

"You know, that was pretty sick. You know you were wrong," Thomlin said.

"Relax. I'm sure she'll be fine," Ward replied. "What do you want me to do, go back and apologize?"

"Forget it. You're hopeless."

Thomlin struggled for the right words before leaning back into the seat. He could feel Dougall still staring at him, but he did not face him. The driver was still laughing. Abruptly, the sick laughter stopped as something ahead caught the driver's attention. Thomlin silently prayed that it was not another schoolgirl.

The road ahead leading to Munsan split into two and Thomlin started to make out someone lying on the pavement at the fork. As the vehicle neared the divide Thomlin could clearly see an old, overweight Korean woman covered in red lying spread eagle, face up. Her long, dark hair was matted to the side of her face and to the asphalt. The long cloth skirt she was wearing was hiked up, revealing one of her fleshy thighs. On the side of the road a large blue terminator was parked, the driver leaning against the front, smoking a cigarette. Hyundais and Daewoos sped by without slowing. There were no police racing to the scene or blaring sounds of incoming ambulances. The Humvee passed slowly so the driver could rubberneck and observe the scene in more detail.

"Wow. That's what you call road kill," the driver snorted.

"Shut up," Thomlin said. "Just keep your eyes on the road and keep moving."

Both Thomlin and Dougall focused their attention on the passing scenery as they continued on through Munsan. Munsan was a slightly upscale city compared to Dongducheon or Pobwon-ni. The streets were wider, the buildings a little more modern, and the area somewhat cleaner. And not a foreigner in sight, Thomlin thought.

The Humvee rolled to a halt in front of the one-lane bridge spanning the Imjin River, known as Freedom Bridge. The Koreans and Americans jointly controlled access to the bridge, carefully monitoring all traffic coming and going. Since the Imjin River was one of the few natural barriers that could slow a North Korean advance, the Koreans only had a few bridges spanning the distance and most were used strictly for military purposes.

"According to the popular rumor, which I believe," Thomlin leaned over and said to Dougall, "the bridges can be quickly rigged with explosives and dropped to the water to deny the enemy the advantage. The land beyond the river is void of large populations except for farms, rice paddies, ROK outposts, and U.S. Army training areas."

Dougall scanned the immediate area to his left and noticed the Korean tourists teeming around the Korean War monuments and small museum. They were dressed in what appeared as their Sunday best, enjoying the outing. This drew a cynical smile on Thomlin's face. Thomlin wondered if they were really aware that less than five miles from them there was no monument or museum, just armed guards and soldiers of an enemy nation that would like nothing better than to finish the job they failed to complete almost 50 years ago. His American mind could not comprehend what it would be like to live in a land where your enemies were so close and continuously posed a threat to everything you lived for. The smiling Korean families seemed immune to the danger they had known since their youth. A military vehicle loaded with ROK troops, all locked and loaded with live rounds, or a U.S. military convoy drew no special attention.

Thomlin noticed Dougall checking out the monuments. Thomlin leaned toward him and said, "It's not even worth spending the time to walk around it."

Dougall nodded his head. He stared at the long, slender gingko trees with their erratic branches lining the walkway. The manicured boxwood hedges ringed groups of brightly colored flowers. The large rounded crimson petals of Chinese peony bloomed next to the dark pink Japanese roses. Near the entrance of the museum, hydrangeas packed with white petals grew as tall as small trees.

"It looks pretty at least," Dougall said.

"I once went there and saw the whole scene," Thomlin continued. "It was all bullshit. They had this exact replica of an M1A1 Abrams tank, except it was called a K1 or something. There was an inscription underneath it in Korean and English that said something like, 'This is the K1A1 Korean tank, the most power-ful tank on the modern day battlefield. The Americans copied this design in order to develop their own.'"

"Unappreciative bastards, Sir," the driver chimed in from the front seat.

"You would think the Koreans would have some sort of moral appreciation for us," Ward said. "It's like what we did five decades ago didn't mean much. You would think that they would welcome us wherever we went."

"Maybe it's pride," Dougall said quietly.

"What do you mean?" Thomlin asked.

"I mean, our presence is a constant reminder to the Koreans that their nation is not completely self-reliant. Back in the States I watched the news showing Korean college students protest-ing the American military. Maybe it's, like, an insult to keep U.S. troops in the country. Koreans have some pretty strong feelings of national pride and all that."

"They need to read their history books," Ward snorted. "They're in self-denial. They need us."

"One thing is for sure," Thomlin said, "the younger generation wants us to leave."

"Again, they need to read some history or talk to the older gen-eration that felt the pain of war. Young Koreans have a problem. War is not real to them."

Dougall sat back and gave up the conversation. Thomlin was silent too and stared at the Korean families walking into the mu-seum. Thomlin wanted to agree with Ward but couldn't bring himself to say it.

"I don't know," Thomlin said looking at the window. "I guess I can't speak for them. I'm not Korean."

9

TENT CITY

A few miles north of the Imjin River, Private Ko went through his daily routine, checking his watch every few minutes. Only a few weeks prior Ko had heard rumors about a famous tree in the midst of the DMZ checkpoints. At a section of the DMZ where the two Korean elements were at their closest to one another, there was a full-grown Daimyo oak tree on the North Korean side. The long branches from the 70-foot tree extended into the southern perimeter. From the chatter of the older soldiers, Ko overheard the rumors that the tree was the one sure way to communicate with someone on the other side of the DMZ.

Several soldiers had been caught leaving notes in the branches that were most likely retrieved by North Koreans. The soldiers were given mere administrative punishment for their actions, convincing Ko that the chain of command really didn't care about communicating with their northern counterparts.

After days of observing the tree and noticing other soldiers leave notes in the branches, Ko decided to do the same. It was easy to leave and retrieve notes without being caught. The initial notes he pulled from the branches seemed generic, one asking for American-made equipment and another asking for information on personnel.

Ko dismissed these messages and almost gave up on the idea of communicating the northern side until one evening he read the message he had been searching for. Earlier in the day he plucked a note from the tree and stuffed it into his uniform pocket. He almost forgot about the note until later that night when he was writing a letter home. He pulled the message and smiled as he read the note.

The words on the slip of paper depicted the daily routines of a North Korean soldier. I knew it, Ko thought, he is no different than me. The note was signed with the soldier's initials and the next day Ko used the initials to leave a personal note to the soldier. Ko asked for more details of what life was like in the North and made up initials to sign the note to avoid discovery in case someone else were to read the message.

Soon, Ko looked forward to exchanging messages with his North Korean counterpart more than anything else. Ko eventually disclosed how much he hated being in the army and how he wanted their country to be unified again. Then one early afternoon he found a message with instructions on how he could help his northern comrade.

■ ■ ■

Thomlin's vehicle rolled slowly toward the bridge. There were three Korean soldiers, all locked and loaded with live ammunition, waving them through the entrance as they neared the first checkpoint. Standing next to the Korean soldiers were three American soldiers from the lieutenants' sister battalion, the 2-77th Infantry, with unloaded M16s.

"Stands alone," the American soldiers saluted and spouted off their battalion motto as the vehicle passed.

"Yeah, but you sleep together, you bunch of homos," the driver yelled as he hung out the window.

"Nothing like a little camaraderie and cohesion among American fighting soldiers," Thomlin laughed.

The Humvee tires seemed to rattle the bridge as the driver carefully drove over the old wooden planks. The bridge itself was a mammoth steel structure for Korea, sitting almost 100 feet over the Imjin River on large stone pillars. The floor of the bridge was wooden and always created the impression that a heavy vehicle could plunge through the middle at any given moment. Dougall silently hoped that the supposed explosives were not currently attached to the structure. Large spotlights were fixed to each side of the bridge at regular intervals to prevent anyone from messing around during hours of darkness. At last, the vehicle hit pavement again, passing the guard post on the far side as the driver repeated his performance of screaming profanity as they rumbled by.

"How many units are over there?" Dougall asked as they rolled passed the home of their sister battalion, Camp Guardian.

"Just the 2-77th. Camp Guardian is tiny compared to Kayes. Guardian only houses one battalion and no other major units," Thomlin said. He pointed to buildings behind the chain linked fence and concertina wire. "All that's there is the barracks, a small pizza shack, a few other buildings, and most importantly, the liquor store. Although the camp is small, the soldiers at Guardian put down more alcohol on an average weekend than all of Camp Kayes combined. You can usually see the large, white eighteen-wheeler full of Budweiser drive up through the gate on an average Thursday afternoon. The whiners on Kayes that work nine-to-five jobs always complain about the living conditions, but they have no right to complain compared to the soldiers stuck at Guardian. The soldiers there can only entertain themselves by either working out or drinking beer. Because they are north of the Imjin River, only a small percentage of the unit can take pass at any given time. Usually, soldiers of the 2-77th come down to Camp Kayes to party and see how the other half live."

"Check it out," Thomlin quickly pointed out Dougall's side of the vehicle.

On the opposite side of Camp Guardian, Thomlin could barely see the red flag of North Korea hanging in the distance.

"That's pretty hardcore," Dougall said. "If you were assigned up here you'd get up every morning and stare at the North Korean flag."

"I'm not sure if it makes a difference," Thomlin said.

"You don't think you would view things differently from up here?"

"What? Like, a greater sense of purpose?"

"Yeah. I mean, you can see right into enemy territory."

"No," Thomlin thought out loud. "I'd probably end up a complete alcoholic rather than just a weekend drinker if I were up here."

"It doesn't matter anyway," Ward piped up from the front. "The wartime mission of the 2-77th is to blow all their buildings and head south as quickly as possible."

Soon they were out of sight of Camp Guardian and passed near the last village separating them from Tent City.

"Is that that Camp Guardian's version of downrange?" Dougall asked, pointing to the village.

"Off limits," Thomlin said and didn't bother with any details. He had never learned the name of the village, but he knew that it was off limits to all U.S. personnel. He heard much talk that several years before he ever sat foot in country a young Korean girl was raped and murdered. Thomlin didn't remember hearing any big trial or scene like when a few marines in Okinawa raped two young schoolgirls, and he couldn't even remember if the suspect was ever caught or convicted. To Thomlin, it didn't matter. Deductive logic would indicate that if a girl was raped then it would have to be an American GI, since rape in Korea was almost unheard of.

On either side of the road Korean workers had plowed the earth flat for as far south as the men could see. Unmanned tractors and equipment were left in the distance toward the center of the cleared area.

"What are they building this far north?" Dougall asked.

"I heard rumors that the Koreans are actually building a real highway. A highway by American standards is unheard of this far north. Look how wide it is. It's large enough for two or even three lanes."

Dougall stared at the smoothed surface and said, "It looks like it heads straight toward the DMZ."

"The South won't need to finish the project because the North Koreans are probably already geared to use it." Thomlin could picture tractors and equipment on the north side of the DMZ poised ready to complete the endeavor of the South Koreans. It was hard for him to imagine that the South Koreans believed in the inevitable unity of their peninsula so fervently that they were building highways to link them with the North.

The vehicle finally pulled into Tent City, the unit's second home. Tent City was somewhat of a disappointment to anyone seeing it for the first time. It was only a couple of acres of land wrapped by a chain link fence and concertina wire. The two-story guard tower at the front gate was the only structure of its size in the area. The gravel path within Tent City forked, one direction heading toward the dining facility and the other toward the living quarters for most of the soldiers. All of the soldiers lived in the half-dozen rows of 16 by 32 foot tents. Each of the tents sat on top of a concrete slab used as the flooring and housed approximately 20 soldiers. Two rows of cots lined the inside of the tents. Although the cots were older than most of the soldiers that slept on them, it was a luxury compared to sleeping on the ground. The thick olive drab colored canvas easily held off the rainwater, but was ineffective against the local mosquitoes. In the winter time, stoves were erected inside the tents for some form of warmth against the cold Korean air.

At the far end of the compound a few permanent structures had been erected. The dining facility was the largest of three buildings, but could only be occupied by a couple of platoons at a time. Next to the dining facility was the compound's Post Exchange, a converted trailer that had been turned into a convenience store for the soldiers. On the other side of the dining facility was the cantina. It was a small concrete building where soldiers could go and relax when they were done with the daily activities. It was also the only place where soldiers were allowed to drink alcohol. Each soldier had a nightly two-beer limit on the 40-ounce Korean beers that were sold at the cantina, although who actually enforced the rules was a mystery.

The Humvee rolled to a stop in front of Alpha Company's designated tents. Thomlin and Dougall stepped out, grabbed their field gear, and headed to the tent that would house their respective platoons. After dropping his equipment, Dougall headed to find Thomlin.

Taking a seat on the opposite cot from Thomlin, Dougall asked, "So, about the whole black box thing… What's the big deal?"

Thomlin glanced around to ensure no one else was in earshot. Wilson had most of the younger soldiers move out of the back opening of the tent to perform some duties outside. After thinking for a few moments, Thomlin answered, "As I told you, we lost it the last we came to the field. We only spent two days searching for it. Suddenly, we stopped and then went home. The last unit on Kayes that lost a sensitive item was out in the field for over a month looking for it, and yet, we only spent about 48 hours. It was like, everyone just gave up."

"Why?" Dougall asked.

"Slicky Boy," Thomlin answered in defeat.

"What?"

"Slicky Boy," Thomlin repeated. "Haven't you already heard the rumors about Slicky Boy? Why do you think every piece of equipment is tied down to every soldier? Some say that North Korean Special Forces are required to infiltrate into South Korea and return with a stolen piece of U.S. Army equipment in order to graduate. You know, like an initiation. I really think it's just the local Koreans. They follow us to the field sneak through the night and take what they can to later sell on the black market."

Slicky Boy reached almost mythical proportions within American units in Korea. To anyone's knowledge, no one had ever caught Slicky Boy or even had any sort of physical evidence that he even existed. Slicky Boy was more elusive than Big Foot. Whenever a soldier lost any piece of equipment out in the field, Slicky Boy was always the prime suspect. Slicky Boy could penetrate American lines with ease, take what he wanted, and silently slip away. Soldiers took great efforts when they went to the field to thwart the Korean enigma. Gear was tied down, guarded, checked and rechecked numerous times, and company canine mascots were even brought to the field. At times, these efforts proved useless as soldiers would awake and find something amiss.

"What do you think happened?" Dougall asked.

"Slicky Boy, I guess. At first I didn't care because we were heading home. Then a couple of weeks later I was slapped with the Report of Survey. Now I have to go through the nut roll of getting all this shit done just so I can determine whether someone didn't guard against Slicky Boy enough or if Slicky Boy was just too good this time."

"But why take the black box? What about a weapon?"

"Weapons are too risky for Koreans. People back home can bitch as much as they want about the new five-day waiting period to buy a firearm, but there's no second amendment in this country. They're not allowed to own any guns and the penalty could be death if they're ever caught with one. It's much easier for them to take something else and try to sell it. I just can't figure out how the black box got stolen. It was a black box from Headquarters Company and I don't even know why one of the soldiers would even have one out here during qualification week."

"I guess that's what you get to figure out." Dougall smiled.

"Lucky me," Thomlin sarcastically replied. "I just can't figure out why the unit gave up looking so easily and why everyone wants the report wrapped up as fast as possible. It's strange even by Korean standards. We have our own playbook here and you can usually rewrite the rules as you go. It's almost unnerving to be expected to follow regulations this efficiently. This is really starting to cramp my personal life."

"You mind if I ask you something? If all you have to do is write a report that says the black box got lost or stolen, why is it taking you so long to do it? Sounds like you could knock it out in a day."

Thomlin stared at Dougall. He knew he was procrastinating, but it was more than that. He found it difficult to explain his feelings even in his own mind.

"I don't know," Thomlin said. There was a touch of irritation in his voice. "Maybe I'm being hardheaded. It's just that I hate being pushed to do anything. You know why Sergeant Wilson and I get along so well? It's certainly not because I'm the most squared-away lieutenant he has ever seen. He knows I'm not just going to nod my head and simply follow every order. He trusts me to call bullshit if there is something that's not right, even if it means every senior officer in the battalion would line up to flame me one at a time. My soldiers know that too. I just feel like there's one easy answer that everyone wants and I don't like it."

Dougall nodded. Thomlin shook his head in frustration. He couldn't wrap his arms around the whole situation; he only knew that he hated the feeling of being pushed to do something. Dougall started to say something but stopped abruptly when he noticed a woman walk through the tent flap.

"Hey, guys," Foster smiled as she walked in. She was in battle dress uniform but not wearing any field gear.

"Well, if it isn't our local intelligence officer," Thomlin said dryly. "What brings you to our neck of the woods?"

"I had to come to Camp Guardian to meet with their battalion intel officer and since I was in the neighborhood, I thought I would visit my favorite group of knuckle-draggers. Besides, the food at Guardian is worse than eating roadkill. My driver and I wanted to grab a bite before we headed back."

"You just can't stay away from us," Thomlin shot back. Before Foster could come back with a remark, Thomlin stood and said, "I have to go check on the platoon. Brent, I'll meet you over at the chow hall."

Foster watched Thomlin exit the rear of the tent before taking a seat on his cot.

"How was the ride up here?" she asked Dougall.

"I guess it was pretty normal from what I've heard. You know, lots of crazy drivers, lots of nice scenery, a dead body in the middle of the road."

"Someone got run over?"

"Yeah, but no one seemed overly concerned."

"Let me guess, the dead body was a woman."

"How did you know that?"

"Because no one was overly concerned." Foster stared at the opening in the back of the tent.

"Would it be different if it were a man? I guess it's tough being a woman in this country."

Foster continued to stare at the rear of the tent and mumbled, "Even tougher to be an American woman over here."

Dougall switched subjects, "So what's between you and Thomlin?"

"Let's see," Foster said turning her gaze directly on Dougall. "Which story did Thomlin tell you? Was it the story that I'm a closet lesbian or was it the one where I was starring in my own porn production?"

"Actually, neither." Dougall blushed.

"I know all you men have this male bonding bullshit causing you to back up what each other says regardless of the story, but let me tell you, don't believe 90 percent of what you hear. Thomlin is far from perfect too. You know, just because I wasn't born with a penis doesn't mean I should be held to a different standard."

Dougall nodded slowly, unsure how to respond.

"I'm going to grab something to eat," Foster quietly said after a brief pause. "Have fun out here. I'll see you when you get back to Kayes."

Foster stood and went out of the front of the tent. Dougall shook his head, still confused about Foster's outburst. Gradually, Dougall unpacked some of his field equipment before leaving the tent and heading to his platoon area.

■ ■ ■

The soldiers at Tent City barely noticed the afternoon blending into the evening as they busily prepared for the next day's activities. Between orders and preparations soldiers found ways to amuse themselves and pass time. It was a process as old as standing armies. In the most austere Roman legions, soldiers were likely to be found playing games of chance to occupy their time while sitting between their temporary shelters. Soldiers in Thomlin's tent huddled around an overturned cardboard box to play a game of Spades. The soldiers, even the veteran noncommissioned officers, were fanatical about the game in which two pairs of card players sat opposite each other and silently tried to play off one another to beat the other team. Occasionally one of the team members would slap a card down and scream in victory while onlookers howled in amusement.

The card game was interrupted only when it was time to head to the mess hall. The soldiers shuffled down the main dirt road dividing Tent City and filed into the dining facility. It was a little tight inside, but soldiers didn't seem to care. Each enjoyed the hot meal and the short time in the air-conditioned building. As protocol required, Thomlin and Dougall were the last to eat, after all the members of their respective platoons grabbed a tray full of food. It was a small gesture, but one all officers took seriously. A cardinal sin was committed if an officer were to actually start shoveling food down his throat before his own soldiers had the opportunity. Napoleon first quipped that an army lived on its stomach, but there was more truth to the statement than any civilian would ever know.

Sergeant First Class Wilson sat at a corner table in the dining facility. Between gulps of food he barked orders at the soldiers.

"Five minutes, second platoon," he roared. "Stop your jaw-jackin' and hurry up."

Wilson was fixated on the younger soldiers and didn't notice Captain Watts standing over him with a tray full of food.

"Evening, Sergeant. You mind if I join you?" he asked as he pulled the chair across from Wilson.

"By all means, Sir," Wilson obliged. He stared at his commander for a moment and thought Captain Watts looked worn. He wondered what was weighing on his mind. Wilson genuinely respected Watts for the mere fact that the commander didn't give a damn about being popular. Watts was a hard-ass, but he was a consistent hard-ass. There was never any doubt what the expectations were or where he stood in his commander's mind. "Good to be back out here."

"Damn right," Watts sighed as he dropped into his seat. "Garrison is too boring and there are too many opportunities for soldiers to cause trouble. Speaking of trouble, how's your el-tee?"

"Lieutenant Thomlin is doing just fine, Sir," Wilson laughed. "I don't like to tell him, but I'm glad to have him. I don't want him to get a big head. He's squared away and works well with all the NCOs."

Watts nodded slowly and paused before responding, "I just get concerned about his active social life."

"Well, Sir, he lives by the motto: work hard, play harder."

"Yeah, well, he should be working hard on the Report of Survey he was assigned to."

"Sir, I am sure it will done on time and exceed the standard," Wilson reassured.

Watts changed the subject, "I remember when things here were different. You were here in the eighties, right? Back when we still actively patrolled the DMZ. The constant cycle of prepping for the field, conducting the patrols, and then standing down. It felt more real back then."

"Were you down at Kayes or up at Camp Guardian?" Wilson asked nonchalantly. "I think I may have missed you by about a year or two."

"I started down at Kayes and ended up at Guardian."

Wilson knew not to press his commander for details. The admission from Captain Watts that he spent time in two units in one tour had only one logical answer in Wilson's mind. Watts did not voluntarily switch units.

Wilson leaned closer to the captain and offered, "Sir, maybe the el-tee could benefit from your mentoring. Give him some war stories to chew on."

Watts dismissed the thought with the wave of his hand.

"Lieutenants like Thomlin have to learn through their own experiences. Besides, he's in your good hands."

"Absolutely, Sir. You can always count on me," Wilson said. He excused himself by shouting at the few remaining soldiers still eating and quickly left.

■ ■ ■

After dinner was over, Thomlin joined Ward, Nelson and Dougall at the Canteen. Each already had a large bottle of Korean brewed OB beer in their hands as Thomlin took his place. The Canteen wasn't much more than a 20-by-30 foot metal shack, but it was still a luxury to any soldier. Inside, a long bar lined one end and several tables and chairs were scattered throughout. No decorations were hung but a few vintage 1985 pinball and arcade games rested on the back wall. The poor lighting within the building hid the visual effects of those who surpassed the two-beer limit.

"Ready for an uneventful week?" Nelson asked the other lieutenants. "Tomorrow begins qualification week. The soldiers will qualify on their individual weapons for the next three days."

"We going to divide and conquer on this one?" Ward asked.

"Right," Nelson replied. "To make things more efficient, the soldiers in the company will split into groups and sent to the various ranges."

"I got dibs on the anti-tank range," Ward interrupted. "I'll take anything that explodes."

"No problem," Nelson continued, "Bravo Company will run the M60 machine gun range and M16 qualification. Charlie Company will take the grenadiers."

"Good. This will give us a chance to get a full tour of all the ranges," Thomlin told Dougall. And enough time to conduct a few of the mandatory interviews for the Report of Survey, he thought.

After finishing their second beer, the lieutenants left the Canteen and headed back down the road toward their platoon areas. The sun was gone and Tent City was in darkness save for a few lights around the perimeter and the light emitting from a tent as the flap opened from time to time.

"Did you really start a rumor that Foster was a lesbian?" Dougall suddenly asked.

The question caught Thomlin off guard and he started to laugh, "I don't remember starting that one, but I may have had a hand in passing that around. It does make for a nice story. Look, don't feel too bad for her. She brings it on herself. There are a lot of other women on Kayes that can act in a professional manner and don't have to screw their way to the top."

"Still…" Dougall trailed off.

"I'll tell you what I think," Thomlin said. "I think she's got a massive inferiority complex. I remember when she first showed up in country. She was out with a bunch of us. She started flirting with me and coming on strong but at the end of the night it burned her that I went home with a Korean girl I met downrange. Sorry, but I didn't come here to meet American women."

"When in Rome, do the Romans," Ward cackled.

"Ever since that time she's been a real pain in the ass," Thomlin continued. "She tries to take a lot of shots at me and get under my skin, but I give it right back."

"Maybe it's just hard for her to fit in," Dougall said thoughtfully.

"I don't buy it," Thomlin snapped. "Besides, that's her problem. She doesn't have to act the way she does. It's her choice."

Dougall started to say something else but was startled when a PA system suddenly come to life in the distance. A few high-pitched tones signifying the beginning of some program were quickly followed by a woman's voice speaking in Korean. The voice was speaking fast, as if the speaker was rushing to fill the air.

"What the hell is that?" Dougall asked. The noise made him stop in his tracks.

"It's a recording coming from the South Korean side of the DMZ. North Koreans blare propaganda to the South across the DMZ all night long, shouting the triumphs of the People's Republic. The South returns the same," Nelson laughed. The DMZ was almost a mile away but the words were clearly audible.

"At the DMZ the propaganda is played at eardrum popping

decibels to drown out the North Koreans," Ward added. "You'll get used to it."

In some strange way the PA system playing in the distance, in its alien language, was a comfort to Thomlin. The men settled into their areas with the rest of the members of their platoon. Soldiers were constructing netted cocoons around their cots to protect them from the onslaught of mosquitoes as Thomlin entered the tent. Thomlin quickly prepped his gear for the next morning and fell into a dreamless sleep on his cot.

10

RANGE WEEK

Thomlin awoke the next morning to find Wilson's face looming over him.

"Good morning, sunshine."

"Morning, Sergeant," Thomlin replied. "Will you please tell *ahgashi* that I'm ready for my morning massage with my cup of coffee?"

A few soldiers chuckled as Wilson shook his head and walked away. Wilson barked orders at the soldiers as they hurriedly moved in front of the tent. It was 5:30 in the morning and time for physical training. It didn't matter that the unit was in the field or that the rain beat steadily on the roof of the tent; physical fitness was conducted regardless of the terrain or conditions. It was one of the many things that separated the U.S. Army from other militaries around the world. American forces placed huge stock on physical prowess and endurance. For the 1-77th, it was almost a religion.

The entire battalion stood lining the dirt road in Tent City wearing their twelve-pound flak vests. Lieutenant Colonel Gibson stood in front of the battalion and saluted as each company commander gave the morning report. Nearly 400 men stood at attention in complete silence.

"Men," Gibson bellowed, "you know my motto. The 1-77th will not be Task Force Smith."

"No Task Force Smith!" the men yelled in unison. The words echoed through Tent City.

In 1950 when the North invaded, a small American contingency known as Task Force Smith was quickly overrun by enemy soldiers. Many physical fitness instructors, known as Master Fitness Trainers in the Army, used Task Force Smith as an example of why physical training was such a vital component of combat effectiveness.

"The stronger the body, the stronger the mind!" Gibson shouted and the men repeated his words.

Shortly after the North crossed the 38th parallel, American forces headquartered in Japan sent two infantry companies with assorted headquarters personnel and a supporting artillery battery to intimidate the North Koreans into halting their advance.

"General MacArthur once publicly called Task Force Smith an arrogant display of strength. People were convinced that the enemy would turn and run once they realized who they were fighting. They would have no choice but to back down or feel the full military weight of the awesome American power. However, the company was poorly trained and equipped with antiquated weapons. They were mentally and physically unfit for combat."

The average soldier of Task Force Smith was barely 20 years old and had never seen combat. Their commander was young too. Lieutenant Colonel Charles B. Smith, a West Point graduate, was only 34 but no stranger to combat. Smith followed his orders, left Japan for Korea on the first of July, and soon had his men deployed on a main highway between Suwon and Osan. The soldiers were confident. Many felt they would be lucky if they even got to fire a few rounds before the North Koreans turned and ran.

On the sixth of July, columns of T-34 tanks began streaming toward the American unit. The outdated antitank weapons were useless against their enemy and the tanks rolled by without engaging. The tankers dismissed the mild resistance as a minor roadblock and continued their advance. As tanks rolled toward the artillery battery many American soldiers abandoned the howitzers, leaving officers and NCOs to man the guns themselves. Soon, a six-mile-long column of enemy soldiers headed for Smith's position. The confidence among the American soldiers was now replaced with fear.

"There is an inherent link between physical fitness and psychological fortitude," Gibson went on. "Mental stamina is vital and it is only possible after a soldier has the physical stamina to withstand the challenges of war."

After taking a few dozen casualties, Smith had no choice but to withdraw. In modern army doctrine there is no mention of the word retreat. The word implies a disorganized, frantic, if not cowardly, run to the rear. Withdrawals are tactical. Units leapfrog in reverse to better fighting positions. However, Smith's tactical withdrawal that early July quickly became a chaotic mess. Soldiers left machine guns, recoilless rifles, and mortars for the enemy. The dead were left on the battlefield along with those too wounded to walk. Leaders lost track of their men. Units stopped leapfrogging for fear of being left behind and promptly turned to save themselves. Heavy casualties were sustained. Some soldiers were not found for days. Smith silently cursed the inexperience of his men, the poor equipment, and the poor intelligence. His unit was lost.

Gibson continued, "The soldiers of Task Force Smith only lasted seven hours in combat. That will never be us. For those of you who have not spent a winter here in Korea, let me tell you, it's pretty damn cold."

Some of the men chuckled. During the winter months the battalion could be found running down the main street on Kayes bundled to protect them against the piercing cold wind and snowfall.

"We will train regardless of the conditions, regardless of where we are," Gibson stated. "I don't care about the monsoon rains, the heat, the snow, or the cold. We will always train. Are you with me?"

A loud cheer came from the ranks. The soldiers were motivated and ready to punish their bodies. After rendering honors to the flag the soldiers turned and headed out of Tent City for a five-mile run. Within minutes, the soldiers were soaked with rainwater and sweat.

After the morning physical training, soldiers crammed into the small latrines to shower and change. Thomlin knew the day would be fairly routine. After breakfast and personal hygiene the soldiers would divide into their respective groups, board trucks, and head to the firing ranges. Thomlin quickly headed to the tent that housed Headquarters Company. Thomlin knew he would need to interview the company armorer for the Report of Survey since the armorer typically issued sensitive items and weapons to the rightful recipients.

Thomlin asked for the first soldier he found sitting on a cot, "Who's the armorer?"

"Sir, that would be Specialist Wickersham," the young soldier responded.

"Okay, where can I find him?"

"Kayes," the soldier responded. Seeing that Thomlin was puzzled at this answer, the soldier asked, "Sir, didn't you hear what happened to Wickersham last night?"

"Who the hell is Wickersham?" Thomlin blurted, irritated.

"Sir, Specialist Wickersham came through the gate the night before last covered in his own blood. Captain Hadley had to go pick him up."

"He was covered in his own blood?"

"I guess so, Sir. Captain Hadley has him back on post under watch by the rear detachment."

Shit, Thomlin thought. Without the armorer to talk to, Thomlin would have to wait until he got back to Kayes. He knew Watts would be on his ass but there was not much he could do out in the field. Thomlin shrugged off the thought and left the tent to find Dougall.

■ ■ ■

After the soldiers had departed for their range, Thomlin searched for a driver to take him and Dougall on a tour. As he exited the company headquarters tent he walked into Major Streeter.

"Lieutenant Thomlin, not joining the rest of your platoon?"

"No, Sir. I'm trying to find a driver to take Lieutenant Dougall on the grand tour."

"Well, be careful out there," Streeter smiled as he turned to walk away.

"Yes, Sir, we'll make sure not to run through the minefields."

"No," Streeter laughed. "I meant don't get lost. You're taking a map and a GPS, right?"

"Well, Sir, I've been up here many times before. I know my way around."

"Look, Lieutenant Thomlin, don't get overconfident. I'll tell you a story you can keep to yourself. Once when we were up here, I decided to explore the countryside a bit. Better than sitting around, wasting time with the staff, right? There's a lot of history in these mountains. Abandoned ROK Army fighting positions and bunkers, whatever. Well, my driver and I spent so much time out there that night started to come and we almost lost our way trying to backtrack through these dirt roads. The vehicle was running on empty. The radios went dead. Not a good feeling."

"Hooah, Sir," Thomlin laughed.

"We made it back just as the PA system was playing retreat."

"Sir, no offense, but that's almost a scenario to become a nominee for the Big Boot award."

"Damn right, Thomlin. I can only imagine being marooned on some distant mountain top or rice paddy dike. Call me paranoid, but now I take every precaution—extra radio batteries, GPS, night vision goggles, everything. Anything that may come in handy. I'll let the rest of the staff worry about earning another Big Boot award. Understand?"

"Roger, Sir."

"Hey, you don't have to listen to me, el-tee. I'm sure that boot will look good mounted over your desk."

"Sir, thanks for the advice. Seriously, I'll make sure we take the GPS too."

Streeter started to walk away. He smiled as he said, "And Thomlin, if you mention that story to anyone, I'll mount a plaque over my desk with your nuts stapled to it."

Thomlin laughed and went back into the tent to find a driver. After several minutes of searching, Thomlin finally found a young soldier unfortunate enough to become a chauffer for the next few hours.

■ ■ ■

Thomlin rode shotgun with Dougall in the back seat. A mile north of Tent City, just before hitting the DMZ, the Humvee left the paved road and headed down a wide dirt road. At least the rains were good for something, Thomlin thought. Normally the vehicle would kick up a blinding amount of dust but the rain weighed the dirt down. In the summer, the dust was almost nauseating. Soldiers became almost paranoid with first few documented cases of Korean hemorrhagic fever, a nasty condition that originated with the urine from field mice and rats. It was kicked up in the dust and ingested by an unfortunate few. Then, flu like symptoms set in before the virus attacked other parts of the body.

"Rat piss," Thomlin muttered. It was just one more danger.

Before Dougall could ask what he just said, Thomlin pointed to the thin wire strung along the side of the road decorated with inverted triangles containing Korean symbols.

"Those mark the boundary line for minefields," Thomlin explained. "Korea has one of the largest uncharted minefields in the world. Even Koreans don't know exactly where the mines are."

"Has anyone actually set one off?" Dougall asked.

"Every now and then stories pop up about a soldier stepping over the marker and blowing a foot off," Thomlin said. "Initially, I dismissed the rumors as urban legends, but I wouldn't be surprised if it were true. Units in Korea have a higher injury and death rate than any other unit in the Army. Even the units doing the peacekeeping mission in Bosnia don't have as many injuries and fatalities as we do."

"Well, at least we are number one at something," Dougall joked.

The Humvee wound around the steep hillsides and passed the bright green rice paddies on the valley floor. Families of Koreans worked down the rows of green stalks in knee-deep water, harvesting the rice by hand. Thomlin noticed the tall, white napped Manchurian cranes picking through the far edge of the paddies. The rain slowed as occasional fat drops landed on the windshield.

By midmorning, Thomlin had already showed Dougall a few firing ranges. Most were the same as those in the United States. Soldiers lay on their stomachs, firing at targets posted on the distant mountainside. Thomlin decided to head to the sniper range run by the battalion's scout platoon. Soldiers from this unit were slightly unique in that they used modified M14 rifles with high-powered scopes, compared to the average soldier with an M16.

Scout platoon, the eyes and ears of the battalion, was routinely reserved for the most senior and best platoon leaders. It was a coveted specialty platoon amongst lieutenants, normally granting certain bragging rights to the officer in that position. In reality, the most difficult platoon leader position had to be the support platoon, responsible for the logistical requirements of the battalion. Support platoon required the most brainpower and the support platoon leader was the one who received no praise if things were going well, but the first ass-chewing if things were going badly. On the other hand, scout platoon typically had the most experienced noncommissioned officers and the best soldiers. The scouts were fully capable of running on autopilot in the absence of an officer to lead them. However, the current scout platoon leader was one of the most technically proficient lieutenants in the battalion.

"That's Matt McManus," Thomlin pointed out. McManus was six-foot-three, slender, with a curly black high and tight haircut, and bushy eyebrows. He stood with a slight hunch forward, looking downrange. Thomlin could recognize his stance from a mile away.

"Interesting that the scout platoon leader doesn't even have an airborne badge," Dougall remarked.

"Don't let the uniform fool you. Before attending Officer Candidate School, Matt made his way through third bat," Thomlin replied, referring to the third Ranger battalion of the renowned 75th Ranger Regiment. "Although he never wears it, he's one of the few officers in the battalion with a Combat Infantryman's Badge. He just likes to wear a sterilized uniform, nothing more than his rank, name, and U.S. Army tape."

"Is the bare uniform supposed to give him an air of mystique or something?"

"Hell, no. He's a cheap bastard. Too cheap to have all the badges he's earned sewn on every uniform. You know how much that would cost?"

As the pair neared McManus, Thomlin noticed him squinting; making it look like a caterpillar was crossing his forehead. Matt's lips were twisted in a snarl, revealing a few jagged teeth. There was no hiding it; McManus looked every bit of his 35 years of age.

"What's up, bud," Thomlin said as they approached.

"Goddamn farmers, man," McManus grumbled. Thomlin now saw what McManus was looking at and immediately understood the problem.

"Look out there," Thomlin instructed Dougall. In the distance, approximately 400 yards away, Thomlin could barely see a family of Koreans working around the boundary of McManus' range.

"Why would they have their farms right next to a firing range?" Dougall asked.

"Farmland is precious in Korea," Thomlin replied. "Just look around you. Everywhere you look you can see mountains, no matter where you are in this country. Rural Korean farmers have to use every inch they can."

Dougall surveyed the paddies covering the landscape. He could see that the Koreans constructed their rice fields all the way up to the range boundaries.

"Although we're granted a certain amount of land for training areas and ranges," Thomlin continued, "the Koreans view this as their land too. This happens from time to time. We want to put rounds downrange and they want to tend to their crops."

Dougall watched as some of the workers with large baskets on their heads strolled across the far edge of the range to the imme-diate front, directly in the line of fire. A KATUSA from the scout platoon was desperately trying to clear the range by screaming into a bullhorn trying to warn the Koreans that the Americans were about to fire. The Koreans paid no attention and continued to go about their business.

Thomlin shook his head, "The Koreans know we can't start firing until they're out of the way. Look at them. They're taking their sweet time."

McManus was irate by now and Thomlin guessed that he had probably been scheduled to begin putting rounds downrange about an hour prior. Finally, McManus had enough and turned to one of his noncoms.

"Sergeant Pillatiere, who's the best shot we got in the platoon?"

"Sir, that would be me." The squad leader grinned while rais-ing his sniper rifle,

"Okay, Sergeant. Put a few rounds over their heads. About two to three meters above should do."

Thomlin was a little astonished at the order and couldn't even imagine what Dougall was thinking. The sergeant nodded without questioning and started to lie down in the prone position, looking down his sights. The KATUSA gave one final warning but it had no effect, as the Koreans continued to work, most likely believing it was a bluff. For a second Thomlin also believed that it was merely a trick until he heard the crack of the first round go off. There was a brief pause and then another round was off. Another three shots repeated in quicker succession. Five rounds headed straight above the Koreans farmers.

At the crack of the first round, the farmers didn't seem to pay much attention. As the second and third rounds snapped through the air just overhead, the Koreans dropped their tools and baskets and beelined straight to the nearby rice rocket at almost superhuman speed. Thomlin immediately envisioned himself being cross-examined in a military courtroom. However, it was obvious that Dougall and Thomlin were the only two with their careers flashing before their eyes, as they noticed everyone around them laughing hysterically.

"Holy shit! Did you see those guys move?" one soldier joked to another. Even the two KATUSAs were laughing. McManus remained slightly stonefaced, but a slight smirk gave him away. It was obvious he was pleased that he had temporarily resolved the situation.

McManus gave the order to his platoon sergeant to take charge and get the range started. He turned and walked toward the Humvee with Thomlin and Dougall.

"How's the Report of Survey coming?" McManus asked.

"Jesus Christ," Thomlin spat, "if one more person asks me that question…"

"Look, buddy, I was just looking out for you," McManus said, cutting him off. "You got a seriously fucked up situation on your hands."

"What are talking about?" Thomlin asked. He was surprised at the comment McManus made. Reports of Surveys were not fun but they were more of an annoyance than anything else.

"You didn't hear this shit from me, but I'll tell you what the rumor in Headquarters Company is," McManus explained in a low voice. Scout platoon was technically part of Headquarters Company, making McManus more in tune with what was going on. He stole a glance at Dougall almost as if silently asking if Dougall could be trusted. "I heard the damn thing was lost before coming to the field."

"What?" Thomlin was dumbfounded.

"The story is the black box was lost the time before, when we went to the field almost two months ago."

Thomlin didn't know how to respond. McManus went on, "Before we came to the field for weapons qualifications, we came the month prior for field exercises. We used all the night-vision gear, GPS systems, radios, and everything else. The rumor is the black box was lost at the time and not revealed until we got back to Kayes."

Thomlin was still struggling to piece everything together. "How is that possible?" he asked.

"The black box was lost, either the soldier fucked up and lost it, or Slicky Boy worked his magic. No one reported it, a false report was submitted to battalion, we came back to Kayes, and again another false report was sent to battalion after everything was supposed to be locked back in the company arms room. After a couple of false reports and the fact that we were already back at Kayes, what were they going to do? I mean, we're talking about careers ending here, from Gibson down through Hadley."

Thomlin was trying to grasp the entire scenario. Standard operating procedure called for the physical inspection of every serial number on every weapon and sensitive item locked in the arms room. Then, a final status report was submitted and the unit was released. An inspection that was incomplete or inaccurate was completely unacceptable. It was commonly referred to as a false report, implying a lack of integrity on the one who submitted it. For an officer, such a violation of personal and professional integrity was grounds for relief.

"Hadley is so damn anal, how could he not do a proper arms room inspection?"

"Hadley? No, Greg, the arms room inspection isn't normally done by the commander, it's done by his executive officer."

Thomlin immediately thought of Josh Shelton, the headquarters executive officer. Josh was a good guy. He was squared away, knew his stuff, and had a good sense of humor to balance out Hadley's blank personality. Thomlin thought it would be unlike Shelton to completely screw things up this badly, but maybe McManus was right.

"In extreme circumstances, people do extreme things," McManus said.

Thomlin thanked McManus and slapped him on the shoulder, bidding him goodbye. Thomlin assured him that he would keep the events and the conversation of the past few minutes confidential. With Dougall in tow, Thomlin headed to the vehicle to complete the rest of the tour.

Within minutes, the Hummer weaved its way through the narrow dirt trails between the rice paddies, toward another firing range. The rain had subsided slightly and for a brief moment the sun popped out from between the clouds. The vehicle rolled to a stop behind a concrete shack used as the range control building. Thomlin noticed Ward and his platoon sergeant off to the far right of the building leaning over the hood of a Humvee with their backs to the long line of soldiers that stretched across the front of the range. Each of the soldiers carried a simulated shoulder-fired AT-4 antitank weapon. The actual weapon was too expensive for soldiers to practice with, so soldiers were forced to use a modified version. The long green plastic tube on their shoulder was approximately three feet long and several inches in diameter. Instead of an actual antitank missile, the modified weapon fired a nine millimeter tracer round. The round made a dull thump as the soldiers fired into the hillside a few hundred yards to their front. As one of the soldiers shouted commands over the range PA system, which was as comprehensible as the loud speaker in the New York subway, the low popping of the tracer rounds could be heard over and over.

Ward and the sergeant were in charge of the antitank range. The soldiers on the range were a mix from all over the battalion and Thomlin recognized a few of his younger soldiers. The antitank weapon was added weight to the soldier's already impossibly heavy load so it was typical to find the younger soldiers get stuck with the task. It was also an awkward size. Usually, soldiers strapped the weapon across their rucksacks on their backs, allowing the weapon to stick out a foot on either side of the soldier, ensuring the soldier would get hung up on a tree or bush as he maneuvered through the field. The AT-4 was a pain in the ass to most soldiers and many young privates looked forward to delegating the weapon to someone more junior than them.

Some soldiers nodded as Thomlin and Dougall approached. Ward's platoon sergeant, a young broad-shouldered Staff Sergeant known across the battalion as a rising star, delved his fingers into a can of Skoal and loaded his bottom lip with a large pinch of tobacco before extending his hand to Dougall.

"What's the good word?" Ward asked.

"Just taking a tour," Thomlin said casually. "I heard about the guy over in headquarters that came through the gate drunk and doused with his own blood."

"Oh, yeah?"

"Yeah, the asshole is the company armorer that I need to interview for the Report of Survey."

"Let me guess, you are going to ask Captain Watts to go back to the rear to interview him," Ward laughed.

"Well," Thomlin smiled, "it is necessary to get his statement. Just happens to be that he's in the rear."

"Sure. If he lets you go, I think I need to supervise you on the way back."

Thomlin changed the subject and said in a low voice, "Hey, did you hear any rumor about the black box being lost before we came to the field last time, and Shelton submitting a false report?"

"Before we came to the field? No. Who told you that?"

Thomlin looked around to make sure no one else would hear, "McManus."

Ward thought for a moment before responding, "Don't know, Greg. McManus and Shelton don't exactly play nice together in the same sandbox. Shelton is the company executive officer and McManus does have to go through him to get the support he needs."

"Do you know of anything specific?"

"No," Ward answered, "just that McManus is a cowboy and Shelton shuts down some of scout platoon's plans every now and then."

"That's a pretty big violation of the Lieutenant Protection Agency, don't you think? To set up Shelton like that?"

"Yeah, I guess you're right," Ward agreed. "My only point is be careful who you trust."

As the men talked they didn't notice the smoldering hillside behind them. The tracer rounds launched by the antitank simulators burned hot. Even in the damp environment of the summer rains, the tracer rounds were still hot enough to cause brush fires. Considering that hundreds of tracer rounds had been fired since the time the range opened several hours before, several small fires burned in the distance. The Staff Sergeant briefly turned to see the smoke and then quickly disregarded the scene. Out of control brush fires were not much of a risk during the monsoon season.

As the next hour passed, the small fires multiplied and ultimately converged. Ward finally faced the range and nonchalantly mumbled, "Well, shit, look at that."

The entire hillside was ablaze. The three lieutenants stood in silence watching the flickering landscape. Thomlin wondered why the rain had briefly stopped. The hypnotic beating of the AT-4 simulators drummed a steady rhythm as the bright red streaks flew from the tubes into the fire. The smoke blotted most of the sky in the foreground.

"Maybe I should call a cease-fire" Ward thought out loud.

Ward did not move and, after a long pause, he finally broke the silence. "Well, I hope you two brought some marshmallows for the campfire."

The four men turned back to face the hood of the vehicle. As the fire continued to burn, another vehicle skidded to a stop in front of the range control shed. A short Korean sergeant major jumped out and quickly moved toward the lieutenants.

"This guy looks pretty pissed," Ward's platoon sergeant huffed.

"He has no reason to be," Ward said. "We have this range all day. I checked everything with range control."

"No, Sir, I think he's probably mad about the fire. There's a small Korean outpost not too far from the range."

"Who in charge here?" the sergeant major spoke in a heavy accent. "I want know who in charge."

Ward, only a few inches taller than the Korean, turned and faced the sergeant major. "I am."

"You stop firing. You and your men go put out fire. Now," the Korean shouted.

"Hell, no," Ward said. "No way are we going out onto the range. There are mines out there."

The sergeant major did not flinch. He shouted even louder this time, "No mines out there. Your men go now and put out fire."

Ward was not a cherry second lieutenant. He had been in country for almost eight months and he was not accustomed to backing down. He slowly assessed the situation and then headed toward the range control shed. After a few minutes of talking to the soldier in the shed, orders were shouted over the PA system and the firing stopped. Soldiers began to file back off the firing line and moved toward their gear. Weapons were stacked against their rucksack and the soldiers retrieved their folding entrenching tools.

Noncommissioned officers took control of the soldiers and organized them into groups. Orders were relayed from one sergeant to another as they began to move forward to the blazing brush fire. The ROK sergeant major stood silently with his arms folded, obviously satisfied that the Americans were about to follow his initial command. Ward watched as the other two lieutenants stood motionless watching the scene. The soldiers shuffled their way in the direction of the flames for almost 20 yards before a loud thud was heard in the distance. All the men stopped and looked in the direction of their squad leaders for further commands. Before the noncommissioned officers could give any further direction, another explosion ripped through the air. This one was louder, loud enough to rattle the Plexiglas window in the range control shed and cause the soldiers to collectively lose their breath. Immediately, Ward spun to face the sergeant major again.

"Okay, maybe some mines, but not many," the sergeant major said. He was still standing with his arms across his chest, obviously waiting for the Americans to continue.

"Sergeant Major, kiss my ass," Ward blurted. Since the sergeant major did not understand the idiom, Ward added, "You want the fire out, you go put it out."

Without waiting for a response, Ward turned and ordered the men back on their gear. Frustrated, the sergeant major let out a loud sigh, hopped in his vehicle and left the range. As the vehicle spun its tires leaving the area, the lieutenants burst out laughing. Despite the short delay the soldiers finally resumed their range activities. Dougall was baffled beyond words and could only bid Ward and his platoon sergeant goodbye as he and Thomlin headed for their own vehicle. The ride back to Tent City was quiet and Thomlin had already pushed the incident from his mind as he began to think about the Report of Survey.

11

THE FIELD

First Lieutenant Job Connelly lay on Thomlin's cot thumbing through the latest issue of British Maxim. Connelly's linebacker build caused the cot frame to creak with every page turn. Thomlin came through the tent flap and immediately recognized the shaved scalp behind the magazine.

"Jesus, it's good to see you. How the hell are you? What brings you to the other side of the tracks?" Thomlin asked.

Both had attended the Officer Basic Course and Ranger School together, and both elected to stay in Korea. After Connelly's first tour, he accepted a position as the executive officer of a Korean company stationed in the Joint Security Area within the DMZ. He was the only American assigned to the unit and served as the liaison between Korean and American forces at the Demilitarized

Zone.

The Joint Security Area was a small portion of the DMZ controlled by both Americans and Koreans. For decades after the Korean War both Americans and Koreans actively patrolled the DMZ, with infantry soldiers from units all over the country rotating to the DMZ for a month at a time. It was the closest thing the soldiers in Korea would get to combat. They carried live ammunition and would recon or lay in ambushes waiting for North Korean infiltrators. There were always stories of close calls or even small firefights that would never make the evening news back in the States. In the 1980s the American units handed over the duties to the Koreans and no longer actively patrolled the area with the exception of one platoon, the scout platoon, at the Joint Security Area. Connelly routinely worked with the scout platoon, although his job required him to perform more routine duties including the daily visits to the many manned checkpoints overlooking the DMZ. In many of these checkpoints the South Korean and American soldiers could see the North Koreans off in the distance performing similar duties.

"I had some of the soldiers mixed in some of your ranges today. I thought I would come by and see if you were around."

"You still having fun staring at the North Koreans all day?" Thomlin asked.

"I was until the past few weeks," Connelly said. "You know it's normal for the North Koreans to shout at us over a bullhorn when we do our rounds at the checkpoints, right? Our policy is to completely ignore the verbal assaults. The North Koreans speak broken English and read the nametags on the American uniforms through binoculars. They call the soldiers by name and antagonize them, hoping for some sort of response or at least an acknowledgement.

"Sometimes the North Koreans get a hold of trash or even

discarded letters from our soldiers, and read them over their PA system. It pisses a lot of people off. Some soldiers can't handle the harassment and break down under the circumstances. It's not uncommon for soldiers to be transferred to units further south. Personally, it never bothered me until recently."

"What happened?" Thomlin was intrigued.

"I had just returned from midtour leave of 30 days back home. I began the morning by following my routine checks when the North Koreans began taunting me. This was nothing new so I ignored the comments as usual, until I heard one of the North Koreans shout, 'Hey, Connelly, hope you had nice vacation.' For the first time, they made me stop in my tracks. Those bastards had been tracking me. I knew I was being watched, but I had no idea that they followed me to such a degree that they knew I was on leave. I never turned around or made a verbal response, but they know they finally got under my skin."

Thomlin listened to his friend and sympathized with the daily pressures of what Connelly had to go through. Connelly knew that his presence on the DMZ was more for show than anything else, but he became increasingly paranoid of what the North Koreans might know about him.

"I shredded every piece of information that had my name on it, but I'm not sure it did any good," Connelly said. "I think some South Korean soldiers are relaying information to their northern counterparts. You know, the ROK soldiers render the proper respect to me but I'm still an outcast in this unit.

"You know the tree on the border of the DMZ, where ROK soldiers and the North Koreans trade messages? I sometimes wonder if any of the notes are about me."

The two lieutenants switched to more trivial topics before Thomlin asked Connelly if there was anything else that was bothering him.

"Rape," Connelly said flatly.

Thomlin thought he had misheard him and stared at Connelly with a bewildered expression.

"There's a small post exchange within the Joint Security Area. One of the South Korean workers recently approached me about some oddities," Connelly explained.

Although there were no women at the DMZ the post exchange kept running out of condoms. As Connelly tried to understand what was going on, he learned about a seemingly unrelated bit of information that had come to his attention. The medics were treating many of the younger South Korean soldiers for facial bruises.

"I assumed that the younger soldiers were beaten in a form of initiation to the unit, but then the medics also mentioned that the same soldiers were complaining of hemorrhoids. The soldiers all had the same explanation. The facial bruises and black eyes were due to falling out of their bunks as they slept and the hemorrhoids were because the toilet paper was too rough. Do you know how much the unit has already spent on toilet paper with more padding? Man, I think the initiation goes far beyond the beatings."

"Some form of male dominance, I guess," Thomlin said. "Maybe like the hierarchy in a prison system."

"Yeah, prison rule: the guy on top isn't gay."

Homosexuality was not accepted in Korea, and it was certainly not discussed. Although American soldiers occasionally suspected that most Korean men were gay, it was a misperception among cultures. Korean men did not publicly display affection toward women, and they could be observed walking down any city street arm in arm. Younger men hung on each other and made contact with one another in ways that made homophobic American soldiers cringe. During initial orientations to the country soldiers were briefed that this was Korean society and it did not imply the same meaning as back in the States. Thomlin always accepted this as one of the infinite number of customs that separated the two cultures. He thought it might be due to the way Koreans were raised, segregated from the other gender in their school systems.

"I asked my sergeant major about this and he vehemently denied any such practices," Connelly added. "His defensiveness makes me think even more that something else is going on. Every time I try to pry for more information the South Korean soldiers completely clam up. I'm no use on this one. I don't think I'll ever be able to change the situation."

Thomlin couldn't offer any advice and could only change the subject to get Connelly's mind off the subject. Connelly seemed to lighten up a bit with the change of topic. He finally asked Thomlin, "Whatever happened to the black box you guys lost the last time you came out here?"

Thomlin smiled, "You're looking at the lucky Report of Survey officer."

"No shit?" Connelly laughed. "That should be the quickest Report of Survey in history. Let me guess, it's going to go something like, we came to the field and Slicky Boy took our stuff."

"Damn right. Slicky Boy did his thing all right. I have to conduct a couple of mandatory interviews and it should be done." Thomlin thought about what McManus had told him but decided not to get into it now.

Soldiers began returning from the firing ranges in large, five-ton trucks as Thomlin and Connelly walked toward the dining facility for dinner. Ward and Nelson joined the pair as they returned with their soldiers. After a quick meal in the packed dining facility the group headed to the canteen for their nightly round of beer.

Thomlin turned to Connelly, "So when are you finally going to tell me the secret of the Philippines?"

Thomlin knew that several months ago during Connelly's leave he made a brief pit stop in the Philippines to enjoy some unadulterated fun. Thomlin also knew that Connelly had run into Sergeant First Class Wilson, and there was some deep secret about the extended weekend that he had been holding out on. Connelly had alluded to an incident but never divulged any details, and Thomlin desperately wanted to know what went on.

"Well, you didn't hear it from me," Connelly began with a smile. He gulped the last of his beer and began to recount the story of his second night in a country with more temptations than Korea, the Philippines.

Connelly was half drunk in a topless bar when he noticed Wilson sitting two tables in front of him. Wilson was locking lips with a short Filipino girl as if he was sucking the life out of her. The act was almost obscene but only seemed to encourage Connelly to move to the table next to Wilson to purposefully be noticed by the NCO.

Wilson finally took a break to gasp for more air before spotting Connelly. He was clearly beyond the point of operating any heavy machinery and was not at all embarrassed in front of the lieutenant. Wilson leaned over and shouted, "Hey, el-tee, check out my new bride. I'm going to marry her and bring her back to Korea."

Connelly smiled broadly, trying to withhold any laughter, "That's fantastic, Sergeant."

"Stick around, Sir, she's going to be on stage in a couple of minutes," Wilson commanded. The young woman sat on his lap and mugged Wilson's face one last time before getting up to move to the stage.

As Crystal Waters started to play over the loudspeakers, the woman gyrated across the small platform. She removed her bikini top and leaned over the stage to again plant her mouth on Wilson. Wilson made grunting noises and clearly loved the attention. He elbowed Connelly as if looking for acknowledgement of his new love. Connelly shook his head and tried to appear envious.

The woman continued her dance until the disc jockey switched to an Ace of Base remix. As the loud techno music thumped away the woman reached back to the silk curtain behind her and ripped it aside to reveal a full grown mule. Wilson stopped smiling briefly as if trying to comprehend what was about to happen. Without skipping a beat the woman bounced in front of the animal and then dropped to her knees. Before Wilson's inebriated brain could process the information passing through his retinas, the woman began to orally please the four-legged creature.

Wilson and Connelly both sat in utter shock. A large Australian sitting behind the soldiers who had been watching the entire episode leaned over to Wilson and said in a heavy accent, "I hate to ruin your night, mate, but this is her second show."

The group of lieutenants in the canteen exploded with laughter so loud other soldiers stopped to wonder what was said. Thomlin beamed with the new found details and knew someday it would come in handy.

Connelly stuck around until the group finished their beers at the canteen. As night fell and the propaganda over the loud speakers played in the distance, Connelly left Tent City for the DMZ. Thomlin wished him luck and inwardly noted that Connelly would be happy when his final tour was complete. There would be no more extensions in Korea for Connelly.

When Thomlin returned to his tent he pulled out some paperwork from a small bag. Going through it he noticed that PFC Robert Padilla was the soldier on the hand receipt for the lost black box. Thomlin decided that there was no time like the present, left the platoon area and went in search of the soldier.

■ ■ ■

Private First Class Robert Padilla, the 20-year-old soldier from Phoenix, Arizona, stood watching the nightly game of cards in the headquarters tent when Thomlin walked in. Up until the last field exercise, Padilla was the driver for Major Pierce. He was one of a half dozen soldiers assigned to the battalion operations staff. He was a competent soldier, physically fit and possessed the intellect to do many of the administrative and reporting tasks associated with his job. Prior to the black box incident Padilla's reputation was very positive. He had even won the coveted Soldier of the Quarter award twice in a row. Padilla was fairly short and somewhat stout, and was naturally a quiet person. Since the last field training exercise he had become even more introverted. Padilla made brief eye contact with Thomlin, who walked through the flap of the tent. Padilla immediately knew why Thomlin had come. Padilla's eyes were slightly downcast as he slowly walked over to greet the lieutenant. Thomlin pulled him over to two empty cots.

"Sit down and relax, Padilla," Thomlin said softly. "This is just a routine interview, so it's no big deal. Why don't you tell me what happened during the field training exercise when the equipment was lost."

Padilla spoke softly, never meeting Thomlin's gaze. His words seemed scripted to Thomlin. Padilla described how he signed the black box from the arms room prior to getting the vehicle ready for Major Pierce. The Humvee was equipped with two radios that needed to be uploaded with the necessary information. He signed the hand receipt from Specialist Wickersham, as required by standard operating procedures. The signing of the hand receipt relinquished responsibility of the black box from the company to Padilla's personal care. Padilla mentioned that he tied the black box to the inside of the rucksack with a piece of thin durable nylon rope known commonly among soldiers as 550 cord, signifying the tensile strength of the rope.

"Sir, I went to one of the ranges with members of the unit one evening to night qualify my M16 rifle," Padilla went on. "I grounded my gear with the other soldiers well behind the firing line, just like we're supposed to. The range lasted most of the night."

"When did you return to your gear?"

"Not exactly sure, Sir. It was probably around 0200 hours when the firing finally ended. Everyone conducted a personal physical inspection of all their stuff before leaving, and that's when I noticed that my rucksack flap had been opened and the 550 cord was cut. I looked inside my ruck and the black box was gone. Sir, you know the rest of the story," Padilla stated, referring to the notification and subsequent search for the missing item.

Thomlin listened to the whole story without interrupting and took a few notes on a small pad. He asked a few follow up questions but Padilla recounted the same story, almost word for word as before. Thomlin shifted his body on the cot several times, becoming increasingly dissatisfied with the whole story. Again, he asked Padilla a few questions and again received the same recount. A long pause drifted between them while Padilla stared at the concrete tent floor. Finally, Thomlin broke the silence.

"Padilla, what really happened?" Thomlin said quietly.

"I don't know what more I can tell you, Sir," Padilla replied.

Thomlin decided to take a chance and leaned in close until he was only a few inches from Padilla's nose.

"Bullshit," Thomlin said in a low but demanding tone. "Padilla, I know the black box wasn't lost that way. I know you didn't lose it. The black box had been missing since the field exercise the month before and you never even signed it from the arms room last month. Now tell me what really happened."

Padilla finally looked Thomlin in the face. Padilla looked stunned. Seeing that Thomlin wasn't blinking and was waiting for a reply, Padilla finally spoke. This time his words were deliberate, almost angry.

"Sir, I didn't lose that damn box," he said in a barely audible voice.

"Then tell me who did," Thomlin demanded.

Padilla quickly looked behind him to see if anyone else was listening.

"Sir, I don't know. I was just following orders."

Before Thomlin could ask whose orders Padilla had followed, Lieutenant Josh Shelton burst through the tent flap adjacent to where Thomlin and Padilla were sitting. Shelton immediately noticed the pair and knew what the conversation was about. Shelton plopped down next to Padilla and grinned at Thomlin.

"What's up?" Shelton asked Thomlin. "Going over the infamous black box story?"

Thomlin exhaled in frustration. He returned a smirk to Shelton, knowing he had lost the opportunity to find the truth. Thomlin dismissed Padilla who stood up and returned to the group watching the card game.

Thomlin asked Shelton a few questions regarding the black box, fully anticipating the response. Shelton's story mirrored what Padilla had said moments before. Thomlin decided not to press the issue with Shelton and asked the status of Specialist Wickersham.

"You haven't heard?" Shelton asked. "The Korean police in Dongducheon found a 40-year-old hooker beaten into a coma the morning we came to the field. The woman has a fractured skull. The Koreans immediately went to the military police suspecting the handiwork of an American soldier. Military police quickly tracked down Wickersham because he stumbled through the gate earlier in the morning, drunk, covered in blood. Of course Wickersham wasn't injured, so it wasn't his own blood he was wearing. Apparently it only took 50 minutes to get a confession from him."

"Shit," Thomlin cursed aloud. "Where is he now?"

"Back in the rear still," Shelton replied. "The MPs can't hold him so the rear detachment is still watching him, except this time Wickersham will be easier to monitor. He's now shuffling around from his room to the chow hall in shackles."

"Great," Thomlin said flatly. Shelton was speaking to Thomlin coolly, as if it was almost an inside joke.

"I need to speak to him," Thomlin said but was almost immediately sorry he had said the words out loud.

"Good luck. He's being watched 24/7. You'll probably need permission to sit with him. You shouldn't worry about it though, you can probably complete the Report of Survey without him, I mean, it's a pretty cut and dry case."

Shelton pulled close to Thomlin and asked, "What's the big deal? What's your angle? You can tell me, we'll keep this within the Lieutenant Protection Agency."

Thomlin slowly nodded as Shelton added, "He's a dumb bastard anyway. I heard from some of the folks back in the rear that he's acting like it's no big deal. The guy almost killed a woman and will probably do time in a Korean prison for what he did."

Thomlin knew Shelton was right. Despite the Status of Forces

Agreement, highly visible heinous crimes did not go unnoticed. In such cases, the U.S. military was likely to turn Wickersham over to the Korean authorities, to be tried in a Korean court. In such cases, the trial would be completely in Korean. Wickersham would most likely not know what was going on and would not have the benefit of an American lawyer to represent him. The Korean counsel assigned to Wickersham would likely not make overt attempts to help the American criminal who would be required to prove his innocence in order to avoid prison. Justice would be very swift. Wickersham was looking at ten years in Korean jail at a minimum. Unlike American prisons that occasionally received media attention and were forced to meet high humane standards, Korean jails were brutal for foreigners. Without being able to speak the language, Wickersham would be an exile. Along with the other prisoners he would be fed a rice diet and could be dealt with harshly for minor infractions. Shelton was right, Thomlin thought, Wickersham had no idea what was in store for him.

Thomlin said goodbye to Shelton and returned to his own tent. As he entered the area one of his soldiers mentioned that Captain Watts had requested to see him. Thomlin walked over to the company tent, where Watts sat writing a letter. Watts asked some routine questions about the qualification ranges without ever taking his pen off the paper. After a brief pause, he capped his pen and looked up at Thomlin, who stood silently at attention.

"How's the Report of Survey coming?" Watts asked in a conversational tone.

Thomlin told him that he had interviewed Padilla and Shelton, without including Padilla's additional statements. He also told Watts about the recent developments with Specialist Wickersham. From the look on Watts' face it was obvious that the information had already been relayed to him. Thomlin asked for permission to go back to the rear to interview Wickersham.

"No way," Watts said, "I need you here with your platoon. Don't try to score yourself some free time to screw around back in the rear while everyone else is out here. Find Wickersham when we return in a few days, and if for some reason you can't talk to him, don't worry about it. Just get the report done. The battalion commander has been asking me about the status. Just get it done, okay?"

Thomlin stood for a moment and stared at his commander. He thought about telling Watts the comments Padilla made before Shelton cut him off. Thomlin wondered if it would make any difference, or if Watts really didn't care. He thought it was odd that everyone, even Watts, wanted things done so quickly.

"Yes, Sir," Thomlin finally said and headed back to his tent.

■ ■ ■

The following days of continuous weapons qualification practice passed without incident. Thomlin stuck with the soldiers of his platoon and participated in the qualifications. Range detail was somewhat boring to Thomlin, who looked forward to the three-day tactical field exercise culminating the deployment to Tent City. During the training exercise the companies would leave Tent City and stay in the field, participating in a variety of tactical missions that were designed to simulate what the unit would have to do in an eventual war.

In the early morning, as the soldiers prepared to head to the field in lieu of physical training, Thomlin discovered numerous small strips of paper littering the ground across Tent City. Thomlin noticed Dougall collecting the brightly colored pieces of paper along with a few other soldiers. Without bending down to see what was scrawled on the paper, Thomlin knew that it was.

"It's pretty common to find that stuff up here," Thomlin told Dougall. "There are all sorts of North Korean propaganda at Tent City."

The paper contained small pictures of American celebrities, even the president, with captions written in Korean.

"What do you think it says?" asked Dougall.

"Probably something about the outpouring of sympathy American figureheads feel toward the struggle of the courageous North Korean people. I once had one of the KATUSAs translate one for me. I don't even bother to look at them anymore."

"How does it end up here?"

"That's a real mystery," Thomlin replied. "According to the battalion intelligence officer, North Koreans send helium balloons attached with scores of flyers that are released with timers. Maybe it's one of the Korean kitchen or canteen workers sneaking them in and releasing them."

As soldiers stuffed their pockets with the North Korean souvenirs and boarded the trucks headed to the field, Thomlin thought it was humorous that the messages designed to illicit sympathy and support for the communist regime would find their way into a scrapbook in a Des Moines suburb. Thomlin quickly put the thought aside and jumped into the five ton truck headed five miles to the east for the beginning of the field training.

Before long Thomlin and the platoon were cutting through the thick waist-high silvergrass at the base of a steep hillside. Thick patches of wayfaring trees and wild weigela made the movement difficult and the men soon found themselves in a long file to get through the brush. Thomlin felt relieved when they discovered some pre-dug trenches traversing the hillside to help navigate their way across. He could hear the rain start to patter through the tall Korean pines and sawtooth oaks that covered the hillside, and knew the rain would only bring more humidity. He frowned at the thought but signaled his squad leaders to push onward.

In the garrison, Wilson dictated the actions, but in the field Thomlin ran the show. He issued a brief warning order to his squad leaders on the fly as they disembarked the trucks. Thomlin planned on moving the platoon for several miles before setting up a patrol base. From there, Thomlin would begin the detailed planning, resulting in the issue of the operations order. The operatons order would contain the comprehensive description of the mission to be carried out. The information would be disseminated to every solider in the unit, each one having a part in the coordinated movement to complete the mission.

Five miles to the east, Dougall and Ward were conducting the same series of activities. Each platoon's movement was orchestrated into the larger plan of the company. The lieutenants engrossed themselves in the task, physically and mentally, concentrating on executing the details of the plan while they moved under equipment loads weighing over 100 pounds.

The mission, a simulated deliberate attack on a fixed enemy position, was not complete until the early morning hours the following day. The operation was successful by established standards. The soldiers of each platoon performed without incident. Watts was openly satisfied with the result and commended his platoon leaders and senior noncommissioned officers on their effort. As a reward, the platoons did not have to repeat the exercise. Each unit moved back to their patrol base in the early morning darkness and was allowed to rest for several hours before the start of their next mission. The platoon leaders were exhausted. The physical exertion was only half as tiring as the mental fatigue. It was referred to as the leader's rush. Thomlin had first felt it in Ranger School when soldiers were selected at random for leadership positions for portions of the mission, and graded by sadistic Ranger instructors in order to pass and move onto the next phase. Failing too many patrols meant the unlucky Ranger student would repeat the entire phase, or worse, he would be sent packing to his unit without the sought-after Ranger tab.

There was a flood of adrenaline for Thomlin when he was in charge, knowing that he was personally responsible for the success of the unit. The surge kept him alert and awake despite the physical weariness, but there was immediate exhaustion when the mission was over. He knew that he could be asleep within minutes if he dropped his gear and sat.

Thomlin was not alone in this physical state. Dougall was feeling the same effects in his patrol base several miles away. The men of the platoon were laid out in the shape of a triangle with pairs of soldiers facing outward approximately fifteen feet apart. In the center of the platoon, Dougall, the platoon sergeant, and Dougall's radio operator sat in a small depression among clumps of feather reed grass. The three men took turns monitoring the radio while they lay under a shelter constructed from their ponchos. The shelter hung low to the ground, creating a low silhouette but giving them enough room to slip in and out to check on the rest of the perimeter.

The platoon sergeant was out checking on the patrol base when two soldiers crept up to talk to the radio operator.

"Sir," one of the young soldiers said, "did they tell you to watch out for moon bears?"

"Moon bears?"

"Yes, Sir," the soldier answered. "It's like a small black bear. Pretty common."

"Sir, that's nothing compared to the Korean tiger," the other solider said. The radio operator began to giggle.

"Is that so?" came the voice of the platoon sergeant from behind the pair of soldiers. "I'll tell you what. If you don't get to your positions in a nanosecond, you're going to demonstrate how to dig a full blown fighting position until I'm completely satisfied with the outcome. That should only take the rest of the night."

The soldiers vanished in an instant. Sergeant First Class Lancour slid under the poncho.

"Don't listen to them, Sir. They're just testing you. Trying to play games."

"Moon bears and tigers?"

"At one time, maybe. The Japs cut down every damn tree during the war, which killed off most of the animals. You'll be lucky if you come across a squirrel out here. But, the rodents have to be fast or else they'll end up in some local farmer's stew pot. No, Sir, the only thing you get to see here are the birds and the Jindo dogs with the curly tails."

"Wow."

Lancour leaned forward and whispered with a smile, "Sir, I'll tell you, I love coming to the field here, you know why? There's no snakes. This is the only place I've ever been to that doesn't have snakes. I hate snakes."

Both Dougall and Lancour laughed lightly. As soon as his platoon sergeant made the suggestion to relax, Dougall was fast asleep. He didn't even hear the radio spring to life with the chatter of the excited voices from headquarters.

The platoon sergeant and the radio operator listened intently to the news that came through the small handset. Many miles south of their position, near the city of Osan, the ROK Army was searching feverishly for several North Korean infiltrators. After the Army unit had been tipped off to the whereabouts of the North Koreans through some local inhabitants, ROK soldiers stood poised to capture the insurgents. Surprised at being discovered, the North Koreans were still unwilling to be taken prisoner and opened fire on the advancing ROK soldiers. Gunfire was exchanged in the deserted city streets outside of Osan. One ROK soldier was immediately killed along with two North Koreans. ROK units were able to capture a third infiltrator after wounding him in the leg. The ROK soldiers were convinced at least one other soldier was wounded and trying to evade capture, probably attempting to make it back through the DMZ.

Although the information was relayed from battalion headquarters, there were no instructions at this point. No information was given on how the North Koreans made it to Osan in the first place. Like a breaking news bulletin, the platoon sergeant could only offer new information to his squad leaders without any following commands. As the squad leaders came and went to get updates, Dougall stirred. He could hear the light rain drizzling on the ponchos suspended above and the voices of his noncommissioned officers speaking in heated tones. Dougall could make out their outlines in the dark. He watched for a moment as they came in to exchange words with the platoon sergeant and then head back out to the area along the edge of the patrol base.

"Sergeant Lancour," Dougall whispered, "what's going on?"

"Nothing, Sir. The ROKs caught some infiltrators near Osan and they're looking for a few more," Dougall's platoon sergeant replied casually. For a moment, Dougall thought his platoon sergeant was playing a practical joke on him, but then he too could hear the information coming across the radio net.

"So what are we doing?" Dougall asked.

"Don't worry about it, Sir. This is not our battle to fight. The South Koreans will hunt down the others, if there are any."

As Lancour spoke he was already stretching out on his back on the ground. He pulled the poncho liner over him and rolled on his side, unconcerned about the situation to their south. Dougall was stunned. He couldn't understand why the battalion was not mobilizing immediately. Osan was far south of them. How could the North Koreans get that far beyond their position? It was a long time before Dougall could get back to sleep. While lying awake pondering the possibilities of what this could all mean, he became distinctly aware of the rain drumming on his small shelter and the silence around him. Dougall thought Lancour would be the only one not bothered by the situation until he began to hear the heavy breathing and snoring of the soldiers around him.

12

REDEPLOY

Lee woke when the phone rang, but his daughter picked up before he could answer. Lee's wife was snoring peacefully and barely stirred. It was four o'clock.

"It's for you," his daughter whispered, handing him the receiver.

Lee grunted a few replies before hanging up the phone. He noticed the silhouette of his daughter standing in the doorway.

"What is it? Whoever it was sounded upset," she said.

"Nothing," he said flatly, "just work. One of my co-workers called in sick. They want me to be in Osan in a few hours to pick up some supplies. I'll probably be gone all day."

"I'll make tea," she said and walked to the kitchen.

Lee dressed quickly and joined his daughter at the kitchen table. He lit a cigarette and sat down. His daughter handed him a cup as she yawned.

"Don't do that," he said to her as she reached over to turn on the small television resting on the countertop. "You'll wake your mother."

She nodded sleepily and fell into the chair across from her father.

"So tell me, Yumi," Lee said trying to make small talk, "you never did tell me how your night in Dongducheon went."

"Fine, father," she said, yawning.

"Did you see your friend?"

"Oh, yes. It was okay. I guess you're right about American soldiers. There was too much testosterone in one place. Why do guys insist on fighting?"

"Well, they are young and far from home, I guess," Lee said quietly as he took a long drag from his cigarette before tapping it out in the ashtray.

"I guess," his daughter replied half asleep. Lee stared at his daughter briefly and decided not to press for more details. He didn't have time to engage in a conversation about the behavior of young men.

"I have a long day ahead of me," he said as he rose and kissed his daughter on the head. "Don't wait up for me."

He smiled at her as he slipped on an old green windbreaker and quietly walked out the door.

■ ■ ■

When the sky finally brightened enough to see clearly, Dougall awoke to find his soldiers preparing their gear for the day's exercise. He briefly wondered if he had dreamt the information from the night before but Lancour assured him it was real. Lancour told his young lieutenant not to worry about it.

"Stuff like this happens all the time, el-tee," Lancour smiled. Despite the rain, Lancour was already brewing some coffee over a tiny portable stove. Dougall shook off the thought but was still amazed at how routine this situation had seemed to most everyone around him.

Like Lancour, Thomlin was also unaffected by the news. Thomlin had been monitoring the net when the news broke. He perked up a little to hear the news, like hearing a good piece of gossip. He wasn't afraid of being pulled out of the field or going on alert. The news of the infiltration was interesting and a bit unusual but not overwhelmingly surprising. Thomlin was just amazed at how the South Koreans managed to find the insurgents. Wilson snored lightly on a thin foam mat and Thomlin didn't even consider waking the platoon sergeant to bother him with the news. It could all wait until the morning.

As Wilson brewed his own coffee over a small portable stove, Thomlin relayed the information. Wilson grunted an acknowledgement. When the coffee was finally made, Wilson poured the oil-thick black substance into his canteen cup and took a few sips. He reached over and grabbed one of the limbless, baby Daimyo oaks, snapping it in half. He peeled back the bark on the end and used it to stir some powdered creamer into the coffee.

Leaning back on his rucksack, Wilson said, "Sir, did I ever tell you about the time I was here in the eighties? Back when we still patrolled the DMZ."

"You know what they say. The only difference between a fairy tale and a war story is that the war story usually starts with, 'No shit, there I was.'"

"Well, then, no shit, there I was," Wilson laughed. He began to recount a story of his first tour in Korea years ago. Thomlin listened intently as Wilson described an engagement between

American soldiers and North Koreans that no one ever heard about. He nodded as he listened, not even caring about all of the facts.

■ ■ ■

Thomlin and the rest of the platoon leaders soon received orders from Watts on their next platoon mission that included more long movements across the mountainous countryside. The thick summer air added an additional ten pounds to the soldiers' load and made the movements sluggish. The exercise was similar to the day prior, but Thomlin knew that after today the platoon would dig in and conduct one last defensive mission before heading back to spend their last night at Tent City. After a couple of days sleeping on the muddy, monsoon soaked ground, the cot back in the tent would feel like a down mattress.

The days passed quickly for Thomlin, who engrossed himself in the planning and execution of the missions Watts handed down over the radio. The platoon worked well together despite the fact that the high turnover rate in Korea ensured that almost a third of his soldiers were fairly new and had not worked with each other for more than a month or two. Thomlin had even forgotten about the Report of Survey until the last mission, the company defense. As the soldiers dug their armpit-deep fighting positions, Thomlin began thinking about how he would try to guarantee himself an interview with Wickersham without any supervision.

His thoughts were interrupted when the radio operator came to Thomlin with a message from Captain Watts. The radio operator, a young recent college grad who joined the Army to pay off student loans, informed Thomlin that Watts wanted him to meet with some ROK Army officers.

"Well, Sir," the young soldier began, "apparently a ROK field artillery unit has moved in on our pickup zone. Captain Watts wants you and Lieutenant Nelson to go out there and coordinate with the Koreans. Remind them that the area is ours tomorrow morning for the mission outta here."

Thomlin remembered that after spending one last night in Tent City the unit would march an easy six miles to the area that would be used as a pick-up zone for the air mobile mission back to Camp Kayes. When the entire battalion had reached the pick-up zone they would form a large tactical perimeter around the area and wait for the Blackhawk helicopters to come and transport them back to Kayes.

"This is supposed to be an easy mission," Thomlin said as he approached Nelson and his driver.

"What's that?"

"I said, this is supposed to be a walk in the park. Catch the birds and go home."

"Yeah. A 20 minute helicopter ride beats the hell out of an hour and a half ride on the back of five-ton trucks."

Thomlin didn't like the idea of something throwing a wrench in the plan so he shrugged off the thoughts of Wickersham and the interview.

"Okay, let's make this quick," Thomlin said as he climbed into the backseat. Within minutes, the Humvee rolled down the dirt road toward the pickup zone.

As the vehicle pulled into the large open area Thomlin could see the large, self-propelled howitzers lined up in a row for their own field exercise. Large camouflage nets hung over the tracked vehicles and a small command tent had already been erected near the center of the activity. It was clear that the ROKs expected to be in the area for a while.

Nelson and Thomlin got out of the vehicle and approached the command tent.

"Should we do rock-paper-scissors to see who gets to talk to this guy?" Nelson asked.

"Last time I checked, you're the ranking officer. I believe you get to be the ambassador of goodwill," Thomlin said as he pulled off his helmet.

A Korean officer emerged from the tent and quickly met them halfway. Thomlin noticed the man's rank and saw that he was a major. The officers exchanged salutes, even though it was not common practice for Americans to salute in the field.

"Look here, Sir," Nelson started to explain in a tone of authority, "the 1-77th clearly has priority over the pickup zone. You and your men need to vacate the area for our upcoming air assault mission."

Within seconds Thomlin realized that the Korean officer didn't speak a word of English and probably understood even less. The major bowed his chest out and moved within inches of Nelson's face. The Korean started speaking in a hurried voice, clearly not happy with presence of the Americans in his area. Thomlin silently cursed himself for not bringing a KATUSA with them to translate.

"Sir, let me repeat, my unit owns this training area today. Your unit needs to move out, okay?" Nelson said as he referenced some range paperwork extended in his hand.

Although the two men obviously did not speak the same language, Nelson raised his voice and spoke slower. The major did the same, except he spoke even louder and now started to make wild gestures with his hands. Nelson loomed over the major and started slamming his hand into the paperwork as he screamed at him.

"Goddamn it, Major, what part of my range paperwork don't you understand? The 1-77th. Owns. This. Fucking. Training. Area."

Just great, Thomlin thought as both men were now at full volume, yelling at each other in foreign tongues. While Thomlin was quietly wishing he hadn't been selected for this task, he never saw the major's next move coming. In one swift movement the major had unhooked his nine millimeter pistol from his belt and raised it into the air. The movement was so fluid and so quick it took a full second or two for Thomlin to realize that the major was actually waving his weapon in front of them. The barrel of the weapon was never aimed directly at either of them; it became an extension of his gesturing hand. Nelson was stunned into silence. He was frozen solid as the major continued to scream and curse at ever increasing decibels.

"Dude," Thomlin whispered to Nelson, "his weapon is loaded with live ammo."

Thomlin looked down and became suddenly aware of the bright red blank adapter screwed onto the end of his M16 rifle, a necessary article to fire blank ammunition. He slowly reached over and put his hand on Nelson's shoulder. Nelson snapped out of his state and realized the major was speaking an international language that all of them could comprehend.

Nelson saluted smartly, "Well, major, as I was saying, the training area is yours for the duration."

The Humvee tires spun quickly as the Americans peeled out of the area. Inside the vehicle the men were silent as they rolled down the road. Nelson finally turned to face Thomlin and both men broke out laughing.

"I think I'll nominate you to break this one to Captain Watts," Thomlin chuckled.

"With pleasure," Nelson agreed.

■ ■ ■

Nearly 100 yards away, Private Ko watched the two American officers argue with the Korean major. Ko, along with several other Korean soldiers on a routine work detail, worked shirtless in the summer heat filling sandbags. There was no rain falling but the humid air trapped by the overcast sky wrapped around their bodies. Ko continued to fill and stack the sandbags to repair a small dirt road that eroded under the monsoon rains, but never took his eyes off the event unfolding in the distance.

"What are you looking at?" one of the other soldiers asked Ko.

"Do you see the American officers? I think I recognize one of them. The one that is a little shorter. Not sure, but he looks like the platoon leader I had when I was attached to an American unit," Ko said. His voice trailed as he thought about the short time he spent as a KATUSA.

"You were with the Americans?" another soldier scoffed. "If you were really assigned to them, why are you here? You should have stayed with them."

Ko turned to face the soldier that overheard him. "I was only with them for a short time," Ko said quietly. "They don't think anything of us or our country. They hate being here and take it out on the Koreans in the unit."

A few younger soldiers stopped filling sandbags for a moment and were now staring at Ko. The soldier that initially questioned Ko seemed unimpressed.

"I've met a few American soldiers before," he said casually. "I didn't think they were really that different than any other solders, except not many of them smoke."

"That's not true," Ko said. He was getting defensive as all of the soldiers in the work detail stopped and began to listen to the exchange. "They're not like us. They don't even understand us. If it wasn't for them and their government we would be one country by now."

The other soldier slammed the tip of his shovel into the mud. "That's crazy. You don't know what you're talking about. The Americans have nothing to do with it."

Ko turned his back on the other soldiers and watched the two American officers again.

"They think they are superior to us," Ko said. His eyes lit up when he saw the major raise his weapon. "But they're not."

As the lieutenants retreated into their vehicle and sped away Ko smiled before picking up his entrenching tool to shovel mud into an empty sandbag.

■ ■ ■

By nightfall the final company mission was over and the soldiers headed back to Tent City. The soldiers disembarked the trucks and streamed toward the dining facility for their last hot meal in Tent City. The captains in the battalion operations staff quickly worked to resolve the scheduling problem with the pickup zone area, as soldiers finished their meal and piled into the canteen to max out their two-beer limit. Thomlin and the other lieutenants did the same, all knowing that the beer restrictions would be overlooked if anyone decided to have more than his share. By midnight soldiers were stumbling into their tent to rest for a few hours before the quick jaunt to the pickup zone. The lights in the command tent stayed lit well through the night as several officers remained glued to their radios, staying in close contact with their Korean counterparts to work out a compromise for the training area.

Thomlin woke when Wilson kicked his cot slightly to rouse

him. The first thing Thomlin noticed was that it was already light outside. The original plan called for a tactical battalion road march before dawn. Thomlin immediately knew that something was amiss. As he gathered his gear Nelson entered the tent with the latest update.

"The Koreans have no intention of moving," Nelson told him. "As a compromise, they are going to halt their operations for a few hours and let the battalion march past the training area to an alternate pickup zone. It's just a few miles beyond the original."

"Just great," Thomlin huffed, "when are we supposed to step off?"

"Don't know. Whenever they tell us, I guess."

Thomlin walked out of the tent and could see some of the soldiers already arranging themselves on the road leading out of Tent City. Many sat on the ground leaning up against their rucksacks in what was commonly known as the rucksack flop. Soon, all several hundred members of the battalion were sprawled out waiting for the word to get up and move out. The rain had finally stopped for the first time in several weeks and Thomlin could feel a steamy sensation as the heat rose from the ground into the air.

Hours passed and no orders came down from battalion headquarters. The midmorning sun rose into a cloudless sky as the soldiers began to feel the heat. Many of them fell into a drowsy slumber under the humidity of the morning. Thomlin walked back and forth among his noncommissioned officers making idle chatter. The sweat was already coming through his uniform in patches and it was only ten in the morning. The heavy pressure on his bladder reminded him of the beer from the night before. Dehydration was already setting in and the soldiers had yet to take their first step toward the pickup zone.

Another hour and a half passed before Watts appeared in front of the company formation.

"Mount up!" he boomed.

The soldiers moved sluggishly, dragging themselves to their feet. The sun was directly overhead and bearing its full weight on every soldier's load.

"Get ready, el-tee," Wilson said quietly as he passed Thomlin. "Something tells me this isn't going to be fun."

Thomlin managed a smile. "C'mon, Sergeant. This is a quick walk in the park."

Finally the soldiers began walking through the gates of Tent City onto the hard pavement. Within a mile the pavement was gone and replaced by the dirt road. With every step along the dry dirt more dust was kicked up until it hung in the air in a permanent yellow haze.

"Sir," Thomlin's radio operator mumbled, "I don't feel so good."

"Christ, man," Thomlin answered. "We can still see Tent City. Keep moving."

Only a few hundred yards onto the dirt road, Thomlin's radio operator doubled over and began vomiting. Thomlin could smell the alcohol rising from the remnants the young soldier left on the ground.

"Medic," Wilson called as he quickly marched over to the young soldier. Wilson grabbed the soldier by his rucksack and screamed a few obscenities in his ear.

"Sir," Wilson said to Thomlin, "it's no use trying to make him walk any further. Let the medic take care of it."

The platoon medic hustled over, sat the soldier down on the side of the road and stuck an intravenous needle into his arm. The needle was hooked to a small bag of saline solution to hydrate the heat casualty. The platoon continued along the windy road without stopping. Thomlin cursed the fact there was no shade anywhere to be found along the road, leaving the soldiers to march completely exposed to the sun.

Within a few more hundred yards Thomlin noticed another soldier sitting along the side of the road with an IV dangling from his forearm. The soldier was from one of the platoons ahead in the order of march.

"Another one," Thomlin said to Wilson.

"Check your two o'clock, Sir," Wilson said, pointing to another fallen soldier. "Medics are gonna have their work cut out for them. There's more IVs out here than at a drug clinic."

"Hang in there," Thomlin shouted to his men as he felt streams of sweat pour over his face. He could feel the pit of stomach turn as he looked ahead and could see other soldiers lying off in the brush every few hundred yards or so.

"Hell, Sir," Wilson cursed, "this is like Hansel and Gretel. The battalion is leaving a trail of dehydrated soldiers behind in case we need to find our way home."

An hour and several dozen downed soldiers later, the unit had only moved a few miles. Soldiers had already drained what little water they held in their canteens and there were no planned water stops to refill. They could only push on until they reached their destination. Medics ran out of intravenous needles. Soldiers were left on the side of the road to wait for some imaginary trucks to pick them up. A few more of Thomlin's soldiers went down despite the encouragement of their NCOs. Thomlin was not immune to the effects of the heat and began to feel nauseous.

"Look," Wilson called to the men, "we're at the halfway point. Halfway home."

"Only halfway?" a soldier cried and immediately fell straight to the ground.

As Thomlin crested a small hill he saw AJ Fox on a stretcher lying buck naked on his side. It was obvious that Fox was more than dehydrated; he was suffering from heat stroke. Medics were spraying Fox down with his water to bring his body temperature down.

"Shit, that's more of Lieutenant Fox than I ever wanted to see," Wilson breathed.

"You know, I can't even remember a road march that made me feel this bad. Even in Ranger School, the movements weren't this bad," Thomlin said so only Wilson could hear.

"This is the goddamn Bataan Death March," one soldier whispered to another. Thomlin instantly knew that the incident would later become legend in the battalion folklore, even after all the soldiers currently on the march had rotated home.

A young soldier trotted up to Wilson. "Sergeant, we just lost third squad."

"The squad leader?" Wilson snapped.

"No, Sergeant. All of third squad just went down."

"All of third squad?" cried two soldiers in unison before collapsing and rolling off the side of the road.

"Holy hell," was all Wilson could say.

Thomlin and Wilson were helpless against the elements. The march degenerated into every man looking out for himself. They could only order their squad leaders to hold their squads together. In turn, the squad leaders delegated down to their team leaders, young corporals in charge of two to three men. By the time Thomlin neared the pickup zone he could notice entire squads sitting by the side of the road. One entire platoon from Charlie Company found the only tree within miles that offered enough shade for the whole platoon, and hovered around the trunk.

Thomlin briefly thought of throwing the towel in when he pulled his head up long enough to see the entrance to the pickup zone.

"We're here," Thomlin shouted in relief. He briefly put aside his pain and increased his gait. Wilson also stepped it as the two men finally reached the end of the march. Thomlin noticed Major Pierce and the captains from operations running back and forth trying to gain control. Thomlin and Wilson realized they would get no help from battalion staff and decided to attempt to collect the members of their platoon themselves.

Underneath a small tree the pair rested on one knee and tried to get some form of accountability.

"I don't believe that no one planned to put one drop of water for the soldiers on this entire goddamn route." Wilson shook his head in frustration.

As members of the platoon gaggled to their position, they pulled them together and redistributed the remaining water.

"This is going to take hours before the entire battalion is here," Thomlin said. Wilson only stared at the road.

Trucks materialized and made several trips to pick up the stragglers. Soldiers too sick to continue were trucked back to Camp Kayes.

As the sun finally set and relieved the men, Nelson passed Thomlin's position. "I hear over a third of the unit fell out. You believe that?"

"Unfortunately, I do."

"Everyone here from your platoon?"

Thomlin surveyed the panting bodies strewn across the area. "Most. I think only a half dozen soldiers were trucked back to the rear."

As night set in and Watts finally came to their position to issue more orders for the evening, Wilson muttered, "What a clusterfuck."

Thomlin grunted his agreement. However, the helicopters

were still scheduled to pick them up and airlift them back home. Thomlin gathered his squad leaders, relayed the orders from the company commander, and slowly moved his men into positions around the perimeter of the pickup zone. Clouds moved back into the open sky and a light drizzle fell, cooling the soldiers. Before long, the battalion had its game face back on. Units were now moving in a tactical manner, resuming the original mission. Hours passed. Thomlin and the men of second platoon tried to forget the road march and focus on the last piece of the field exercise that would take them back to Camp Kayes.

■ ■ ■

The entire pickup zone was silent. The rains had temporarily stopped but there was too much cloud cover to reveal any illumination from the stars or moon. It was barely light enough to make out the outline of the soldiers hovering around the perimeter. Off in the distance, toward the center of the open area, a red chem light swung in wide, slow circles. A soldier was standing at the edge of the landing area ready to signal the birds that were still too far in the distance to hear the blades cutting through the air. The sound of crickets and the shining red circle seemed to be the only signal of life in the immediate area.

Lieutenant Colonel Gibson felt a mixture of anger and fatigue. He was still fuming over the debacle of a road march. He knew that in a stateside unit the fiasco earlier in the day would have been enough to seal his fate. "What commander lets so many men fall out?" he asked himself.

"You know, Major Streeter," Gibson whispered to Streeter kneeling beside him, "the combination of events between losing the black box and the botched road march is almost too much to take."

"I know, Sir," Streeter agreed quietly.

Gibson sighed and then pushed all the negative thoughts from his mind. "Focus on the current mission. Salvation always lies in concentrating on flawlessly performing the task at hand and not dwelling the past."

"Yes, Sir."

"This air mobile mission, right now, is what it's supposed to be about. One hundred percent tactical. No one moves, no one makes a sound. This is gotta be the payoff to a successful field exercise. All the other admin bullshit is frustrating, but events like this, the simulated combat conditions, will prepare the men."

"Sir," Streeter whispered, "did you hear that?"

To Gibson's far left he heard a faint, high pitched sound.

"Oooh, seeee…"

Gibson cocked his head to hear more. The sound began to grow louder as whatever it was drew closer. The noise soon became distinct syllables as it grew louder.

"What the hell is that?" Gibson asked. Streeter shrugged.

"Oooke. Epseeee…"

Gibson scratched his ear to ensure that he was not hearing things. For the first time he could notice the barely audible noises of soldiers to his left and right rustle the nearby brush as they shifted their weight. The whine, which was clearly a woman's voice, became even louder as it cut through the silence like an oncoming police siren.

"Coooke. Pepsiiiii."

What in the hell? Gibson thought. Murmurs rose from the men around him. Everyone seemed stunned at what they were hearing. Although the darkness of the night was thick, Gibson identified the outline of what was obviously a short, overweight Korean woman with a bucket of sodas on her head strolling 50 feet to his front.

"I don't believe it." Gibson shook his head. "The most technologically advanced and technically proficient army the world has ever known, operating in a tactical, airtight defensive perimeter, has just been penetrated by a 100-year-old ajoomma with a twelve pack of bottled Cokes on her freakin' head."

Old Mama Lee glided around the opening without the need of a $13,000 pair of night vision goggles. She moved close to each position uttering the few English words she knew. Before, Gibson could hardly hear those around him, but now he could easily hear the younger soldiers giggle and the officers openly curse.

"At this point, I'm almost ready to just pull out my wallet and buy some drinks," said Gibson

The loud rotary hum of approaching Blackhawks was finally audible, but it didn't matter now. The operation had lost any sense of realism. Even the glowing arch of the signaling red chem light seemed to be off course for a few rotations.

Streeter's whole body shook. "Sir, let's just get the hell out of here."

Gibson silently agreed.

■ ■ ■

The 20-minute flight back was a relief to Thomlin. The air blasting through the open doors of the helicopter made him feel completely awake. Even in the darkness of the helicopter he could see the faces of the other soldiers with him. They were worn but also visibly relieved that the exercise was over. The birds landed within the compound of Camp Kayes, across from the battalion area. The men unloaded their gear and walked the short distance to their platoon area.

Thomlin found Nelson in the company area. "Same drill as always?"

"You got it. Let the soldiers clean the gear for a couple of hours, then let's plan on turning everything into the arms room by zero-one hundred."

"We releasing the soldiers after that?"

"No. Let me do the arms room inspection twice, unless you want to do it with me. We'll wait until the final status is sent to Brigade. Then, everyone can hit the rack."

"Okay. Can you convince the commander to make first call at seven? They'll get five hours of sleep that way."

Nelson barely nodded his head, already feeling sleepy. A few hours later, in the early morning hours, Nelson, Dougall, and Thomlin drifted back to their Quonset huts after their soldiers had settled down in their bunks.

13

PROTEST

Thomlin and the rest of the lieutenants slept late the morning back from the field. There was no physical training and Thomlin knew the next few days would be routine cleaning and re-cleaning of equipment and weapons. For Thomlin, it was Wilson's show. Wilson and the rest of the squad leaders would take complete control over the platoon's activities now that everyone was back in garrison. The lieutenants would be needed only to spot check and inspect at the request of their sergeants. It was routine and boring to Thomlin, but a necessary evil to ensure everything was ready and operational for the next deployment.

The lieutenants emerged from the Quonset hut and lazily moved to the dining facility before heading to their company areas. Still tired from the few hours of sleep and dehydration of the day before, the conversation among the group of lieutenants was light. AJ Fox had already returned to the unit and joined the men sitting for breakfast. Fox had recovered fully and showed no damage from the heat stroke. Unfortunately for Fox, his condition was not serious enough to prevent him from becoming the butt of more than a few jokes from the other lieutenants. In an Army infantry unit sympathy only extended to those who were dismembered or dead.

After breakfast, Thomlin immediately went to check in with Wilson. As he entered the company barracks he drew his attention to the chalk bulletin board posting the latest information. A message was scrawled in large, bold letters, warning soldiers not to go outside the front gate of Camp Kayes until at least 1800 hours. The word "protest" was written in even larger letters and underlined several times. The drunken act of Specialist Wickersham had drawn attention from the entire Korean community of Dongducheon. Hundreds of Koreans would post themselves outside the main gate of Kayes to protest the Status of Forces Agreement, the American presence in Korea, or whatever else they were upset with the Americans about. Soldiers did not want to be caught outside the gate during this time for fear of becoming an unwitting target of a foreign mob. However, the posting on the bulletin board did not serve as a deterrent for soldiers wanting to observe from within the base. They would grab their cameras and video recorders, and head down to catch a glimpse.

With everyone distracted between the required maintenance and the protests, Thomlin thought the timing was perfect for his interview with Wickersham. He headed over to the headquarters billets and found a young sergeant sitting outside Wickersham's room reading a magazine. Thomlin walked with a determined pace toward the room and carried a clipboard with paperwork to make the visit look official.

"I need to speak with Wickersham."

"I'm sorry, Sir," the sergeant said, "but it's the company commander's orders that no one can talk to this guy."

"I understand, Sergeant, but I am the survey officer for the ANCD investigation," Thomlin spoke with authority. "Right now you're impeding progress. The battalion commander wants this done ASAP. By regulation, I need Wickersham's sworn statement in order to bring this to closure."

The sergeant frowned. He paused for a moment as if unsure how to take the whole situation. Thomlin knew that he was not intimidating but counted on the sergeant to at least believe part of what he was saying.

"Sir, no one mentioned to me that you were stopping by," the sergeant said. He sat in silence, scrutinizing Thomlin. Thomlin switched tactics.

"Look, Sergeant, I know the last thing you need is some lieutenant coming by and making your life difficult. I just need five minutes to get his statement and then I'm out of your hair. Just let me talk to him. You can take a break for a couple of minutes, can't you?"

"Sir, I'm going to grab some coffee, but I'll be back in a few minutes." The sergeant shrugged before standing up and stepping aside.

Thomlin thanked him and walked into the room. Wickersham's room was typical of any soldier's room. It contained a wooden bunk with a dark green wool blanket, a desk, a wall locker for uniforms and gear, and a small refrigerator placed next to the desk. The walls were painted white, barren of any posters or pictures. It was remarkably plain and ordinary by any standard.

Specialist Kenneth Wickersham leaned back on his bunk with his head resting against the wall and his feet firmly planted on the floor. He was a lanky six-foot-two, wore his hair length to the edge of Army regulations, and had sideburns that might have looked better on Elvis. Thomlin guessed he was no older than 21 or 22. Wickersham's hands were chained together about twelve inches apart, as were his feet. A long chain connected the bindings on his wrists to the chains on his feet. Although Thomlin didn't expect Wickersham to get up and greet him, Thomlin was surprised that Wickersham didn't even acknowledge him. Thomlin pulled a chair from the desk and sat across from Wickersham.

"Specialist Wickersham, I'm Lieutenant Thomlin, the Report of Survey officer," Thomlin said, looking Wickersham directly in the eye. "I need a statement from you regarding the lost black box from Headquarters Company."

"Why the hell do you need a statement from me?" Wickersham lifted his eyes to meet Thomlin, revealing a smug expression. "The last time we went out to the field, I signed over the black box and the other weapons and sensitive items to everyone in headquarters. We went to the field and Padilla lost it. End of story."

Thomlin ignored Wickersham's lack of military courtesy, but became increasingly irritated at the look on Wickersham's face.

"Is there something funny, Specialist Wickersham?"

"Why do you ask?"

"You're smiling. I want to know what the joke is."

"The joke? This whole situation is one big joke, you know that?"

"Let's cut the bullshit, Wickersham," Thomlin said coldly. "The black box wasn't even signed out for that exercise. It was lost during the previous move to Tent City. You fucked up, didn't conduct the arms room inspection as you were supposed to when the battalion returned from the field, and then noticed it was lost the next day. When you noticed it was finally missing you decided that the easiest thing to do was to wait until the next field exercise. Then, you faked records signing it out and had Padilla report it missing before the end of the field exercise."

Wickersham's expression never changed as Thomlin spoke. Thomlin was heated and on the edge of the wooden chair.

"What I can't figure out is why Padilla agreed to go along with it. What do you have over that kid?"

"Sir, you got nothin' on me." Wickersham leaned forward and smiled broadly.

"Wickersham, you're about to be convicted and put in a Korean jail. Why don't you come clean and tell me what happened?"

"I'll never do time. Who gives a shit about an old Korean whore?"

"Apparently, a few hundred Koreans in Dongducheon. They're protesting outside the main gate because of you."

"I'm not worried."

"You seem pretty impressed with yourself."

"I have friends in high places who owe me a favor."

"I sincerely hope you have naked pictures of the division commander."

"Like I said, Lieutenant, I'm not worried." Wickersham spoke with such arrogance that it made Thomlin flinch.

"Perhaps, you should tell me the truth about what happened. After all, what do you have to fear? At least you'll have a backup in case something doesn't work out for you."

"I'm not stupid, el-tee," Wickersham scoffed with an exaggerated facial expression. "I don't need any contingencies."

Thomlin ignored Wickersham's bad attitude and focused on the sequence of events. Something was missing and Thomlin couldn't put his finger on it.

"Why Padilla? Why screw over a good soldier like that?"

"Padilla will be fine, Sir, don't worry about that kid. At most he'll lose one month's pay, go back to the States and forget about the whole damn thing."

Thomlin could feel the blood flooding his face. He thought of Padilla and wanted to make Wickersham's head a permanent fixture in the wall. Just as Thomlin was about to ask another question, Major Streeter opened the door. He stood in the hallway and did not enter the room. Everyone exchanged glances for a brief moment before the battalion executive officer spoke.

"Excuse me, Lieutenant Thomlin, may I have a word with you?"

Thomlin got up and walked in the hallway, closing the door behind him. Major Streeter put his hand around Thomlin and walked with him down the hall.

"Greg, no one is supposed to talk to Wickersham after what he did. The battalion commander would probably have a fit if he knew you were in there."

"I was just getting his statement, Sir. I appreciate your understanding for slightly bending the rules."

"I'll tell you what. Leave the form with me and I will make sure that piece of garbage writes down a full statement for your report. I'll have it to you by tomorrow morning."

"Not sure how much good it will do, Sir. Wickersham seems pretty adamant about his position."

"Well, I wouldn't worry about this too much, Greg. It seems to everyone that this one is pretty straightforward. The black box went to the field, Slicky Boy arrived, and it ended up missing."

Thomlin nodded his head as Major Streeter talked. He finally reached the end of the hall and thanked the executive officer before heading back to the company area.

■ ■ ■

When Thomlin returned to his company area he found Dougall and Nelson with a video recorder.

"Hundreds of protestors are packing the streets outside the main gate of Camp Kayes," Dougall anxiously explained. "Nelson and I don't wanna miss the fun so we're going to get some live footage of a potential riot."

"I could use a distraction right about now," Thomlin replied. He could still see Wickersham's smirking face in the back of his mind. "Okay, I'm in."

After several minutes at the bus stop the three lieutenants boarded a bus and got off at the last stop before the main gate. Dougall stepped off first and was openly disappointed that several dozen other soldiers also had the same idea. Groups of soldiers with cameras and camcorders lined the area before the main gate trying to get pictures or video.

"I can't see a damn thing," Dougall complained. He stood on his toes to see what was happening on the other side of the gate through the crowds of onlookers. The three lieutenants maneuvered their way through the mass of bodies for a better vantage point.

"This is the definition of irony," Thomlin said.

"How's that?" Dougall asked.

"Hundreds of Koreans are over there protesting the presence of Americans, yet their demonstration is drawing even more Americans who think this is entertaining."

"What do you think they're shouting?" Dougall asked.

"The usual. The mob is probably showing their hatred for policies that grant Americans preferential treatment in their country," Thomlin answered.

Many shouted slogans and brandished signs. The crowd was mostly made up of men, but Thomlin could soon notice college-aged women. He assumed that many of the protestors came all the way from Seoul. For students, protesting, whether it was against the American presence or their own government, was an integral part of their college experience. Unlike the popular views of university students in the United States, young Koreans considered public demonstrations part of their civic duty.

A middle-aged Korean man standing on top of a car was shouting something through a bullhorn. He screamed something unintelligible and the crowd of Koreans would respond in unison. The man gained momentum with each shouted phrase. The people surrounding him were all standing, shouting, and raising their fists. American military police began forming a line at the inside of the gate, ordering the observing soldiers to back away from the gate. The American personnel largely ignored the MPs and looked for spots to snap more photographs.

Somewhere beyond the gate a whistle blew. As the sound grew louder, Thomlin saw the ROK police marching toward the main gate in full riot gear. Their bodies were covered in thick black padding over dark blue uniforms. Each of them carried a long black metal riot shield in one arm and a three-foot-long baton in the other. They quickly formed a barrier three rows deep in front of the main gate. The military police let out a collective sigh as the ROK police arrived. The situation would soon be under control.

"Get the cameras ready," Thomlin said, "I think we're about to see some action."

The protestors continued their demonstration for another ten minutes. They did not dare come toward the main gate and did not seem to turn violent, but the ROK police decided the demonstration was over. With a sharp whistle blow the ranks of blue and black clad officers suddenly burst forward with batons raised. Tear gas canisters exploded and covered the area in a white haze. The Korean protestors turned in all directions and ran in a panic. Anyone not fast enough to move away from the Korean police suffered repeated blows. The young policemen were skilled in the use of riot control tactics and wielded their batons with expertise. Political ideology in the minds of the protestors quickly gave way to thoughts of survival. The screaming flurry of people broke off in all directions. The ROK police peeled off into smaller groups and ran through the city streets chasing the fleeing demonstrators.

Dougall and Nelson laughed hysterically while trying to catch everything on film. The MPs no longer tried to hold back the crowd of Americans, and many poured into the streets after the ROK police.

"Let's go," Nelson yelled and Dougall and Nelson followed the crowd. Nelson acted as the combat anchorman and Dougall played his cameraman. Thomlin made no effort to join the pair. He had seen demonstrations like this before. In Seoul, the protestors were usually more resilient, and sometimes more violent.

Before leaving the scene, Thomlin perked his ears after overhearing part of a conversation by one of the uniformed soldiers next to him. Thomlin turned and noticed a young corporal talking to some other soldiers.

"I'm sorry for eavesdropping, but what did you just say?" Thomlin asked.

"Sir, I said this should bode well with the new pass policy," the young soldier replied.

"What are you talking about?"

"Sir, the Koreans in TDC are already pissed at us for some dumbass soldier in the 77th beating up one of their women." The corporal frowned, obviously not enjoying that he was forced to explain something to a lieutenant. "Now they're going to be even angrier when they find out that the post commander has just changed the pass policy for everyone on Camp Kayes. From now on, only ten percent of each unit will be allowed to be outside the gates after midnight. Every battalion is going to have to issue passes for anyone that is going downrange past twelve, otherwise they're not going to be able to get back in the gate until the next morning."

Thomlin was in shock. He saw his social life flash before his eyes. The soldier continued with more bad news.

"I hear that the Koreans are pretty upset because all the bars and nightclubs are going to lose a shitload of money. Supposedly, all the business owners are to shut everything down in protest when the pass policy goes into effect next week. Every single place is supposed to close its doors until the post commander changes the policy back, and you and I know that's never going to happen."

Downrange on strike? Thomlin asked himself. It was inconceivable. He wanted to break down and weep, but decided to flag down a taxi and head back to the battalion area. Thomlin pushed aside the thoughts of the Report of Survey again and focused on the upcoming weekend. His single thought for the next 24 hours would be to pass the weapons and equipment inspections and secure a weekend pass to head down to Itaewon, the section all foreigners went to in Seoul.

14

ITAEWON

The weekend arrived. The unit passed the numerous required inspections and the soldiers, including the officers, would have some time to themselves. The rumored pass policy restrictions had become official, and in response downrange shut down. Soldiers were bitter at the turn of events but vowed to move their plans to within the limits of the base. Thomlin was surprised when Watts casually approved his weekend pass and plans to head south to Seoul. Thomlin imagined that Watts must have believed Thomlin would do less damage far from Camp Kayes versus sticking around the company area. Dougall, Ward and Nelson also managed to secure passes for themselves and joined Thomlin.

"How are we getting there?" Dougall asked.

"A couple of options," Thomlin said, internally debating their mode of transportation before leaving the confines of Camp Kayes. "Seoul is only about 40 miles south. Buses leave every few hours from the main gate but make a few stops along the way, guaranteeing a two-hour trip at a minimum."

"Let's go with a taxi. It's the fastest way. We can be down there in 45 minutes," Ward suggested.

"No way. Too expensive," Thomlin said. He turned to Dougall, "If you thought driving through Terminator Alley was scary, you've never driven in a civilian taxi."

Thomlin remembered a trip when he sat petrified in the passenger seat as the taxi careened around the streets at insanely high speeds, narrowly missing oncoming traffic.

"That leaves us the train," Nelson offered. Thomlin knew that the most efficient way was by train. They could catch the train that ran every hour out of Dongducheon and get off in Uijeongbu. In Uijeongbu they would switch from the train to the subway that would take them all the way into Seoul.

The first leg of their journey was uneventful and only lasted 30 minutes. The four boarded the rickety train that looked several decades old and stood in the open compartment at the rear. The train was only partially occupied but the four opted for the open air instead of the rows of seats and stale air of the enclosed cars.

"I think this train is older than some of the relics sitting in the seats," Nelson joked.

"I don't know which smell is worse, inside the cars or out here," Ward added.

They stood watching the scenery pass as the train rolled through the rundown towns and local villages to the south of Dongducheon. The one-story homes looked like metal shacks, each with a large satellite dish on the roof. Everywhere they looked they could see rice paddies and mountains in the distance. Eventually, the towns grew larger and pavement began to replace the rice fields.

Unlike the station in Dongducheon, the subway platform in Uijeongbu was packed with Koreans. The four pale white Americans stuck out in the crowd. They moved through a swarm of foreign faces to make their way to the ticket booth.

The line before the booth was long and the men jockeyed for position as older Koreans cut in front of them, keeping the Americans to the back of the line. Dougall's expression showed his frustration. He was baffled by the rudeness of the people maneuvering in front of him and was tempted to blurt something out to give the people around him a piece of his mind.

"Don't get upset," Thomlin said, sensing Dougall's annoyance. "In many Asian societies there's an unspoken caste system. Koreans are brought up this way since their youth and naturally respect their elders and people in positions of authority. Many Koreans don't understand how to treat Americans in regards to the community structure, and simply decide to ignore us or pretend we're not there."

Thomlin noticed Dougall frown and relax his shoulders. "That's a weird custom."

"Younger soldiers are usually offended by this, and sometimes voice their thoughts. But this only reinforces the perception in the minds of some Koreans that Americans are rude and disrespectful."

"We're the rude ones?"

"Just do yourself a favor and shrug it off as the price of being a foreigner."

The Seoul subway system was a complex, metropolitan mass-transit system. Unlike the vintage train that took them from Dongducheon to Uijeongbu, Seoul's subway system rivaled other modern nations. To inexperienced travelers, the map posted on the walls of the subway platform was nothing more than colored lines and hieroglyphics. Thomlin helped his friends navigate to their destination and they blindly followed.

"Thank God for Thomlin," Ward said. "Master of the Korean subway system."

Thomlin led his group through a train change and several stops. Within an hour, the four lieutenants emerged almost a quarter of a mile away from the main U.S. Army post in Seoul, Camp Yongsan, headquarters for the Second Infantry Division.

It was almost ten o'clock and Thomlin had no intention of stopping at the Army post. Even in the evening darkness he could make out the silhouette of the city. He noticed the Seoul Tower rising almost 800 feet above the skyline and it reminded him of the Seattle Space Needle. The wide city streets were jammed with traffic and the sound of horns and accelerating engines filled the air. Thomlin smiled. This was his favorite place in all of Korea, the center of activity, and the only place in the country where he felt slightly at home.

■ ■ ■

Seoul, the native Korean word for "capital," had played an integral part in Korea's history for centuries. The city was located on the downstream of the Han River that cut across the central part of the Korean Peninsula. For Thomlin, it was almost overwhelming. Home to over a fifth of all South Koreans, the city boasted a population of over ten million. There were huge high rises and modern buildings stretching toward the sky, yet there was also poverty that could not be overlooked. On the hillside beyond some of the recent buildings Thomlin could see small apartments, almost like shanties, stacked up on each other. It was a mix of both modern and old, progress and the stagnant.

Over the centuries, the city seemed to grow exponentially. By the seventeenth century the population was already over 200,000. The ruling king established city districts and organized a complex bureaucracy to administer the growing populace. An additional population spurt came in the nineteenth century when the country opened itself to foreign powers and the establishment of foreign missions in Seoul.

Thomlin admired the fact that the city had withstood the test of time. With each passing invading force, Seoul had been ransacked and sometimes burned to the ground. In the twentieth century, it was the Japanese who invaded. Starting with the annexation of Korea in 1910 and decades of Japanese rule through the end of World War II, the suffering continued when the North Koreans invaded only several years later. The city, like the people, had been beaten back only to rebuild and rise again.

"We're almost in Itaewon," Thomlin said. The men continued to walk almost a mile beyond the Army post to a small section of the city. During the daytime Itaewon was the shopping district for foreign travelers, and at night it was the best place to party until the sun came up. "Itaewon is Korea's way of keeping all the foreigners in one area."

"You kidding me?" Dougall asked.

"When we've tried to go out to other sections of the city Korean bouncers always refuse to let us in. The bouncers will flat out tell you that they don't accept foreigners, only Koreans. But, it doesn't matter because Itaewon has enough for every tourist and foreign national living in the country. Soldiers, tourists, English teachers, visiting performers, businessmen and anyone else not born here hangs out in Itaewon."

"And everyone in Itaewon hangs out at the Hill," Nelson added in reference to the infamous Hooker Hill. Stretching only a few hundred yards in the center of town, Hooker Hill was a steep, narrow road lined with bars and nightclubs.

"Oh, please no more midgets," Dougall groaned.

"I promise you the initiation period is over," Thomlin laughed. "A decade ago the Hill was covered with brothels. Prostitutes openly solicited customers, competing with one another for the cash of anyone that walked by. This place is legendary. I've met people who've never even set foot on the continent who ask me about the Hill. Over time the brothels were replaced with bars, but every soldier still knows it by the name that made it popular."

The four lieutenants rounded a corner past a large neon-lit McDonald's and headed down the city street that ran perpendicular to Hooker Hill. Turning up the street to the Hill, Thomlin could see the nightly party had already started. The rise of the small knoll was so steep that it made the buildings appear as if they were almost stacked on top of each other, like a giant staircase. Many of the nightclubs had different themes targeting specific tastes in music or dress. As the men continued upward they could hear Pantera, George Straight, and the Spice Girls, all blaring out of different clubs. Many of the bars had no theme, as they were barely large enough to hold a dozen occupants.

The street cutting up through the center of the hill was completely jammed with people. Thomlin guessed that the clubs were already packed, along with the sitting areas just outside the nightclubs, leaving standing room only in the street. Voices with Australian and European accents blended with other unfamiliar dialects. American soldiers barely made up the majority of the partygoers. Thomlin pressed on toward the top of the hill with Ward, Nelson, and Dougall following close behind.

"There's a successive order to the bars on the Hill," Thomlin said. "The higher up the hill, the larger the bar and the better the clientele."

Thomlin pushed on until they reached the entrance of the King Kettle House, his favorite drinking spot on the Hill. Beyond the door was a narrow, poorly lit hall that led into the main bar. A long bar stretched along the side of one wall with an open dance floor in front. Against the opposite walls a few tables, chairs and couches were strewn about in no particular order. The back wall was mostly glass, overlooking the main street of Itaewon off the backside of the hill. Speakers tucked in the corners of the room were cranking out Oasis as the men walked in. Already, cliques of people were standing in their groups across the floor in front of the bar. Thomlin knew that the floor would be completely packed and impassable within the next few hours. The open floor would become a makeshift dance floor.

Nelson walked over to the bar and shouted a music request to the short Korean man standing next to the record players. Nelson's request immediately triggered a violent response from the shorter man, who immediately lunged across the top of the bar and was a few inches from Nelson's face.

"You want to get rowdy?" the man was screamed at Nelson. "I will throw all of you out."

Dougall was completely unaware of what was going on, but Thomlin was openly laughing.

"It's an inside joke," Thomlin explained. "Nelson must have requested 'Safety Dance' by Men Without Hats. For some reason, the song elicits mass chaos and always promises to cause a riot."

"Why's that?"

"No clue. It's a tradition that began long before our arrival in country."

Ward was quick to make his way to the bar, buying several

40-ounce bottles of beer from a tall, blond bartender sporting a thick Australian accent. Thomlin wasn't sure if the bar was Korean owned or not, but the mix seemed to draw a very diverse crowd.

Unfortunately, not diverse enough, Thomlin thought. He glanced over and noticed Nicole Foster standing with Josh Shelton and a few other lieutenants from Headquarters Company. Thomlin cringed. He thought Foster was obnoxious even if he wasn't sure if she was drunk yet. Thomlin put his back to Foster and hoped she wouldn't notice him as the place began to quickly fill up. Two beers later, Thomlin couldn't even notice Foster through the sea of faces that swayed back and forth. The King Kettle House was close to maximum capacity but more people trickled in.

Thomlin scanned the faces in the crowd several times before suddenly stopping to stare at a Korean woman near the bar. He squinted hard for several seconds as he examined the woman's features before finally recognizing her. He smiled when the woman turned her head in his direction and caught his gaze. As Thomlin cut through the crowd he noticed the woman's face hardening to granite. It was the American woman Thomlin met at Crossroads after the Hail and Farewell.

"Hi there," Thomlin smiled broadly. "I remember you. I don't think we had proper introductions back in Dongducheon."

"Unfortunately, I remember you too. Are you and your friends looking for another nightclub to trash, or did you just come over to practice more of your broken English?"

Thomlin forced a laugh, brushing off the comments.

"You probably won't believe this but I came all the way from Dongducheon just to try to find you."

"You're right. I don't believe you."

"Look, I just wanted to apologize for our first meeting. Honestly, I didn't mean to offend you. As a peace offering, let me buy you a drink."

"Oh, please," the woman rolled her eyes. "You can do me a favor and just leave. I'm sure after a couple of drinks and a few weeks of therapy we'll both forget that we ever met each other."

Thomlin was beginning to enjoy the banter. He extended his hand and said, "Well, that's just it, we never formally met. My name is Greg."

She ignored Thomlin's outstretched hand and tried to stare him down.

"Just what do I have to do to make you go away? If you look directly behind you there is a very drunk Korean national. She's right up your alley."

"I'm really not like that. But since we are on the subject, just what type are you looking for? Once again I find you in a bar inhabited by a lot of American soldiers. I think you're in denial."

"It just so happens that I am with someone. And I also came here because I know most of the bartenders."

"Whatever," Thomlin smiled, mocking her. "Since you're alone at the moment and the friendly neighborhood bartenders are ignoring you, why don't we buy each other a drink and continue this conversation?"

"Did I forget to mention last time that you are a complete ass?"

Thomlin was undeterred. The woman's sarcasm only seemed to encourage him. He started to parry this with a quick retort when a short, blond-haired girl wedged between the people around them and stood by her side. Thomlin could see the expression of victory on the Korean-American girl's face as she introduced her.

"This is my friend Sam." She then leaned close to Thomlin and said with a smile, "I'm sorry, but like I tried telling you, I'm not interested."

With that, she grabbed her friend by the hand and headed for the door. As she headed out Thomlin noticed two of the bartenders waving good-bye. Thomlin was still unable to move as he felt a hand slap him on the back.

"Way to go, hero," Nelson laughed.

"Maybe you should stick to the cheap women outside of Kayes," Foster screamed over the noise of the crowd as she joined Nelson. "They're more in your league. The women down here have probably heard all your pick-up lines."

Thomlin chose to ignore the words even though he was quite sure the people around him would not be able to do the same. Thomlin scanned the room for Dougall and Ward. Thomlin thought the both of them might have also enjoyed his blundering attempt to pick up a woman. The pair of lieutenants, oblivious to Thomlin, was standing at the end of the bar, up against a wall.

A short, darkly painted wall spanned the distance between the end of the bar and the large glass windows lining the back of the nightclub. Unlike the other walls of the club, this one was completely barren of any decorations or pictures. Dougall was surveying the entire bar scene when he leaned his body back against the wall. Under his body weight a hinged section of the wall gave way, causing Dougall to lose his balance and stumble through. Dougall lurched forward to regain his footing before realizing he had stumbled into a hidden room. Dougall figured the room was only about four feet wide and fifteen feet long, covering the distance between the bar and the edge of the nightclub. At the same moment Dougall calculated the approximate dimensions of the room he discovered he was not alone. In the tiny corridor a half dozen naked couples were busily working in various sexual positions. Dougall straightened and stood in shock, having just

stumbled into a moving, living demonstration of the Kama Su-
tra. The thrusting and gyrating abruptly stopped with Dougall's
intrusion. One of the men shouted at Dougall in a thick foreign
accent to get out, and followed it with a string of profanity-laden
shouts. Startled, Dougall backed his way out of the room and the
door was slammed shut behind him. Dougall stood at the closed
section of the wall for a moment or two, still thinking about what
was taking place on the other side.

"It looks like you've found the secret room," Ward said over
the music.

Dougall was dumbfounded. He wondered how many others
knew of this secret passage.

"I wouldn't go in there alone again," Ward added. "The bouncers will toss you down the hill."

Dougall shrugged off the incident but couldn't help stealing
glances at the wall. He thought he might catch someone going
in or out. Thomlin made his way over and joined Dougall and
Ward. Before Dougall could ask Thomlin about the hidden door,
Dougall saw a large soldier on the other side of the bar shove
someone to the ground. Dougall momentarily forgot about the
past few minutes and pointed the new development out to Thomlin. Thomlin turned and shook his head in disgust as he watched
the fight unfold.

Foster flirted with a stranger and once she had him fully engaged she positioned herself in the middle of the path of another man headed for the bathroom. When the oncoming man
brushed against her, Foster exaggerated the contact as if she had
been shoved. Foster made a scene as if she was physically hurt,
causing the man she was flirting with to defend her. A fist immediately went into the air, knocking the bladder-full patron to
the ground. Friends and onlookers quickly picked sides. Within
seconds, almost every person in the bar burst into action. Arms

were flailing toward the face of the nearest stranger. It was every man for himself, as the initial fight turned into a full bar brawl.

Thomlin could see Nelson fighting his way toward the front door and decided to do the same. Ward and Dougall towed behind Thomlin. Thomlin met Nelson just outside the club and quickly checked to ensure Ward and Dougall had joined them. The fight had already poured into the street on the hill and spread into neighboring bars. It appeared that everyone was fighting each other as several Koreans were on their knees trying to crawl through the action.

Thomlin could feel the burning glare of the Korean-American woman standing just outside the club.

"Again?" she shouted with a look of disgust. "What's wrong with you? One bar wasn't good enough so now you want to tear apart all of Itaewon?"

Thomlin desperately wanted to deny any involvement but the woman and her friend raced away down the back of the hill. Thomlin was about to pursue her when he felt a tug on his arm.

"MPs," Dougall shouted to Thomlin.

American military police started to make their way up the Hill, grappling with those on the outskirts of the larger conflict. The mob of brawlers was quick to notice the presence of the military police and suddenly the crowd unified against the oncoming uniformed soldiers. Like a drunken tsunami, the tidal wave of bodies pounded the American police as they tried to force their way up the hill. Many of the soldiers were knocked to the ground and rolled downhill toward the bottom. Others were picked up over the crowd like fans at a rock concert and surfed to the bottom. The military police regrouped at the bottom of the hill and made another attempt but met the same result. Thomlin could hear the laughter and shouts from the crowd with each attempt from the military police to get to the high ground.

"Are they actually playing Men Without Hats?" Dougall asked, still able to hear the music from the King Kettle House.

Before Thomlin could respond, he was caught by a sudden silence. All the noise on the Hill had stopped. Blue flashing lights could be seen on the street. Everything was quiet until a piercing voice rose from the bottom of the hill.

"ROK police!" a voice shrieked out, causing immediate panic.

People ran in every direction trying to get away from the Korean cops. Even Thomlin was hit with a splash of fear. There was no such concept as police brutality in Korea and every American soldier knew this. Ironically, the Korean police did not carry pistols or tasers, only their long, deadly batons. But it was the baton every drunk feared. Even bystanders tried to get away as fast as they could. If an onlooker was accidentally beaten, the Korean cops would probably say the bystander shouldn't have been there in the first place and therefore had it coming.

Within minutes the street halfway down the Hill was empty. Everyone was screaming and running. Even the crowd at the top turned to run. The bar brawlers completely dispersed. The four lieutenants also ran for safety, heading down the steps on the backside of Hooker Hill. They cut through traffic and moved to the opposite side of the main street through Itaewon to catch their breath.

"Well, fun's over," Nelson said.

"Helluva grand finale for the night," Thomlin added.

"That was supposed to be fun?" Dougall asked. "What now?"

"You remember the walk of shame, right? Think of this as the extended version with taxis, buses, and trains. It's the long trip back home," Thomlin said.

The men turned down the sidewalk and headed to Camp Yongsan.

15

MOTEL FOOD COURT

"Anyone for some meat on a stick?" Thomlin asked as he headed for the small, three-wheeled cart.

"Nasty," Ward panted. "Where do you think that meat comes from? When was the last time you saw cattle in this country?"

"Yeah, but the sweet barbecue sauce can make anything taste good," Thomlin said as he eyed the thin strips of beef hanging on wooden skewers. "I think I'll just go with the *kimbap*."

The vendor nodded at Thomlin and quickly scooped the food into a paper bag.

"What is that, a rice doughnut?" Dougall asked.

"Something like that. It's the most popular dish in the country," Thomlin said. Carrots, spinach, cucumber, sausage, radishes and other ingredients were spread over a layer of cooked rice, then rolled into a tube and sliced into thin pieces.

Thomlin and Dougall quickly swallowed the food before heading to the nearby Army post. Twenty minutes later the four men were walking through the security checkpoint at the main gate.

"It'll be several more hours before the buses or trains start running," Thomlin said. "We can either stay out here and sweat, or go to the only place on post open 24 hours."

"Yup, it's another night at the food court in the post exchange," Nelson said as the group followed.

Most of the booths inside the food court were already littered with the unconscious bodies of American partygoers. Ward and Dougall increased the count of motionless bodies by two as they slumped into an unoccupied booth. Nelson stumbled into the buffet area where some food was still available, leaving Thomlin in the middle of the dining area. Thomlin almost followed Nelson until he caught sight of a few women sitting in a nearby both.

Unlike most of the late night regulars of the food court, the women were engrossed in conversation. Thomlin would have ignored the women for the cold leftovers of the buffet except that he recognized one of them. It was a short blonde girl chatting away with another brunette that caused Thomlin to start firing the synapses in his brain. He was having difficulty recalling who she was but knew the alcohol-induced cloud on his memory might part briefly for a quick flashback. Finally, it came to him. Her name was Sam, the friend of the Korean-American girl he had unsuccessfully tried to connect with earlier. Since the young woman Thomlin wanted to talk to was nowhere to be found, Thomlin approached the blonde instead.

"Hi there. You're Sam, right? I'm Greg. We met earlier this evening. I know you met a few of my friends at the same time so I'm sure you didn't catch my name the first time around. Look, I was hoping I could to talk to your friend who was with you. I forgot her name."

Sam sat silently with a bewildered look on her face. She seemed a little embarrassed that she couldn't remember the man standing in front of her. Thomlin hoped that the only thing she could do to break the awkward silence was to offer the name of her friend. Just as Sam was about to speak her friend appeared from behind Thomlin with a tray of coffee and food.

"Wait," she blurted, suddenly remembering Thomlin, "you're the jerk that talked like an idiot to my friend back in Itaewon."

Thomlin didn't get the chance to explain before he was staring into the eyes of the Korean-American girl he had insulted only a few hours earlier. She looked at Thomlin with an expression that said she obviously had not forgotten who he was. It was also obvious from the giggling coming from two other girls seated at the table that Thomlin had been a topic of discussion. As Thomlin searched for the right words, a woman from the food court came up to the table with a handful of change. Thomlin distinctly heard the older woman speak Korean to the girl in front of him and use the name Yumi. Luckily, Thomlin knew the common English translation of the name.

"Look, Michelle," Thomlin started, "I just wanted to apologize again. I was rude and I insulted you, and I wanted to find a way to make it up to you. Do you mind if I sit down?"

Michelle was caught off guard when Thomlin used her name. Thomlin noticed the tray of junk food she was holding.

"At least let me buy you a cup of coffee or a Ho-Ho to make up for it."

"You're like a bad cold I just can't seem to shake," she said dryly. At last she cracked a smile. "If I offer you a seat is there any chance that you'll leave me alone afterwards?"

"When the sun comes up, I promise to go home," Thomlin offered. "So how did a nice American girl like you end up in Korea?" he asked as he took the seat across from her.

"Just your average story," she again said with a dry sense of humor. "Both my parents originally left Korea when they were kids, right after the war, and moved outside Seattle. Their families knew each other and matched them together when they were of marrying age."

"Sounds like the typical American romance."

"My two brothers and I were obviously born and raised in the States. Did I mention that I have two older brothers? Large, overprotective brothers, I might add, who are prone to violence."

"When is their parole date from prison? I'll send a postcard."

"My father worked at Fort Lewis as a government contractor," she added. "He got an opportunity to do a rotation over here in Uijeongbu several years ago and my parents have been back here ever since. After I graduated from college, I had some difficulty putting my hard earned liberal arts degree to good use, so I jumped at the chance to join my parents. I got a job tutoring English and that's what I've been doing for the past year and a half. The money is okay, but it's not the real reason I came back."

"So why did you come?"

"It was about getting back to my roots, so to speak. I know that sounds hokey, but I was brought up to speak both Korean and English and my family is still a traditional Korean family, even if only by American standards. Growing up I only knew of Korea through the stories of my parents and I wanted to see the country myself. So that's me, what about you?"

"Oh, nothing special," Thomlin said nonchalantly, "I had a standard, conventional childhood in suburbia, buried in the middle of Maryland. It was a typical Beaver Cleaver upbringing."

"Brothers? Sisters? Parents?" she asked.

"No other siblings. My parents divorced when I was a teenager and then I was raised by my father."

"What about your mother?"

"I don't have any contact with her," he said, slightly shifting in his seat.

"What?" Michelle asked a little surprised.

"When I was fifteen, my dad caught her in bed with a tennis pro, then after they reconciled I caught her sleeping with the garbage man."

"The garbage man?" she exclaimed. She almost choked on her drink.

"Yeah, can you believe it? For a while I wondered why the garbage truck was making rounds in my neighborhood five days a week."

"Funny, I don't remember seeing that episode on *Leave it to Beaver*," she said.

"Well, things happen, right? Anyway, it's no big deal. I was almost out of the house by that point."

She nodded and changed the subject, "Why go into the Army?"

"Believe it or not, I was very idealistic going into college and joined ROTC," Thomlin smiled.

"You don't say," she responded cynically.

"Yeah, but I lost all of that freshman year," Thomlin said. "I actually enjoyed the training and wasn't sure what I wanted to do. I think I enrolled in ROTC just to do something different. My father wanted me to be a lawyer and my friends were all prepared to go into the corporate world. I've never been one to go with the flow, so I thought the Army would be a good fit. See the world, do interesting stuff, that sort of thing."

"Let me get this straight," she smiled, "you wanted to rebel so you chose to join the most restrictive institution possible. Makes perfect sense. That's the craziest thing I've ever heard."

"It was either that or become a priest, and I don't look good in black. Look, I never said I'm the most rational person in the world."

As they spoke, Thomlin began to feel that she was reforming her opinion of him, maybe thinking that he was an intelligent person who didn't take himself too seriously, and not the arrogant buffoon she first made him out to be. The early morning hours passed quickly as Thomlin and Michelle passed the time trading stories. Michelle's friend Sam had long since fallen asleep in the corner of the booth. Thomlin did not feel any need to sleep, completely engaged in conversation. The darkness outside the food court began to fade as the first light of dawn poked through the window. Thomlin looked at his watch and couldn't believe it was close to seven in the morning. Staring at Michelle he began to think that he would trade all the one night stands he would ever have during his tour for another opportunity to see her.

"So, if you don't think I'm such a bad person, I would like to talk to you again sometime," Thomlin finally suggested.

"Are you trying to get my number?" she laughed.

"Look, I know I'm as sly as a bulldog, so let me just ask and get it over with. I really enjoyed this and I would like to see you again, okay? Would you like to go out sometime?"

"Well, you are mildly cute," she said, smiling.

"Was that an actual compliment?"

"Let's not get ahead of ourselves," she smiled again. For a moment she didn't say a word and then pulled a napkin to write her phone number. After she was done writing, she handed it to him and said, "Let's just keep this as friendship, okay? You can call to talk any time."

Thomlin thanked her and they said goodbye. As Thomlin walked over to find his three friends lying on top of one another in a nearby booth, he smiled to himself. He gently shook Nelson awake and started to rouse Dougall and Ward. The group stumbled out of the food court and into the daylight. Without uttering a word, they all headed toward the bus stop.

■ ■ ■

As the group of lieutenants left the food court, none of them noticed the piercing stare of Nicole Foster from several booths behind them. For the past hour she watched Thomlin and the young Korean woman intently. Foster had never seen the Korean woman with Thomlin before and knew she must be a new target for him. When the pair exchanged what seemed to be phone numbers, Foster felt a gnawing feeling in her stomach.

"So, have you said anything to Thomlin about the Report of Survey?" Josh Shelton asked from the seat across Foster.

Foster turned her attention from Thomlin to the lieutenant sitting in front of her. Shelton was an inch shorter than her and bone thin. His Polo shirt hung loose over his arms. Foster thought for a moment that Shelton was at least slightly attractive. His thick eyebrows and dark eyes made him appear at least a couple of years older than the other lieutenants.

"You haven't said anything, have you?" Shelton pressed.

Foster frowned. She readily agreed weeks ago to prod Thomlin about the Report of Survey. Shelton asked, almost begged her for help. Any reason to needle Thomlin was worth it, she thought. Besides, Shelton would owe her. Now, she was tired and Shelton was becoming a pest.

"I heard you the first time," she said. "Why do you keep asking me? Are you afraid that for some reason the Report of Survey is going to make you look bad?"

"I don't want anyone to look bad. This whole thing is stupid. Thomlin knows what he needs to do. It's an easy report. He could just knock it out in an hour or two."

"Wasn't the missing black box from your arms room?"

"So what?" Shelton replied. "It still doesn't explain why Thomlin is taking his time. All of sudden he's on a high horse?"

"He's probably just dragging his ass on it."

"Didn't he tell me once that you were jealous of the women downrange and started charging a small fee for sex? I mean, I never believed it, but Thomlin always did have wild stories."

Shelton glared at Foster. Foster fought the urge to toss her hot coffee into Shelton's face.

"You know, I don't feel like taking the bus back to Kayes. Why don't you go to the taxi stand and get us a cab," Foster suggested.

"We're going to take a cab all the way back?"

"That's right. I'm going to talk with Thomlin's new friend. Go on. Now."

Shelton slowly stood up. Foster sipped her coffee and didn't acknowledge him as he turned to leave. When Shelton was out of sight she quickly finished her coffee. She watched Thomlin and the other lieutenants walk out the door before approaching the woman Thomlin was speaking to.

"Hi," Foster said abruptly as the Korean woman looked up to her, "I'm sorry, but were you just talking to Greg Thomlin?"

Michelle hesitated at the intrusion and then said, "Yes, his name was Greg. I'm afraid I didn't get his last name."

Foster instantly noticed that the woman spoke without any hint of a Korean accent. She originally suspected the woman was a Korean national, able to get on post freely because she worked somewhere on Yongsan. The lack of an accent meant that she was an American. I bet she's a dependent, Foster thought, maybe her father is a colonel. Foster immediately changed tactics.

"Well, I'm so sorry to bother you, but I just thought I should come and warn you," Foster said in a meek voice. She exhaled deeply and tried to well up tears in her eyes. "I know you don't know me, but I just didn't want another woman to become one of his conquests."

Michelle stared without saying a word. Foster tried to read the woman's face but only saw a blank expression. Does she believe me? Foster wondered. Feeling an uncomfortable pause, Foster went for an over-the-top move to sway the woman.

"Greg and I used to date," she lied, "and, well, one night after we both had been drinking… he almost date-raped me."

Foster put her head down as if silently weeping but was unable to conjure up any tears to go along with her story. She expected any moment to feel the woman's sisterly touch trying to console her in some way and instead felt nothing. With her head bowed, Foster began to feel embarrassed. Without saying anything more, she slipped away from the Korean woman and left the food court.

As Foster felt the thick, moist summer air she already started to lose the uncomfortable feeling. She smiled as she headed to the bus stop. It didn't matter if the Korean girl didn't completely believe her, a seed had been planted. Foster knew that regardless of how hard Thomlin tried to chase the girl, she would always wonder if there was at least some truth to the story. One way or another, Foster thought, Thomlin would learn some respect her.

■ ■ ■

The main post in Seoul served as a sort of central hub for traveling military personnel within the country. A large parking lot not far from the Post Exchange contained rows of buses that moved between the different military installations, shuttling soldiers to and from Seoul. The outbound buses that started running after seven o'clock in the morning on weekends were usually packed to capacity with the bodies of hung-over and passed-out soldiers. The interior of the bus was filled with the stench of alcohol that was more than mildly offensive to any sober individual who dared to board. Thomlin could already see a line forming in front of the next bus marked for a return to Camp Kayes. Some soldiers swayed back and forth in the line, still drunk from partying only a few hours before.

Thomlin immediately decided that he didn't want to accompany the other 50 or so soldiers waiting to board, and told the other three men that he would take the train. Nelson and Ward merely nodded in acknowledgement. Neither man planned to argue. Both Ward and Nelson inwardly wished they were sober enough to do the same. Dougall was the only one who spoke up and decided to join Thomlin.

The pair walked out the main gate and headed to the subway station. They navigated the subway system and found themselves standing on an empty train platform in Uijeongbu within an hour's wait of the train home. Thomlin and Dougall stood alone at the end of the platform. The sun was out and high in the midmorning sky. It was already getting hot and both lieutenants could feel their bodies begging to be hydrated. Thomlin checked his watch and realized it was about another 30 minutes before the train arrived. He cursed to himself and thought about the bus Ward and Nelson were now riding. There was nothing he could do but wait for the train.

After a few minutes of silently milling around, an older Korean man wandered near them. He had black and speckled gray hair and was wearing a blue dress shirt under a dark blue sports coat. Thomlin noticed the man out of the corner of his eye and thought he was inconspicuous, except of course for the burn marks on right side of his face and neck. The flesh was pinkish and wrinkled and almost forced the man's eye into a squint. He stared at Thomlin and Dougall for a moment before approaching the pair. The man was trying to speak to them but he spoke with the forced effort of someone trying to remember something lost.

"You American military?" he asked slowly, carefully selecting each word before he spoke in his thick Korean accent. Dougall slowly nodded in affirmation.

"That good," he said, smiling and nodding. "Very good. American military, good. Good for Korea."

Thomlin turned toward the man and bowed slightly. *"Kamsahamnida,"* he said, thanking the man in Korean. He felt awkward and wasn't quite sure what the man wanted.

"Some people no like American here," he said, obviously intent on getting his message across. "But they no remember. I remember. American military, good thing."

Although Dougall still looked a bit puzzled, Thomlin knew what the man was trying to say. Thomlin thanked the man again, who returned his bow this time, smiled, and slowly walked away.

"I sometimes forget there's an entire generation of Koreans who remember the war," Thomlin said to Dougall. "That man is probably old enough only to have lived through the war as a child. I bet he can still has some vivid memories."

Thomlin realized that for all the protests and animosity, there was perhaps a small minority of people in the country that truly appreciated the presence of their American allies. Thomlin could feel the hangover setting in and suddenly became overwhelmed with guilt for getting drunk the night before. Thomlin certainly didn't try to win the hearts or minds of any of the Koreans he ran into. The partying and gratification was justifiable to Thomlin, a price for being sent 13,000 miles from home. Now, he wasn't so sure. He was not one for ideals and he hated the intangible concepts that came with being a part of something larger than him.

"Maybe being a *migukin* is more than just being an American man," Thomlin thought aloud.

Thomlin lost himself in thought and was brought back to reality only when he heard the sound of the oncoming train. Within minutes, Dougall and Thomlin boarded the train and moved to the outdoor compartment at the back. With a jerk, the train lurched forward and began the ride home.

■ ■ ■

The doorknob turned slowly but Lee Min Yong heard the sounds of his daughter finally coming home. He was busy collecting a few items in his bedroom as Michelle quietly closed the door. He frowned as he came up behind her, realizing she was trying to slide into the apartment unnoticed.

"Good morning, Yumi," he said softly.

Startled, she turned to face her father, "Sorry, I didn't want to wake you."

"It's okay, your mother left earlier to pick up a few things and I am leaving for work soon."

"But it's Saturday," she said.

"Unfortunately the Army does not take the weekends off," he replied with a smirk.

"Why do you have to work today?"

"Munsan," he said, "they want me to go up to Munsan to make a delivery."

"At least, let me make you some tea." She walked toward the kitchen. Lee followed and sat down at the kitchen table. Michelle quickly boiled some water and prepared the tea.

"How was Osan?" she asked.

"Osan?"

"Yes, Osan. You left early the other morning and spent all day down there. What was the emergency?"

"Oh, yes. Osan. I must have forgotten because I was so tired. Yes, I had to go to Osan to help a colleague," Lee said and brushed the question aside. "It was nothing. Just a lot of traveling."

"Why are you going to Munsan? What's up there?" she asked.

"You're like your mother with all the questions," Lee chuckled. "I am going because that's where they ask me to go. You know our family is from there?"

"Really?" she asked sincerely. "Do you remember it?"

"No, I don't have too many memories from then," Lee lied. "I was just a boy when I left there."

For a moment, he considered telling her about his childhood. Maybe then, she'd begin to understand, Lee thought. He wished he could share the painful memories he still had, especially his thoughts of June 1950. Ultimately, he could not bring himself to pass these images on to his daughter.

The small shacks of homes that littered the town of Munsan were quite different back then. Lee remembered the sound of rain drumming on the tin roof above his home early one morning, beating the slow rhythm of sleep. Occasionally, the rumble of distant thunder stirred him as he lay in bed. The booming of thunder sounded different for some reason and he could hear his parents talk hurriedly while moving about the house. The thunder was man-made. Lee could now hear the high-pitch whistling and loud crashes as metal fragments and shells splattered through neighboring metallic huts. His brother and sister rushed to the window to see droves of mustard colored uniforms streaming through the streets. North Korean soldiers poured onto trains heading south toward Seoul.

Lee's parents rushed the children from the house with little belongings, knowing full well what would become of the city. Lee watched as South Korean soldiers attempted to fight tanks barehanded, strapping demolitions to their backs, and throwing themselves under the tanks to slow the assault. The explosions and body parts hurdling through the air had no effect on the enemy. He and his family ran as the Russian made T-34 tanks crashed through the city, grinding the debris and rubble under their steel treads.

"No," Lee repeated softly. "I don't recall much. Besides, there's not much up there."

"I could come with you," Michelle offered.

"Maybe not this time," he said. "You need your rest. I am sure you had a busy night in Itaewon. Tell me about some nice American soldier you met."

Michelle's mouth hung open, "And what makes you think I met an American soldier?"

"Itaewon is a popular spot for them. I may be getting old, but I am not senile," Lee smiled, "at least, not yet."

"If I did meet a nice young American soldier, I would be afraid to tell you. I know you would disapprove." Michelle thought about the strange woman who approached her in the food court, and decided not to tell her father about the young man she met.

"You don't understand," he said. "I don't dislike soldiers. I work around them most of the day. Most are good, a few are not, but most are good men. I always say that we owe much to the Americans. They have given us a life."

He stared at her for a few seconds struggling with the right English words to explain his feelings. Lee did not want to confuse his daughter and carefully chose his words. "The problem is not with American soldiers but how the American government looks at Korea. We are still two countries to them. Their treatment of Korea has not changed since the war. The best thing they could do for Korea is to help push for unification, not try to force Pyongyang into a corner."

Michelle listened silently as her father spoke. After thinking for a few moments, she asked, "Do you think the U.S. military should just leave?"

"No," he answered, "I don't know what the solution is. To use an American expression, maybe it would be better if the field was flat."

"I think you mean, level the playing field," she laughed.

"Yes," Lee exclaimed. "That's it. I am so glad I have you around."

The two laughed together before Lee got up from the table. He grabbed his green windbreaker and a small bag and then headed for the door.

"Get some rest. I'll be back late tonight."

16

HIP POCKET TRAINING

Only a day passed before Thomlin decided to call Michelle. She was a little surprised that he actually initiated the phone call and even more surprised that Thomlin carried a full conversation with no blatant attempts to make a pass at her. The more she talked to him the more she found herself at ease. He listened well and didn't seem overly interested in talking about himself. She began to think that she initially misjudged him. As she said goodbye, Thomlin asked if he could call her again. She didn't hesitate to open the door and let him call again anytime he wanted, but she half expected to never hear from him again. She was happy to have misjudged him again when he called the following night. And when he called again the night after that.

Their phone conversations increased from several minutes to

hours. She could only imagine what his phone bill was like, but she was afraid to ask and give him an excuse not to call. She found herself telling him all about her life, growing up in the northwest, her college experiences, her family, or whatever else came to mind. Michelle was never bored and always acted a bit shocked when she looked at the clock and realized how long they had been talking. She began to look forward to the nightly phone calls. Most of all, she liked the fact that Greg could make her laugh with his somewhat sarcastic wit. There was only one thing that bothered her. She could not shake the lingering memory of the blond woman who approached her the night she met Thomlin.

"Greg, I have to ask you something," she began, "the night we met in the food court, a woman spoke with me after you and your friends left. She said she knew you. She was one of your past girlfriends and she claimed you…" she trailed off not wanting to accuse Thomlin of anything, "you were pretty aggressive with her."

"I've never considered myself aggressive. Who was she?" Thomlin asked without being defensive.

"I don't know. She was American though," Michelle answered.

"That's pretty interesting since I've only dated Korean women since I've been here," Thomlin said flatly.

Michelle didn't notice any tension in his voice. She wanted to believe him.

"She was a tall blonde," Michelle continued, "with large breasts. At first I thought she might be your type, but the whole thing just seemed a little weird. Almost like she was putting on an act."

"Oh, hell," Thomlin said, "I think I know who it was. Look, she's another officer here on Kayes and we pretty much can't stand each other. She probably saw me with you and wanted to make sure I didn't have any chance with you."

"But why would someone do that? Are you sure she doesn't have a thing for you? I mean, that's how she came across."

"That would be pretty sick considering the way I openly despise her," Thomlin laughed. "By my estimate she has slept with half of the officers in the battalion, but I assure you, I'm not one of them."

"I still think she may want you."

"I admit I haven't figured her out. I think she feels everything is one big mind game. Maybe because I've never gone after her, or maybe it's because I've been around longer than most, and my time in country gives me a little stature. Who knows?"

Michelle switched the topic to other things and soon said goodnight. As she hung up, she again thought about the blond woman from the food court and what Thomlin had told her. She didn't sense anything in Thomlin's voice that would cause alarm bells to ring. When the American woman in the food court told her story and put her head down, Michelle almost expected the woman to break out in laughter at any moment and tell Michelle it was all a joke. Michelle shook the memory off and went to sleep.

■ ■ ■

Thomlin looked forward to the end of the day when he would eat dinner with Nelson and Dougall and then head back to his quarters to get on the phone. Gradually he could feel Michelle opening up to him. As she talked more about growing up in Seattle, he told her what it was like being a lieutenant stuck at Camp Kayes. Foster's concocted story at the food court didn't seem to have a lasting impact on Michelle. She asked him many questions about Army life but never probed too much into his personal life, which he was thankful for. He made a personal resolution to himself that he was going to be completely honest with her, even if she did want to know his personal exploits.

As days slipped by and Thomlin made no progress on the Report of Survey, he started to feel it weighing on his mind more and more. Thomlin thought about the confidentiality of the situation but needed to vent. What does it matter if she knows about this stuff, he thought.

"I have to write a report," he said matter-of-factly. "It's more like a small investigation. One of the units lost a piece of equipment, something to do with the radios, and I have to figure out how it was lost and who is responsible."

"I guess this thing was pretty expensive?" Michelle asked.

"Yeah, but it's more than that. It's a very important piece of equipment and no one is supposed to lose this sort of thing," he explained. He tried to keep it simple.

"I have to admit that I'm not quite sure I understand, but in my mind the Army is a world unto itself with many strange rules and customs that I'll probably never fully comprehend. My father has worked for the Army his entire career and I still can't even tell you exactly what he does. I wish I had some words of advice to ease your mind."

"I know, it's okay," Thomlin responded. He could hear the sympathy in her voice and was thankful for the mere fact that she listened intently as he recounted everything.

"So what are you going to do?" she asked softly when the conversation had quieted down.

"Don't know," he said. "I'm still not done investigating. I asked the company commander for an extension and I was shocked when he agreed without giving me a bad time or a 30-minute lecture."

"You mean the captain you mentioned before? What's his

name? Watts? Maybe he's not such a bad guy," she offered.

"Don't hold your breath," Thomlin laughed.

"Well, you could just take what you know right now and write this stupid report."

"I know," Thomlin replied and then paused before adding, "but I'm just not done yet. I know there's more to it and I can't finish it until I really know what happened."

"But where could someone sell this thing if that's what you think really happened? It's not like you see this stuff posted in a department store window in Itaewon."

"There's a place in Dongducheon, an alley, where some Korean vendors sell American military equipment," Thomlin responded without even needing to think. "When soldiers are leaving Korea, they have to turn in all the equipment that was issued to them when they first arrived. If they are missing something, like a canteen or sleeping bag, they can go to one of these stores and buy it a cheaper rate than having to pay Uncle Sam."

"So where do these shops get their stuff?" she asked.

"From other soldiers," he said, briefly remembering Dougall's first day in the battalion. "Some soldiers end up with extra equipment, either by luck or by stealing it in some cases, and then they sell it to make a few bucks. The area is off limits but everyone knows where it is. The only way these places can possibly stay in business is by the constant flow of gear from American soldiers."

Michelle wished him luck and said goodnight. It was close to midnight and Thomlin knew he would have to be up in a matter of hours.

"Can I see you? It would be better to talk in person," Thomlin finally asked.

She hesitated at first but then said, "I'm coming up to Camp Kayes next weekend to see an old friend."

Thomlin was surprised that she was coming but started to feel a little excited that she would be there regardless of the reason. Thomlin said goodnight and hung up the phone. Again, Thomlin found himself looking forward to the weekend and tried to fill the routine, monotonous days of garrison life.

■ ■ ■

Garrison duty was usually relaxed, a fact that seemed to drive commanders crazy. From a soldier's point of view, the comfort was reward for the time spent in the field and during the refit period upon return. In the soldiers' minds, they were entitled to easy, eight-hour days. Commanders, however, hated to see an idle soldier. Soldiers should always be busy training in one form or another, they thought. After all, commanders rationalized, that was what they were paid to do.

In order to resolve this conflict of interest, commanders pushed the need for what they termed hip pocket training. Hip pocket training was a form of training that noncommissioned officers could execute on the spot without the need for elaborate equipment or a large training area. Typically, this training revolved around the individual tasks soldiers were expected to be proficient in, according to the Army's common task manual. As the name implied, junior leaders could pull this training out of their proverbial hip pocket at any time. Commanders didn't expect to see soldiers milling around waiting for some required detail. Commanders expected to see a sergeant with his team in an organized semicircle to his front walking the group through how to properly don a protective mask or use proper radio procedures. No task was too small for recurring training. If soldiers were standing around waiting to get into the latrine, then they could at least be arranged in some sort of formation reciting the

Code of Conduct.

Occasionally, garrison training was a bit more complex, as company commanders tried to increase the tempo and make training more realistic. Alpha Company had decided to do just that. In the small wooded area behind the battalion area, Ward created a training lane large enough for a nine-man infantry squad to maneuver through. The squad training exercise would test the small unit on their ability to execute commonly practiced battle drills, such as how to react to incoming artillery or what to do when initial contact was made with enemy soldiers. The soldiers were in full gear and carried blank ammunition, while Ward and his platoon sergeant stood off to the side to evaluate the squad as they rotated through the lane.

"Sir," Ward's platoon sergeant began, "you're smiling. I don't trust a lieutenant that smiles too much."

Ward laughed. He turned to his platoon sergeant and spoke with a serious tone. "Sergeant, professionally speaking, it's good to be able to watch the soldiers as a detached third party observer to gain a new perspective on how these small groups interact. I also look forward to observing how the junior leaders conduct themselves on the simulated battlefield."

"Sir, if you keep up that line of bullshit you're guaranteed to at least make major someday," the platoon sergeant grinned. "I'm sure your smile has nothing to do with the full bag of artillery simulators you're carrying."

"Well, it is a necessary part of my function here," Ward said. He tried hard not to laugh. Ward planned to throw the artillery simulators at the tactically moving units as they neared his position. The artillery simulators were no ordinary firecrackers. It was an M80 on steroids. It was small enough to comfortably fit in Ward's hand but let out a searing whistle and a deafening boom only a few seconds after Ward pulled the small string to activate

the device. The force was strong enough to blow Ward's hand off
if for some insane reason Ward decided to cook the device before
throwing it.

"Looks like it's time to carry out my duty," Ward smiled again
as he pulled the string and tossed the simulator. Dirt and debris
were kicked into the air due to the small explosion. The squad of
men dropped their gear and dove to the ground as if expecting
incoming artillery barrages. Then, the squad leader jumped to
his feet and shouted a direction and distance to the rest of his
team. The squad snatched their gear and sprinted in the direction ordered, moving out of the kill zone, and regrouped once
far enough away. As the team reformed and accounted for all its
members, Ward launched more artillery simulators, sending the
squad off at a double time once again.

"Sir, has anyone ever told you that you're a sadistic bastard?"
the platoon sergeant joked. "I'm going to guess that you threw
firecrackers at frogs and fish when you were a kid."

"How did you know? There was a pond right next to my house
when I was growing up."

"Tell me, Sir, just between you and me, which is more fun, the
simulator or making the squads run their ass off?"

"That's a good question. I honestly don't know which is better."

Ward could barely contain his own laughter as he waited for
the panting squad leader to radio in a simulated situation report
to higher headquarters before again pulling the small string that
released a small puff of smoke that came with a dull popping
noise. The slight pop was the only thing that gave away what was
about to happen. A few seconds of silence preceded the piercing
shriek and echoing roar of the detonation.

Maybe it was the dirt and leaves that flew through the air that
made Ward so happy. Ward loved hearing the whistle, then see-

ing the bright flash a split second before the blast. It didn't matter to him that it had not rained in over four days and the ground was completely dry. In fact, Ward's mind never even made the connection between the dry brush and the explosive incendiary device.

Ward crouched behind the thick bushes on the edge of the squad training lane so he would not be easily observed. As a new squad appeared and approached his position, Ward tugged the small, white cap attached to a string along the cylindrical device until he heard the slight popping noise. He tossed the simulator a few yards in front of his position and waited gleefully for the whistle.

"Incoming," several soldiers screamed as they hit the ground. A flash and bang followed. As expected, the squad leader was the first to his feet and shouted for his soldiers to move in a forward direction for a few hundred yards. The men quickly picked themselves up and ran straight ahead.

Ward waited for the men to pass his position before grabbing another artillery simulator and breaking into a trot behind the rest of the soldiers. He didn't bother to notice the smoldering device he was leaving behind. The empty shell of the simulator lay beneath the leaves, still burning hot from the explosion it released.

Only a minute later, Ward was approximately one hundred yards away, standing behind the squad as the small unit checked their status.

"Killer six, this is Killer one-two," the gasping squad leader barked into the handset of his radio. He was using the company call signs to notify the company commander the squad leader for second squad, first platoon was calling. "Killer six, this is Killer one-two, prepare to copy, over."

Ward listened intently as the squad leader reported the squad's level of ammunition, casualties, and equipment. Even if he were closer to the growing brush fire behind him, he would probably not even have noticed it. Ward scribbled notes down on a notepad attached to an old wooden clipboard until he heard a voice rise from somewhere in the distance.

"Holy shit. Look at that fire!" someone screamed from behind.

Ward and the rest of the soldiers quickly spun around to see four-foot flames almost 100 yards away. Ward tried to quickly calculate how long it had been since he threw the simulator in an attempt to mentally exonerate himself from initiating the small forest fire. For a moment, everyone stood still like Boy Scouts watching a campfire built on a cool summer night. It wasn't the first time a fire had been created by the artillery simulators, but Ward was amazed at how fast it was growing. Finally, Ward felt a slight gust of wind against his face and knew the breeze was force-feeding the flames.

Now the men broke into action. Soldiers dropped their gear and quickly unfolded their small collapsible entrenching tools to help throw dirt on the fire. Some soldiers took off their top uniform tops and were swatting at the flames. Soon it was too hard to see more than 20 feet due to the smoke created by the blazing wall of fire. Ward turned and stared at the ensuing flames. The landscape was painted in crimson and blinding orange.

"Move back," Ward ordered. He repeatedly yelled at his men to secure their equipment and move away from the advancing fire. Ward gained accountability of all his soldiers, ensuring each one was okay, when he heard the sirens approaching. A fire truck pulled near the soldiers huddled by the road that cut through the battalion.

Korean civilians ran the fire station on Camp Kayes and responded quickly to the call made by a neighboring unit startled by the glowing red smokestack nearby. The fire truck was like any other truck, but the firemen struck Ward as a little odd. As the truck rolled to a stop, a short Korean fireman jumped out from behind the wheel. He was just over five feet tall, middle aged, and had a long cigarette hanging out of his mouth. Two of his partners soon joined him, all brandishing cigarettes. However, it was their uniform that stuck out the most.

"Are they actually wearing polyester body suits?" one of the soldiers asked.

Sure enough, all of the firemen were dressed in what appeared to be 1970s era leisure suits. No rubber boots, no fire retardant protective gear, just five men in total, all dressed like they were heading to a disco. To cap it off, the firemen each grabbed a tool, whether a shovel, pickaxe or ax, and then headed toward the flames. Ward wondered why they weren't grabbing hoses and using water. He was so stunned that he didn't even think to ask them.

17

DITCHED

Thomlin stood outside his company area observing his squad leaders demonstrate how to administer first aid for the 800th consecutive time when he first heard the fire engines barreling down the road. Then, Thomlin noticed the rising smoke behind the battalion area. He initially didn't think anything of it. In his two years at Kayes he had seen numerous small forest fires behind the battalion area and quickly surmised that it was the work of some pyrotechnics gone awry.

"Hey, we need some help. First platoon needs help," a young soldier was screaming as he approached Thomlin's soldiers. "There's a fire. It's huge. We need some help putting it out."

Anxious to get away from the daily hip pocket training class, soldiers immediately grabbed their entrenching tools and headed toward the blaze behind the fire truck. The squad leaders trailed behind them somewhat nonchalantly as Thomlin shrugged off the whole scene and quickly decided how to best make use of his time. As Thomlin stood frowning, surveying the battalion area, his eyes fell on the buildings that housed Headquarters Company. The sight quickly sparked an idea in Thomlin and he moved quickly in that direction.

■ ■ ■

Major Streeter sat in his office staring at the maps covering his desk, barely hearing the light tap on the doorframe to his office.

"Sir, do you have a moment?"

Streeter looked up from his desk and motioned for Lieutenant Foster to come in. "What can I do for you?"

Foster took a seat in front Streeter's desk. She leaned back in the chair and crossed her legs.

"Sir, I was hoping I could talk to you about your missing equipment."

"So this is now my equipment?"

"Well, Sir, I mean the battalion's missing equipment."

"Of course." Streeter smiled. "By the way, how are the encryption guys handling this?"

"Everything, at least all the damage control stuff, is done. That's not why I'm here. I came to talk to you about the possibility that the ANCD wasn't lost."

"What are you talking about?" Streeter shifted slightly in his chair.

"Sir, is it possible that this thing wasn't lost? Or at least, that it was lost intentionally?"

"Go on." Streeter propped his elbows on the armrests and lightly locked his fingers in front of his face.

"I'm not sure you're aware, but I've been involved in several of the past IG inspections around Kayes," Foster said casually, referring to the highly visible, potentially career altering audits led by the Office of the Inspector General.

"I've also helped write many of the policies that most of the arms rooms across the post use as a basis for their standard operating procedures," Foster continued. "I know how sensitive items are supposed to be handled. And I also know that this particular item is never taken to the field."

"I wouldn't say that it is never taken to the field. That's not true."

"Okay, Sir, it's just a little unusual."

"First of all, Lieutenant, if you've come here to tell me the unit screwed up, we're already well aware of that. Second, I think our internal battalion policies shouldn't concern you."

"Sir, I'm just anticipating that Brigade or perhaps Division headquarters will eventually ask me to review your internal policies on handling sensitive items."

"You're probing, Lieutenant." Streeter again shifted in his chair.

"I'm just saying that the incident is unusual. In my experience, most sensitive items don't usually get lost. Did you ever hear of the incident over in the tank battalion where they supposedly lost three sets of night vision goggles in one night?"

"You mean they weren't lost?"

"Hardly. Some young soldier cooked up a plan and stole them. Stashed them out in the woods someplace. Probably planning on recovering them at some point and selling them downrange. After a couple of months in the field, the soldier came forward, but the unit never recovered the goggles."

"They never found them?"

"Either the soldier forgot where he buried them or someone

else with the same idea recovered them first. Perhaps the infamous Slicky Boy."

"Well, I think Slicky Boy had his way in our situation." Major Streeter paused for a moment, then added, "Who knows. If you're right, then maybe we have a chance to recover that little black box. Maybe someone will come forward, or even slip it right back into the arms room where it belongs."

"Sir, I think that would be a little problematic. It would probably raise more questions."

Streeter stiffened a bit. "What do you mean?"

"I'm just saying, Sir, that if Slicky Boy didn't take the box then others, higher up, would really start looking at this unit to figure out what happened. Losing a piece of equipment in the field is bad enough, but do you think it's worse if it's stolen or if the unit is incapable of proper accountability?"

"You're saying that this is better off gone."

Foster smiled, leaned forward and shook her head. "Sir, I'm not saying anything, although it certainly becomes a much easier case if it's just lost. I guess we'll have to wait to read the results of the Report of Survey."

Streeter sat motionless and did not respond. Foster took the silence as her cue to leave.

"Sir, I'll give you a heads-up if I hear anything in regards to a surprise audit on your arms room," Foster winked as she stood. "In the meantime, if there is anything I can do, please don't hesitate to give me a call."

Streeter thanked Foster and waited until he could no longer hear her footsteps down the hallway. He swiveled around and slumped low in the chair while staring at the blank wall behind his desk.

■ ■ ■

Thomlin stepped into the Quonset containing the Headquarters Company arms room. It was no different than any of the other huts except for its steel-reinforced inside door. The steel door was propped open, signifying that the armorer was obviously occupying the room. With Wickersham turned over to the Korean authorities, the new armorer, a stubby Irish kid from the northeast, sat in an old wooden chair with his feet kicked up on an open drawer, reading a porn magazine. Seeing Thomlin standing in the doorway immediately caused the armorer's face to turn a shade closely matching his hair. He flipped the magazine into a drawer and jumped to his feet.

"What can I do for you, Sir?" the armorer asked, more than just a little embarrassed.

"I need to see the arms room log," Thomlin said robotically. Every arms room contained a log that soldiers had to sign when drawing weapons and equipment from the room. Soldiers always drew the same weapons and equipment. The logs were pre-filled with serial numbers so the soldier only had to quickly sign their name to the document to expedite the process of getting equipment from the arms room racks and into the hands of those that needed them.

The young soldier looked confused and stood motionless until Thomlin quickly explained that he was the survey officer. Satisfied, Kelly grabbed the log and handed it to Thomlin. Thomlin rifled back through the log until he was in the midst of the paperwork from the field exercise before the black box was lost. He found Padilla's name next to a serial number for an M16, night vision goggles, and one automated network control device. Thomlin then paged forward to the next field exercise and again found Padilla's signature. The signature was repeated, next to the serial numbers of his designated M16 and night vision goggles. However, the serial number for the black box was different this time. Thomlin had to flip back and forth a few times to convince himself that the two numbers were distinctly different. Thomlin asked himself, why would he sign out equipment different from what he always drew?

"What's that, Sir?" Kelly asked moving toward Thomlin. Thomlin suddenly realized he had been talking to himself out loud. He quickly popped the three-ring spiral bound apart and pulled the sheets out.

"Does everyone in this company draw the same equipment?" Thomlin asked.

"I guess so, Sir. I mean, why wouldn't someone draw the usual stuff? I've always signed for the same weapon."

"What about sensitive items?"

"Yes, Sir, including all sensitive items."

"What if someone wanted to draw out a different piece of equipment?"

"What do you mean, Sir? Unless their equipment is damaged and they have to sign out a different item, everyone should be signing for the same stuff. No one gets to just pick and choose."

"Is that standard operating procedure for Headquarters Company?"

"Of course, Sir, is it any different in Alpha Company?'

"Just let me ask some routine questions, okay?"

"Roger, Sir. Everyone typically signs out the same stuff and signs it back in just the same."

Turning the pages even further back to previous field exercises Thomlin discovered that Padilla always took the same black box from the arms room. The only serial number that was any different from rest was from the exercise when the infamous Slicky Boy supposedly stole the black box. Then another thought came across Thomlin's mind.

"You said sign in. I don't see any signatures for when we came back in from the field and turned everything."

"We have a separate binder for the sign-in sheets." Kelly rummaged through the desk and handed Thomlin another thin, three-ring binder.

Thomlin quickly found the serial number for the black box. As expected, there was no sign-in signature next to it, since it had never been turned in. Thomlin flipped back and forth looking for older documents.

"You're missing some paperwork."

"Say again?"

"You're missing the sign-in sheets from the field exercise before last." Thomlin turned the binder so Kelly could see it. The armorer quickly thumbed through the pages.

"You see? Why are the sign-in sheets missing?"

"I dunno, Sir. I just took over since Wickersham is gone. I guess he didn't keep good files."

Thomlin grew frustrated but realized Kelly could not tell him much more. "I need to make copies of the sign-out log ASAP. I'll get it back to you in 30 minutes."

Before the soldier could protest, Thomlin was out the door. On his way over to the Xerox machine in the battalion operations office, Thomlin again asked himself why Padilla would not draw his usual equipment. As he walked he checked the serial numbers again. Then it hit him. There was something about flipping through the paperwork that reminded him of the conversation with Wickersham.

"I'm not worried. I have friends in high places who owe me a favor," Wickersham had said.

Thomlin stopped halfway to the battalion operations office and began searching previous field exercises for the serial number that matched the lost black box. After a minute or two he found it. Thomlin felt a knot in his stomach when he saw the battalion executive officer's signature. It was unusual for the battalion executive officer himself to sign for the equipment, but Thomlin knew Major Streeter was a hands-on person and didn't like the formalities of having someone else sign for equipment he would use during the exercise.

"Why would he need an ANCD?" Thomlin asked aloud. Then he remembered what Streeter told him at Tent City. Streeter took any device that might be useful if he got stranded while taking one of his personal tours of the landscape. The black box might come in handy if he needed to synch the radios.

Thomlin started to wonder if Wickersham screwed up the order or if he intentionally signed out different equipment. Thomlin knew he didn't have enough information to make the call either way.

"But why didn't he sign it back in?" Thomlin shook his head and wondered if the missing paperwork was also connected. Once he finally reached the copy machine, Thomlin made two copies of the log and stuck one set in the cargo pocket of his pants.

Before leaving the building, Thomlin heard the deep voice of the battalion operations officer, Major Mike Pierce, a couple of rooms away. Major Pierce was obviously reacting to a joke in his signature laugh that sounded a lot like the Jolly Green Giant, except a bit slower. It was ironic to Thomlin that the major was pale and almost skeleton thin. Thomlin had never warmed up to the operations officer and always felt that Major Pierce had the personality of napkin holder. Unlike Major Streeter who was lively and outgoing, Major Pierce was distant. He didn't get to know many officers in the battalion beyond those with whom he had direct contact. Thomlin did his best to avoid Pierce, not out of fear, but out of sheer awkwardness. Talking to the operations officer was as much fun as a proctology exam. No time like the present, Thomlin begrudgingly thought, and headed in the direction of the major's voice.

As Thomlin walked down the hall toward Major Pierce's office, he passed by a larger office housing the captains of the operations office. Major Pierce was the only officer on battalion staff with several captains, noncommissioned officers, and soldiers reporting to him. Battalion operations typically contained a staff of approximately a dozen officers and soldiers due to the scope of the job responsibilities.

The men in battalion operations were responsible for just about everything the unit did in regards to training, planning and strategy. From planning the field training exercise to arranging the battalion Christmas dinner, battalion operations had a large piece of it. The three captains in operations were some of the more junior captains in the battalion. They would bide their time doing staff work, waiting for an opportunity to take command of one of the companies, or more likely, they would spend their entire twelve months shuffling paperwork waiting to rotate home to take command somewhere in the States. Taking a company command in the battalion meant an additional twelve months of service in country from the moment they took charge, which explained why many were content to deal with administrative tasks for a year before going home. Perhaps this was the reason for their nasty disposition and bad attitudes. The captains, frustrated with the perpetual uselessness of their role, amused themselves by picking on lieutenants and other younger soldiers.

Thomlin moved quickly past the open door and caught a glimpse of the captains from the corner of his eye. The captains were in their usual positions. One was reading a magazine with a story about a sheep named Dolly, while another was busy typing a letter on the office computer, and the third captain drew obscene pictures on a dry erase board. Underneath a stack of magazines on the desk of one of the captains was the daily copy of *Stars and Stripes*. The top news story covering the front page was about a North Korean submarine that had been grounded in South Korean waters. Most of the crew was dead but the ROK navy captured several survivors and was currently trying to figure out how much information the sub crew had gathered on its apparent spy mission. The news was big enough to make the evening broadcast back in the States.

Thomlin purposefully did not make eye contact to invite any unnecessary harassment, but it was no good. Like a bunch of high school bullies waiting by the bike racks after class, the captains spotted Thomlin and immediately began shouting for him to come into their office.

"Lieutenant Thomlin," one of the captains shrieked. "Get in here. Now."

Thomlin froze in his tracks halfway down the hall en route to Major Pierce's office and debated whether he should follow the orders of the captains calling his name. He could hear the voice of Captain Ditch Anderson, the worst of the trio, over the other two captains. Ditch received his infamous nickname for plastering his face along the side of a turtle ditch in a drunken stupor one evening. Across the battalion, cement trenches cut through the battalion area to prevent any flooding during monsoon season. During the monsoon season, the trenches were filled to capacity with fast moving water that flowed from the hillside behind the battalion area into a nearby stream. In the dry season, the drains were empty and largely unnoticed. The deep gutters usually posed a safety hazard to new personnel, the turtles, who did not pay any attention until they sank their foot into one and fell on their face.

In most cases the troughs were only a foot or so deep and a foot across, however, some of the trenches were much larger, eight feet across and seven feet deep, requiring a small bridge to walk over. It was one of these large turtle ditches that Captain Anderson decided to leap over one evening, earning him a new nickname and a Big Boot Award.

In a mindset that could only be induced by several consecutive shots of soju and a six-pack of Budweiser, Anderson decided that he possessed the kind of superhuman jumping abilities that would make an Olympic athlete jealous. Without the need for a long running start, Anderson leapt across the width of the turtle ditch only to discover how thick the cement wall on the far side really was. Fortunately for Anderson, his attempt was made during the dry season. Rather than being whisked away in the strong rain current, Anderson rolled to a stop at the bottom of the ditch. Several soldiers who were standing nearby heard the thump of his body, along with the subsequent high-pitch cry, and they rushed to the scene to help. After a brief ambulance ride and visit to the post hospital, Anderson was returned to the unit with a broken nose and a few chipped teeth. Thomlin credited this accident and the subsequent ridicule for Anderson's ill will toward everyone around him. No, Thomlin thought to himself, he was probably an asshole before the accident.

Thomlin reluctantly turned and headed to see the captains. He knew they would catch him on the way back if he blew them off and the result would be even worse than what he was potentially in for now. As Thomlin stood in the doorway, the captains immediately focused their attention on him. Thomlin was silent and waited for the incoming verbal assault.

"Hey, lieutenant, that's not an acceptable way to come into our office. Lieutenants have to low crawl to come in here," Captain Ditch Anderson barked. The other two captains giggled in the background.

"Sir, I haven't come into your office, so there's no need for me to low crawl," Thomlin said with a straight face.

Ditch Anderson flapped his arms in an exaggerated fit. He bellowed, "That's unacceptable. Completely unacceptable. I am ordering you into the office."

Thomlin again replied with robotic logic, "Sir, are you ordering me into your office or to low crawl? I believe I have a medical profile that prevents me from any bending or crawling."

Now all the captains were roaring. Ditch came from around his desk and stood a few feet from Thomlin yelling, "When I was a lieutenant, I didn't mouth off to my superiors. I did what I was told. Back when I was a lieutenant, things were tougher. We had to earn our keep, and that meant following every order regardless of what it was. We didn't have any bogus medical profiles or any other sorry-ass excuse to keep us from low crawling."

Thomlin imagined Ditch in a t-shirt with Greek letters scrawled across his chest. Every fraternity house in college had the one guy who was assigned the task of torturing new pledges during rush. Ditch was the type that would have looked forward to the task all year.

Thomlin tried to keep a straight face but couldn't help smirking when he said, "Well, Sir, I guess times are changing."

Ditch shook his head in mock disbelief while the other two captains standing behind him started chanting, "Get the lieutenant in the front leaning rest position. Smoke him, Ditch, smoke him."

Just as Ditch leaned forward to get in Thomlin's face a voice from the hallway called, "Hey, what's going on here?"

The captains looked up and Thomlin turned around to see Major Streeter walking toward them. Thomlin knew that Major

Streeter wasn't much for these games and didn't like to see such a level of unprofessional behavior among the battalion staff.

"Captain Anderson," the battalion executive officer said as he walked in between Thomlin and the captains, "I was just talking with Major Pierce about the status of the ranges for next month's training exercise. Has that been done yet?"

"Yes, Sir. Well, Sir, I mean, I'm on it. I've been working pretty hard with range control to make sure we're all set. It's been a pretty lengthy process and it's taking a lot of effort," Ditch responded as he walked over to his desk and began rearranging some of the stacks of paper that were piled up on top.

"Sure," Major Streeter responded coolly, "but I'm sure you'll have no problem getting it done by the end of the day."

Major Streeter turned toward Thomlin and said, "Lieutenant, I think I have something for you. Why don't you come with me?"

As Thomlin followed the major he mentioned that he needed to get a statement from Major Pierce. Major Streeter nodded as if he expected that was the reason for Thomlin's visit to battalion headquarters. Both men walked into Major Pierce's office finding the battalion operations officer pouring over some maps.

Major Mike Pierce was a sixteen-year Army veteran. He had been to combat once during the Persian Gulf War, when he was a senior captain attached to the division staff of the 1st Calvary Division. He spent most of his time riding in a vehicle and was awarded a Combat Infantry Badge and a Bronze Star. He was pushing 40, divorced, and had no hobbies that Thomlin knew of. Thomlin immediately started to feel uncomfortable standing in Pierce's large office and was almost glad that the battalion operations officer didn't even look up from his desk. Major Streeter called the operations officer by his first name to get his attention. Major Pierce finally tore his attention away from his maps and stared blankly at Thomlin.

"What can I do for you?" Major Pierce asked.

"Sir," Thomlin began, "I am conducting the Report of Survey on the lost black box, and since Padilla was your driver, I was hoping you could give me some insight on the situation or on Padilla."

Major Pierce leaned back in his chair and looked up at the ceiling.

"Padilla's a good kid," Pierce said as if he were talking to himself. "It's an unfortunate circumstance. It could have happened to anyone, but ultimately he signed for the piece of equipment, and he was responsible for safeguarding it, even against Slicky Boy. However, I do hope you go easy on him. He's already punished himself enough over this."

Thomlin quickly realized that Major Pierce believed everyone had already concluded that the Korean apparition stole the black box and Thomlin simply had to write a report saying Padilla did or did not properly take the necessary precautions. Thomlin didn't respond immediately and a brief, yet awkward, pause came between them. Thomlin tried to judge the major's emotionless demeanor and notice anything that would indicate the major knew something more. The major was as hard to read as a Korean physics textbook, so Thomlin thought he would cast a line to see if Pierce would bite.

"Sir, I just thought it was a little unusual that Padilla wouldn't sign out the same black box as he did every other time we went to the field. Would you know if there was any specific reason why he would do this?" Thomlin asked.

Major Pierce didn't flinch or even show any sort of reaction, he just stared blankly at Thomlin. Thomlin imagined that if he could hear Pierce's thoughts, it would sound a lot like white noise. Although Pierce did not respond, Major Streeter broke the silence.

"What's that, Greg?" Streeter asked.

Thomlin quickly explained what he found in the arms room log and showed both majors the copy he held in his hand. Streeter gently took the copy from Thomlin and scanned the pages slowly. Somewhat detached from the conversation, Pierce stared at both Thomlin and Streeter for a few seconds before returning to his maps.

Pierce said without looking up, "Lieutenant, it doesn't sound like a big deal. Who cares if Padilla signed out the same piece of equipment? I thought the only thing that mattered was whether soldiers signed out the same weapon. Really, it sounds like Wickersham or someone else in the arms room shuffled some of the equipment around. Padilla should have safeguarded all his sensitive items regardless, right?"

Thomlin couldn't argue with Pierce's logic. The question was rhetorical. To Major Pierce there wasn't much of an issue. Padilla signed out a piece of equipment, it was lost, and it was up to Thomlin to fill out the paperwork. End of story. Thomlin started to feel a bit heated. This time it was out of irritation with the major's nonchalant attitude over the potential consequences of a young soldier who was busting his ass to best serve him. Before Thomlin could say anything, a soldier from the operations shop burst in the room.

"Sir, ah, gentlemen, we have a slight problem," he tried to say calmly. Sweat was trickling down the side of his cheeks and it was evident that something bad was happening. He turned in Major Pierce's direction and stammered, "Sir, there's a fire. One of the Alpha Company platoons was training and started a very, very big fire."

Major Pierce frowned at the news but his body language showed that he wasn't overly concerned. Streeter exchanged glances with Pierce and the nervous soldier and then decided to dismiss Thomlin.

"Greg," Major Streeter said, "let me investigate this one with Captain Hadley and Specialist Wickersham. I think Major Pierce is correct, though. This all sounds like Wickersham did his usual half-ass job and signed out the wrong black box to the wrong person. By the way, I have Wickersham's sworn statement on my desk. You can swing by and pick it up on your way out."

"Yes, Sir," Thomlin said and turned to leave the office. He let Major Streeter keep the copy of the arms room log and picked up the statement as the major suggested. As Thomlin walked across the battalion area back toward the company area, he read over Wickersham's statement. It was short, only three paragraphs long, and didn't take up the full page. Wickersham's written words mirrored the story he had given Thomlin. Thomlin frowned as he reread the document. He wanted to pay Wickersham another visit in the near future.

18

REGRETS

For the first time since the whole series of events began, Wickersham was scared. He was sitting in the corner of a barren, six-by-five foot cell in a police station in Dongducheon and he knew there were no Americans here to help him or even understand what he wanted to tell them. It happened so fast; the handover caught him off guard. Wickersham hadn't even thought to blurt out the things he was hiding in order to save himself. Now, he was alone and knew it was unlikely that he would ever go back to Camp Kayes. He pulled his knees into his chest, wrapping his arms around his legs, and wept silently.

During the prior evening, Wickersham waited in his room for his escort to arrive and bring him to dinner after all the other soldiers had left the dining facility. As he shuffled out of the barracks in his shackles, Wickersham noticed a Humvee waiting outside. The sergeant at his side told him that they were going to the military police station near the front gate for a few more questions before he would be allowed to eat. Wickersham rolled his eyes as the sergeant helped him into the back of the vehicle, but he wasn't too worried. Earlier that day, when the sergeant watching over him briefly left his post for some reason, Wickersham's mentor visited him and told him everything would be over soon. Wickersham immediately relaxed upon hearing the confident voice of his partner.

"Relax, Wickersham," the voice had told him. "This will be done in the next few days. Just do yourself a favor and roll with the punches. Keep your mouth shut and just do what you're told. Everything will work out fine."

When Wickersham arrived at the military police station he climbed down from the back of the vehicle and was told to wait in the back seat of a parked, unmarked Hyundai.

"What's going on?" Wickersham asked.

"Don't know," the sergeant standing in front of Wickersham said. "The two holding cells inside the station are full and there is nowhere else to put you. Wait here until you're told to go inside."

Wickersham was more inconvenienced than suspicious. He sat in the back seat as he was told and rested his head. He closed his eyes briefly until the front doors opened and two large Korean men jumped into the front seat. Before Wickersham could utter a word the driver started the engine and spun the car toward the front gate.

"What's going on?" Wickersham demanded. He could feel the first tinge of fear settling into his stomach. The middle-aged Korean in the passenger seat turned slightly and shouted something that was unintelligible to Wickersham.

"Wait. I'm not supposed to leave the post," Wickersham pleaded as the vehicle quickly left the front gates and maneuvered through the streets.

Wickersham turned to look out the rear window and could see the front gate of Camp Kayes getting smaller in the distance. Then, the vehicle turned and the image was gone. Wickersham felt the sudden urge to urinate. His mind quickly raced, trying to find an explanation of what was going on. He could hear the words "roll with the punches" echoing in his head and thought that the trip must have been anticipated. "This is a mistake," he thought, "I'll be back at Kayes as soon as they figure this out."

Within 30 minutes of weaving through the city streets, the car stopped in front of the main Korean police station in Dongducheon. The two men exited the vehicle as two uniformed police officers came to the vehicle, grabbed Wickersham under his arms and pulled him from the car. Wickersham again appealed to his captors but discovered they too did not understand any English.

Inside the station the officers took Wickersham to a back room that resembled an empty closet. Another police officer walked over to Wickersham and handed him a pair gray pajamas, which reminded Wickersham of hospital clothing. The guard motioned for Wickersham to change into his new uniform.

"*Chigeum,*" the officer said. "*Ahgashi, gesseyo?*"

"What the hell is this? What's going on here?" Wickersham protested and refused to move.

The Koreans exchanged glances and a few mumbled words. Wickersham thought he was intimidating them until one of the officers pulled his baton and poked Wickersham in the ribs. Wickersham brushed the baton aside with his elbow and bobbed his chest like a roster before a cockfight.

"Don't touch me, man. You know, I'm protected under the Status of Forces Agreement," Wickersham shouted.

The Korean cop let out a loud yell before slamming the baton into the side of Wickersham's knee. The Korean's scream startled Wickersham and he was momentarily reminded of an old Kung Fu movie until he found himself suddenly lying on his back with his legs above him. The throbbing pain quickly set it and Wickersham gasped loudly. Looking up at the police officer, Wickersham saw the man gesture for him change into the garments.

"*Chigeum. Ppali,*" the officer shouted

Still stunned from the blow, Wickersham lay motionless on the ground.

"I'm an American. *Cheoneun migukin ipnida,*" Wickersham cried.

The Korean police officer became impatient. Wickersham watched the baton arch high into the air and come swooping down toward him.

"No. Wait," Wickersham screamed as the baton crashed into his side. He let out a loud yelp and was spurned into a flurry of instant movement. He tried desperately to change his clothes before being reminded again. Unfortunately for Wickersham, he knew he wasn't fast enough as he glimpsed the baton coming down again.

Hours later, Wickersham found himself alone and sobbing uncontrollably. He felt abandoned. He imagined what Korean prison was like and started to feel sick. He hated his partner for lying to him and knew he had been set up. Wickersham berated himself for not creating a contingency plan. He thought about Lieutenant Thomlin and his suggestion of having some insurance by telling the truth. Wickersham knew he couldn't have written anything in the sworn statement or else it would have disappeared before reaching Thomlin. Wickersham cursed himself for not anticipating this.

■ ■ ■

The phone rang in Thomlin's quarters for several minutes before he finally answered. He looked at the ringing phone with annoyance until he picked up the receiver and heard Michelle's voice.

"Greg, there's stuff all over the Korean news about a fire at Camp Kayes, are you okay?" she asked and sounded genuinely concerned.

Thomlin was relieved to hear her voice. "Let's just say that it's been a long day on many fronts. One of the platoons in my company started a fire by accident and five Korean firefighters lost their lives. Thankfully, I had nothing to do with this one."

"Thank God," she said. "The Korean news is talking about the carelessness of the American soldiers and the valiant way the Korean firefighters struggled to save you guys before giving their life."

"Well, leave it to the unbiased Korean press to report this one," he said. He heard about how the Koreans were equipped when they arrived on the scene but decided not to mention it to Michelle. Thomlin briefly recounted what he heard earlier about how the fire was caused. It took several hours before the fire finally burnt out. Although Ward's soldiers suffered no injuries, Ward was slightly despondent over the whole incident. After the fire was over Ward's soldiers helped put the Korean firefighters in body bags and bring them out of the wooded area. Thomlin left out the gruesome details.

Thomlin also omitted the conversations that occurred in Ward's room that evening as several lieutenants gathered to talk about the situation. They all knew there would be no investigation over the matter. Nobody would lose his career. Most likely, it would be shrugged off as another ugly, unfortunate scene in a strange land that seemed oceans away from any reality. Some of the lieutenants stood in silence as if in deep reflective thought about the lives that had been lost, while others made off color jokes.

"Who the hell wears a polyester body wrap into a forest fire? Those idiots might as well streak through the flames in flip-flops and a light coat of kerosene," AJ Fox was there to joke.

"I don't know, man," Ward said as he gulped a beer from his couch and stared at the floor, "I should've said something. If I'd known it was the last time anyone would ever see them alive, I could've reasoned with them."

"What could you have said?" asked Nelson. "Hey, why don't you grab a pale of water before heading directly into the sea of flames."

"Don't know, man," Ward sighed.

"Dude, don't think too much about this. This is Korea," Nelson said as most of the lieutenants filed out of the room. He appeared to be tired about mulling the situation.

Before Thomlin left the room he gave a look back at Ward.

"You know, I've heard that phrase a thousand times in the past year. It's all bullshit," Ward said without looking up.

Thomlin nodded and silently admitted how many times he had also used the phrase to accept the many things the unit had done that would not have been tolerated in units serving in the States. Sometimes it was used to justify behavior, such as going around proper protocol, or other times it was stated to ease the conscience. Thomlin remembered when AJ Fox once made the grave mistake of letting artillery land outside established boundaries and into civilian farmland. Despite the fact that no one had been hurt, such a mishap would have been grounds for relief. Instead, commanders slapped Fox on the wrist and quickly forgot the incident. "This is Korea," one commander had said. Things were expected to be different, if not outright contradictory to the rules that governed other domestic units.

"How long do you think it will take everyone to forget the fire and the dead firefighters?" Ward asked softly.

"Days, probably," Thomlin replied. Soon, the fire would become just another story soldiers relayed to the newest members of the unit as they came to the country to start their own yearlong tour. The turtles would listen to the recounted version, sure to contain many embellishments, and stare wide-eyed in disbelief. In turn, the story would be passed down long after Ward or anyone else that had been present left Korea. It would become part of the battalion lore that many incoming soldiers would either not believe or at least not dwell upon.

"We really fucked up," Ward whispered before opening another beer. Thomlin did not make an attempt to console Ward. He patted Ward on the shoulder and slipped out of the room.

Thomlin knew he could not explain this to Michelle in any way that would make her understand what soldiers were like, so he made a weak attempt to change the subject. He did not want her to think he was callous.

"I'll be up tomorrow night," she said after a brief silence. Thomlin couldn't be sure but he thought he detected a little nervousness in her voice.

"You okay?" he asked.

"Oh, everything's fine. I just need to take care of something, to see a friend, before meeting you."

Since her father was a U.S. government contractor and she was his dependent, Thomlin knew she had no problem getting on or off any military installation. She promised to meet Thomlin at the main post club the following evening and then said goodnight. Thomlin went to bed early that evening and drifted to sleep thinking of seeing her again.

■ ■ ■

At nine o'clock on Friday evening Thomlin stood alone at the bar of the main post club. It was still fairly early, but the club was over half full. A Shania Twain song was blaring as couples two-stepped across a dance floor that resembled an oversized boxing ring. Thomlin slowly drank a bottled Budweiser and fought the anxious feeling in his stomach. He was surprised at himself for feeling this way. It had been a long time since he inwardly longed to see anyone and he made the conscious effort to resist checking his watch every few minutes. As he finished his beer and turned to order another round, he felt a hand gently placed on his arm. It was Michelle.

Michelle was smiling as she greeted Thomlin, showing off her bright row of perfectly straight teeth. She was wearing a black, sleeveless button-down shirt and a short denim miniskirt. Her dark hair draped around her shoulders and it looked as if she had just been to the salon. Thomlin fought the urge to give her the once over, but he couldn't help himself. The outfit revealed an athletic figure and tan skin that Thomlin couldn't help but admire. She smiled again as if she had caught Thomlin gawking and was not the least bit offended.

"Hi," Thomlin said, "did you get a chance to see your friend?"

"Yes, I did," she said, as the smile disappeared momentarily. She quickly changed the subject. Thomlin briefly wondered what happened and who she had come to see. He decided not to press the issue and bought her a whiskey sour before moving over to a nearby table. He leaned over the table to talk over the shrieking country music and made conversation about her trip up to Dong-ducheon. Thomlin was careful to stay away from any questions about why she came to Camp Kayes, even though he was dying to know. He hoped that she would eventually offer the information and quell any fears that were bubbling in his head.

As Thomlin talked with Michelle, he couldn't help but stare. Michelle tossed her hair slightly over her shoulder as she laughed lightly at Thomlin's jokes. As the main post club filled to capacity, Thomlin noticed many of his soldiers, as well as others from his battalion, moving back and forth through the crowd. Dougall and Nelson arrived and approached Thomlin. Both of the men eyed Michelle as they said hello.

"Hey, you two, what's up?" Nelson slurred.

"Yeah, what's up?" Dougall echoed.

"We're on an alcohol cost savings plan," Nelson said.

"Really?" Michelle said, slightly amused. "What's that?"

"Well," Nelson tried to explain, "the beer here is too expensive. It's almost two bucks a bottle. So, rather than waste our money here, we both decided to ensure that our livers were well stocked before leaving the barracks."

Thomlin started to shrink into his chair. He noticed their slurred speech and was afraid of an embarrassing scene if they hung around the table any longer. It was obvious that their pitiful attempt at small talk was a simple excuse for both Nelson and Dougall to check out the woman Thomlin had been mentioning nonstop over the past few weeks. Thomlin did not offer them a chance to sit down and gave the pair a silent signal with the cock of his head to leave them alone.

Nelson and Dougall staggered back to the bar on cue, barely recognizing Foster standing with her arms folded, watching Thomlin intently. Foster had her hair up in a pony tail and wore jeans and a dark, low cut v-neck. She frowned as she squinted in Thomlin's direction.

"Let it go, Nicole," Nelson said in her ear.

Foster turned, noticing Nelson for the first time. She stared at Nelson without saying a word.

"Whatever the history is, just do yourself a favor and let it go," Nelson said tiredly.

Foster remained motionless as she studied Nelson and finally relaxed her shoulders. She glanced at Dougall. She gave a smirk before finally reaching a hand behind Dougall's neck.

"I like your shirt," Foster said. "Brand new?"

"Yeah," Dougall managed to get out.

Foster yanked a small price tag from Dougall's collar and held it in her palm in front of Dougall's face.

"You're not going to impress many women, even the women downrange, if you leave this sticking out."

"Oh, thanks," Dougall said. "Ah, you know, we're on an alcohol savings plan."

Foster laughed and shook her head, "Yes, I've heard that one somewhere before. I'll tell you what, I'll buy you two a beer so you can maintain your cost reduction scheme."

Foster flagged down the bartender and ordered a round. As she grabbed the beers to hand to Nelson and Dougall she almost slammed into Shelton.

"I see Thomlin still has his new Korean girlfriend," Shelton whispered.

Foster was more irritated than startled. She pushed Shelton aside to hand out the beer.

"You're drunk. And you smell like a rice paddy."

"Did you ever say anything to him about the Report of Survey?"

"Give it a rest, okay?" she said.

"No problem. Just admit one thing for me?"

"What's that?" Foster sighed.

"Admit that you are all talk, no action. Thomlin has always blown you off. You've never been able to get his attention."

"Get away from me," she hissed. "I may decide not to help you with your little problem. I've been thinking about why you want this report done so badly. Let me guess, you didn't do an arms room inspection. Did you pencil whip the report or did you call it into battalion headquarters and tell them you were 100 percent?"

"You don't know what you're talking about. If it weren't for my incompetent armorer, I wouldn't be in this mess. It was his screw-up. I don't want to sit around and get pinned with something that's not my fault."

"Yes, but he works for you which makes you just as incompetent as your armorer. Tell me, how many days went by before you noticed you were missing something?"

"Does it bother you that you rank below every Korean girl from downrange?" Shelton's face contorted in anger.

Foster flinched. Her eyes pierced Shelton.

"You don't know anything. Go back and crawl under the rock you came from. Just get away from me."

Shelton grinned and stumbled away from Foster. When he drifted back into the crowd Foster turned and stared hard at Thomlin and Michelle.

"We're going to grab a table," Dougall said. "You wanna join us?"

"I'm sorry," she said, "maybe later."

■ ■ ■

Thomlin resumed his conversation and out of the corner of his eye noticed Major Streeter walking by their table. The major was in civilian clothes and was therefore not on Courtesy Patrol. Streeter was close enough to see the couple and stared at them as he walked by. As he crossed behind Thomlin, Thomlin caught Michelle looking past his shoulder. Thomlin casually turned around as if surveying the scene, saw Streeter standing with his back to the bar gazing intently in Thomlin's direction. At first Thomlin assumed that Streeter was struck by the beautiful woman Thomlin was with, and was probably wondering how Thomlin had managed to meet her. It was almost an ego boost to Thomlin's sense of male pride. He knew he was sitting with a gorgeous woman and did not mind others admiring her beauty. But as Thomlin turned his attention back to Michelle he noticed she was returning the look to Streeter.

The smile was absent from Michelle's face even though she kept making small talk. Her whole expression had changed. Her posture closed up slightly as she crossed her arms and turned her body slightly. Thomlin could almost feel her becoming a bit colder, but her eyes never left Streeter. Suddenly, Thomlin was jolted with a realization.

"How do you know Major Streeter?" Thomlin asked. Michelle's eyes snapped back and leveled on Thomlin. There was a brief pause before she said anything.

"Yes, I know him," she said flatly. She seemed unsure of what else to say. It was obvious that she had given herself away and there was no sense in denying it.

"Was he the friend you came here to see?" Thomlin probed.

Michelle shifted in her seat. She appeared uncomfortable even though Thomlin tried to be nonchalant. Michelle leaned over and placed her hand on top of Thomlin's while asking him to step outside. Thomlin took her hand, led Michelle past the swarming soldiers outside and stopped when they were just outside the entrance.

"Did you come up here to see Major Streeter?" Thomlin had

to press.

Michelle looked at the ground for a moment and then stared Thomlin directly in the eyes before answering.

"I met Jeremy a while ago. He seemed like a nice guy, so we dated briefly."

"The guy is married with, like, two kids," he blurted. Thomlin was in shock.

"I didn't know that. He wasn't even wearing a wedding ring," she said slowly, but sternly. "As soon as I found out I broke it off."

"But why then did you come see him?" Thomlin was still reeling.

"I still had some of his… stuff," she said.

Thomlin was speechless. Streeter's act of infidelity didn't seem to bother Thomlin so much as the fact that it somehow had tarnished his vision of the woman he wanted. He was unsure how to respond, but Michelle could read his thoughts.

"Look," she said slightly irritated, "I haven't judged you, have I? When that woman approached me in the food court I didn't jump to any conclusions without hearing your side of the story. You have no right to throw stones from the little glass house you've created. Now do you understand why I find military guys so creepy?"

Thomlin knew she was right. He sighed loudly and nodded his head. On the karma scale Thomlin knew he was definitely on the lower end.

"I'm sorry. You're right. I was wrong for thinking anything wrong of you," he said finally.

He shook off the image of Michelle and Streeter together and walked with her away from the main post club. As they returned to the entrance of Camp Kayes they both tried to shift to other topics of conversation. Thomlin began to grow angry toward

Streeter for leading Michelle on. He admitted to himself that Michelle must have been the victim in this case. He could not fault her for becoming involved with a married man since there was no way she could possibly know.

When they reached the entrance to Camp Kayes, Michelle hailed a cab to take her to the train station.

"Look, I apologize again for judging you," Thomlin said. "I would still like to see you again."

"I'll call you. Maybe you can come down to Seoul next time," she said. Michelle flashed a smile at Thomlin and asked lightly, "By the way, you're not married are you?"

They both laughed. The joke helped to lighten the situation. Michelle leaned over and gave Thomlin a hug goodbye. Thomlin felt the same feelings return as when she first placed her hand on him in the main post club. He said goodnight and watched as the cab left Kayes for the train station.

Thomlin walked toward the main post and noticed the streams of soldiers heading for the entrance. Instead of joining the crowd Thomlin kept walking through the night and did not stop until he was in his battalion area. Over and over again he thought about Streeter. He didn't know if Streeter's image would have remained intact in his mind if Streeter's fling had been with anyone else but Michelle. He wanted to believe that it would not have made a difference. Streeter's act had taken him down a notch in Thomlin's mind.

Thomlin had known other married officers and soldiers that had indulged themselves in the temptations that Korea had to offer, but he always felt that Streeter was somehow on a level above the rest. It was a hard fact to swallow. There was an acronym in the Army for temporary duty called TDY, but Thomlin often heard others refer to it as "temporarily divorced for a year," to describe the twelve months in country away from family.

As Thomlin pulled close to his quarters, he noticed an unmistakable silhouette a mere few feet in front of him. He cursed silently to himself as he easily recognized the figure of Nicole Foster. Foster was exiting the billets and walking straight toward him. Thomlin, not wanting to speak to anyone at that moment, especially Foster, cursed again as she slowly approached.

"Thomlin, you almost done with that survey?" Foster asked casually.

Thomlin was a little stunned that Foster would bring up the subject at that hour. Thomlin snapped, "No, as a matter of fact, I'm not. What's it to you?"

"I really don't care," she said. Foster stopped and folded her arms across her chest. "I was just wondering why you're dragging your feet. You think you're going to violate the Lieutenant Protection Agency and pin something on Shelton?"

Thomlin was caught off guard, but quickly recovered. Shelton obviously felt that Thomlin was onto something and somehow engaged Foster.

"Let me guess, Nicole, your man-of-the-week is Shelton and he has asked you to come to me."

"Oh, Greg, are we that different? You have no room to call me a whore. By the way, how is it going with that little Korean dependent you've been trying to hook up with?"

Thomlin could feel the anger rising inside him. He desperately wanted to throttle Foster for trying to sabotage him the night he met Michelle. He knew that if he let his feelings show, she would get the reaction she wanted. He coldly said, "Tell me, do you really like the men on Kayes or is it just the fact that you're in the men's house and this is your way to show that you have some control?"

Foster ignored the remark and moved closer to Thomlin. She

clasped her hands around his neck and drew their faces together. Thomlin could smell tequila.

"C'mon, Greg," she said softly and slid one of her hands down over his chest and ribs, stopping at his waist. "I've seen you look at me before. Don't deny that you haven't thought about it. Why don't we just go to your room now?"

"I would," Thomlin replied as he straightened and stepped back, "but I don't like what I see."

Thomlin pulled away and headed for his room. He didn't notice the expression on Foster's face and didn't care. He wasn't clear on what her motives were. "Did she really want me, or was she doing someone a favor?" he asked himself. He no longer cared what anyone else thought, even if it meant ridicule from his own peer group.

When Thomlin finally reached his room he lay on his bed and tried to forget about Foster and the entire survey. Negative images of Foster quickly shifted to visions of Major Streeter dating Michelle. He thought of her and hoped he hadn't pushed her away. As Thomlin drifted into a half-sleep state, thoughts of Streeter eventually gave way to dreams of Michelle.

19

CROSSROADS

It was Thursday afternoon and both Thomlin and AJ Fox sat in silence in the dining facility having a late lunch. Thomlin clumsily fumbled with the chopsticks as he tried to lift the bulgogi to his mouth. The thin strips of sirloin easily slipped through the chopsticks with each attempt. Thomlin could smell the sweet barbecue sauce the meat had probably marinated in for several hours. The mixture of sesame oil, soy sauce, black pepper, garlic, sugar, onions, ginger, and wine enticed Thomlin enough to keep trying. He was oblivious to everything around him and never noticed Dougall approaching.

"You guys certainly are quiet."

"I'm quiet but Fox is in mourning. He just heard that Tupac got shot."

"Who's Tupac?" Dougall asked.

"Fuck off. Both of you." Fox picked up his tray and left the dining facility.

"You really should try a fork," Dougall said as he sat down across from Thomlin.

"You know, two years in country and I've never really tried to use chopsticks. You believe that?"

"Actually, I do. By the way, Watts is on the warpath for you," Dougall warned.

"What else is new?"

"He really wants that Report of Survey. He's been screaming about it all morning."

Thomlin was avoiding Watts because he knew Watts would hound him for the report. Thomlin didn't want to admit that he had finished some days ago because he was still uncomfortable with what he had written. In barely two days he took all the information he had gathered over the past several weeks and cranked out a brief report. The report would satisfy everyone. It was what everyone wanted to hear. And that's what Thomlin hated most of all.

"Crossroads," Dougall said.

"I'm sorry," Thomlin responded, "what was that?"

"I said, we are all going down to Crossroads tonight. We'll drink here for a few hours and then head straight there. There is a rumor that the club will be open tonight despite the strike. Everyone is going. Well, except for the turtles. They can figure it out for themselves. Are you in?"

Thomlin looked up and studied Dougall for a second. Gone from Dougall's face was the constant look of surprise.

"You're not heading to Tokori? I heard you were quite fond of that place," Thomlin said, referring to the adjacent town to

Dongducheon, known for its prostitutes. Tokori had opted not to join Dongducheon in its strike.

"No," Dougall replied. "Tokori gets boring after a while. Foster says she has an inside source that says some of the clubs in TDC will open."

"Foster? That's interesting. You've been spending a lot of time with her?"

"Hey, don't give me that. I don't think she's nearly as bad as you make her out to be."

Thomlin slowly shook his head, "No, I don't think I'm going to join the crowd."

"That girl from Seoul has really got you whipped," Dougall laughed.

The comment might have offended Thomlin if someone said that to him a year ago, but Thomlin no longer cared. He talked to Michelle every night and finally stopped imagining her involvement with Streeter. The two planned to meet in Seoul during the coming weekend and go to Lotte World, the Korean version of a Disney or Six Flags amusement park. Before Dougall had come into the dining facility Thomlin was contemplating skipping the afternoon session of garrison training and going downrange to buy Michelle a small gift.

"Well, there are more important things," Thomlin replied automatically before realizing what a blasphemous statement he had uttered. The patented look of surprise came back to Dougall's face.

"Are you feeling okay?" Dougall asked. He stood up to leave and was silent for a second or two as if debating what to say.

"What's going on with you?" Dougall pried. "Is there something else wrong? From everything I heard, that report could have easily been turned in by now. Why are you acting so serious about this? Don't tell me that you climbed onto a high horse all of a sudden."

Thomlin thought for a second and looked at Dougall. "Hypothetical situation. You have two choices. Number one, you can just write a simple fairy tale that claims a piece of equipment is lost and everyone is more than willing to believe it, but you know the story is completely false. Or, you write what you believe to be true, although hard to prove, the chain of command gets pissed, your peers may not like you, and you could become an outcast. What would you do?"

Dougall contemplated the situation for a moment. "I was always raised to believe that nothing else matters as long as you can look yourself in the mirror."

Thomlin nodded in agreement

"But in this case," Dougall added, "if I were you, I would just give Watts what he wants."

"Why would Captain Watts want me to rush this? Why does he care about the missing box?"

"Why would he care? This doesn't impact him. The ANCD is not from his company, it wasn't lost by any of his soldiers, why should he care? His only skin in the game is you. You're the only thing that ties him to this."

"But, if that's the case, he should want everything done right."

"Maybe. Or maybe, the sooner it is off your desk, the sooner it's off his. Or maybe, you're just procrastinating. If I were you, I would just get this thing done."

"Thanks for advice," Thomlin smirked.

Thomlin was silent and waited for Dougall to leave him to his thoughts. Thomlin sat back in his chair and shifted his mind from Michelle to the black box.

"Since when have I ever done what was expected?" Thomlin

thought out loud. He jumped out of his seat and decided in an instant moment of resolution to finish the whole thing before the following day. Thomlin left the dining facility and immediately headed toward Headquarters Company.

■ ■ ■

Thomlin walked into PFC Padilla's room without knocking. The room was fairly Spartan with its two bunks, large metal wall lockers, generic wooden desks, and a mini-fridge tucked into the corner. Green wool blankets were pulled tightly into hospital corners and folded neatly under a strip of bright white linen at the head of the bed. A small television set rested on the wooden bureau. The only personal items visible were a few framed family photographs on the desktop.

Padilla and another young soldier were sitting on the floor with their backs leaning up against Padilla's bunk. Their eyes were fixed on the TV screen that sat across from them, and their fingers feverishly worked the control pads of a brand new Nintendo 64. Thomlin stood for a moment watching them and then cleared his throat to announce his presence. The two young soldiers immediately snapped their heads in the direction of the doorway and then jumped to their feet. Thomlin was quick to put them at ease and asked the other soldier to excuse himself while Thomlin talked to Padilla. After the soldier left the room, Thomlin pulled out a form and asked Padilla to write a sworn statement.

"Sir," Padilla said after a long silence, "I don't understand. I've already done this."

"No, Padilla," Thomlin drew close and said evenly, "you've written a statement with the same bullshit story you told me out in the field, but I know what happened."

Padilla's eyes grew wide in disbelief. There was no way the

lieutenant could know what really happened.

"Before Wickersham was handed over to the Koreans, he told me the entire story," Thomlin lied. "The black box was lost and not reported when we came back from the field. Wickersham didn't catch it because he failed to do the arms room inspection properly, so that's when he got the bright idea to wait until the next field exercise and use you as a scapegoat. You signed out the black box even though you never received it and then reported it stolen the day prior to the last day in the field. I just can't figure out why you decided to do it."

Padilla stared at Thomlin for a few seconds before responding.

"I did it for the battalion executive officer, Sir. When Major Streeter and Specialist Wickersham came to me, they said this was the best thing for everyone."

"Wait. Did you just say the battalion executive officer talked to you?"

"That's correct, Sir."

"Both Specialist Wickersham and Major Streeter?" Thomlin was stunned.

"Sir, they told me Major Pierce signed out the black box and lost it, but no one noticed it until they were already back in garrison. Major Streeter told me it was the only way I could help Major Pierce. If I didn't do it, then Major Pierce could kiss his career goodbye. I know losing a sensitive item is a pretty big deal."

This time it was Thomlin staring in disbelief. Thomlin figured Wickersham had somehow convinced Padilla to sign for the missing device. He never imagined the battalion executive officer personally approaching Padilla to solicit his help.

"Did you ever talk to Major Pierce about this?"

"No, Sir. I knew everyone was pretty upset about this and Major Streeter just told me not bring it up. Major Streeter said, 'Major Pierce has always taken care of you, and now, he needs you to help him.' It's true, Major Pierce has always been good to me. He's been great to work for."

"That's a pretty big request, Padilla. If nothing else, that black box is pretty expensive and you could end up paying for it out of your pocket."

"I know that, Sir, but they told me not to worry about it. Major Streeter told me he would take care of everything. If I was blamed for it, then he would make sure Major Pierce reimbursed me."

"Still, what about being blamed for something you didn't do?"

"They told me the report was just a formality. I wasn't going to lose my rank over this. Major Streeter even said I had a good reputation in battalion headquarters and that things like this would be forgotten in a month or two.

Thomlin was silent for a moment.

"Yeah, something like that."

"Sir," Padilla said, "I liked being Major Pierce's driver. I just wanted to do what I was supposed to. What Major Streeter said made sense."

There was only one missing piece. Thomlin wondered why Streeter chose Padilla and not his own driver. If Streeter needed to make it appear that someone had signed out the black box during the field exercise, then it was a good strategy to distance himself as much as possible. Streeter would have no connection to it as long as Padilla kept quiet.

"It makes sense," Thomlin thought out loud.

Thomlin was mad. Padilla was a young soldier who was trying to do right, even if that meant covering up the actions of his superiors. In the end, Thomlin thought, everyone made out, *except* Padilla. Padilla was the one who got screwed. He would be the only one who suffered, even though he was better than those he was serving.

Thomlin leaned forward and put his hand on Padilla's shoulder. Thomlin knew the next words coming out of his mouth would be another lie, but he hoped again that it would serve a higher purpose.

"Padilla," Thomlin began, "the truth about what happened is about to hit the battalion commander's desk. Now, the only way to help Major Pierce is to write another statement. This time, it has to be the complete truth about what happened."

Padilla sighed heavily and nodded slightly before taking the form and pen Thomlin was holding out.

■ ■ ■

Thomlin sat in his quarters rereading Padilla's revised statement yet again. He almost expected the words to change, but they remained there in black and white in front of him. Thomlin had made his daily call to Michelle a little early this evening and poured out all of his thoughts about the situation. He was unsure how much she really understood about all the events but Thomlin was thankful that she was a good listener. She quietly asked him some questions from time to time, asking him what he was going to do.

"I'm not really sure," he told her. "As much as I hate to do this, I think I have to see my company commander and ask his advice."

She wished him luck and told Thomlin that she would call him in the morning. Thomlin said goodnight and picked up the statement to read it one more time before walking to his commander's room and knocking on the door.

Watts opened the door and was standing in a plain t-shirt and gray shorts. His face looked worn and tired and was void of expression. He stared at Thomlin and did not offer any sarcastic remark. For the first time Thomlin wondered how old his company commander was. He guessed Watts was no more than 33 or 34, but the man looked older out of uniform. Without mentioning a word, Watts stepped aside and motioned for Thomlin to enter. Thomlin walked in and stood in the center of the room while Watts walked over to his refrigerator and grabbed two bottles of beer. He handed one to Thomlin and asked him to sit down. Watts sat on a chair opposite Thomlin.

"What's troubling you, Greg?"

Thomlin almost didn't know where to begin. The casual reception was friendlier than what he expected and it caught him off guard. Thomlin slowly began telling Watts everything he knew while Watts listened in silence. Watts never took his gaze off of Thomlin, but Thomlin could see the expression on his face was not as critical as he had expected. Watts appeared concerned as Thomlin reiterated the entire story. When Thomlin was done a brief silence fell between them. Watts did not blink or even shift his body position. Thomlin noticed the thick, gold West Point ring on his commander's left hand. Thomlin thought it was funny how Watts never wore the ring while in uniform; he didn't even know Watts was an Academy grad.

"Sir, you don't look surprised by any of this," Thomlin said. "Did you know?"

Watts sighed loudly and finally said, "Greg, honestly I'm not surprised. I didn't know the extent of what had happened, but I knew something was up."

"How did you know?" Thomlin asked.

Again Watts exhaled and then leaned forward, "You know, you were handpicked for this assignment."

Thomlin was a little stunned. He sat in silence and waited for

Watts to continue.

"I knew there was something more than just a lost piece of equipment as soon as battalion made it a point that you would be the Report of Survey officer. Do you know why?"

Thomlin's head was spinning. He wondered why he had been chosen. Initially he thought he was selected because he would eventually get to the bottom of what really happened, but then Watts spoke and crushed any positive connotations of the intentional selection.

"You know your reputation isn't exactly the best around the battalion," Watts said coolly. "I guessed you were picked because someone higher thought you would cut corners or take the path of least resistance. If there was a bigger story behind what was going on, then someone might have thought you wouldn't find it because you would just do whatever was necessary to get it off your plate as soon as possible."

The words slapped Thomlin. He swallowed hard. Thomlin knew he may have not been the best lieutenant in the battalion, but he thought he had a reputation of being very competent. Thomlin had no illusions of grandeur but the words from his company commander cut right through him.

"Do you know why I am so hard on you? You think I am just some sadistic bastard out to get you, don't you? Greg, I'm the way I am because I see you and the lieutenants you run around with out of control. I want you guys to take your jobs seriously and feel the weight of responsibility of your command. Instead, I see most of you partying and running around like a bunch of college freshmen. You need to start thinking about something more than just when the next time you're going to get drunk or laid."

Thomlin leaned back on the coach. He felt a large walnut in his throat and couldn't speak. Watts continued, "I'm both surprised and impressed that you got this far. Command put pressure on me and I in turn put pressure on you to get this report done as soon as possible, but you did the right thing."

Thomlin finally found his voice, "Do you think the battalion commander knows?"

"I doubt it," Watts replied, "I have a lot of respect for the old man. Sure, Colonel Gibson cares about his career, but he would never have allowed this. I think Major Streeter has convinced him of his story. Do you know what happened to the black box or do you just think it ended up down TA-50 alley?"

"That's the last piece of the puzzle, Sir," Thomlin said. "Without finding the device, or getting someone to corroborate the story, it's going to be hard to convince anyone."

Watts finished the last of his beer and stood up. Thomlin did the same and knew the conversation was over. Thomlin threw the beer bottle in the trash and walked toward the door. As he reached for the doorknob, Watts put his hand on Thomlin's shoulder.

"Greg, do what you have to do. No matter what, realize that you are choosing the harder right over the easier wrong. In the end, that's all that matters."

Thomlin bid Watts goodnight and thanked him for the beer. He walked slowly back to his Quonset hut. The Korean summer was almost over and the air was already starting to change from the oppressive humidity to a cool autumn night.

20

TRAIL OF THE BLACK BOX

Major Jeremy Streeter sat in his quarters drinking a cold beer. The television played a rented movie from the post exchange, but Streeter stared blankly at the screen recounting everything that had happened in the past few months.

Streeter took a swig of his beer and slouched down in his chair. He thought about the black box and the events that followed the whole incident. He sighed loudly, relieved that everything had worked out. He returned to his refrigerator and grabbed another beer. He slowly sipped the beer, waiting until late evening. After everything in the battalion area had settled down, Streeter grabbed his wallet and headed to Dongducheon.

Streeter had a slight buzz from the alcohol when he left his Quonset hut. He walked slowly to the bus stop and waited to be taken to the main gate. His mind had drifted to other things and he never saw the figure walking behind him in the distance.

■ ■ ■

As Streeter boarded the bus, Thomlin flagged down a cab. The taxi was able to pass the bus during one of its many stops and Thomlin s waited near the main gate. When Streeter stepped off the bus and passed through the checkpoint at the main gate Thomlin trailed him in the distance. Downrange was deserted and dark. Except for the few Koreans drifting about, there was no one to be found moving through the streets that were usually filled with intoxicated American soldiers. Thomlin was careful to stay far enough away that Streeter would not see him.

Streeter approached Kim's and Thomlin was a little confused since the bar seemed closed like every other nightclub. Then, Streeter disappeared down a thin alley just before the club. Thomlin quickened his pace and hurriedly reached the opening of the corridor. It was barely wide enough to walk without turning sideways and was obviously used to store trash and garbage. A door opened halfway down the alley, flooding the small area with light as Streeter stepped through the threshold, closing the door behind him. Thomlin, now starting to break a sweat, was slightly amazed. The door was obviously a back entrance to Kim's.

Thomlin crept up to the wooden door and pressed his ear against it. He could hear Streeter's voice loudly talking and laughing along with the voices of a few women. Thomlin guessed which woman or how many Streeter was sleeping with. The voice of Miss Kim was also behind the door, but barely audible. Thomlin wondered how many favors Streeter performed to enable himself access to the backroom of Kim's.

■ ■ ■

"Happy to see you. I didn't know you be back so soon," Miss Kim said as she placed her hands on Streeter's shoulders.

Streeter eyed Miss Kim in her long-sleeve black shirt draping over her dark gray slacks. He briefly imagined what she was like as a younger woman.

"Well, I needed to get out. I thought I would come for a visit. I hope you don't mind?"

"Of course." Miss Kim smiled broadly, bowing her head slightly. She motioned to Streeter to go into the main bar. The bar was barely lit, only the red-green Christmas tree lights on the ceiling blinked. Streeter dropped into one of the worn loveseats along the wall near a couple of broken dartboards.

"You okay?" Miss Kim asked.

"Yes, I'm fine." Streeter breathed heavy for a moment. "This whole thing has been a mess. It really wasn't my fault."

"Of course not."

"I never intended for any of this to happen."

"I know."

"It's just that, well, things happen. Sometimes you end up in a bad situation and have to do what's necessary to clean it up."

Miss Kim was motionless, looking at Streeter. He wanted her to understand.

"When I first came back from the field, I brought everything over to my quarters, as usual, to clean it. My driver swung by and picked up all the equipment for turn-in. Again, as usual. But he forgot the damn black box. I thought he had it, until I almost tripped over it later that night."

"Yes, you see," Miss Kim smiled, "your driver should have take it."

"Well, yeah, but I don't blame him. He's a good kid. The idiot that runs the arms room didn't do what he was supposed to and reported that everything was fine. I waited to see how long it would take them to figure it out and two days went by. Nothing. No one came looking for this thing. If there was any grace period to correct their mistake, they went well beyond it."

Miss Kim moved to the loveseat next to Streeter, sitting on one leg and resting her elbow over the back of the seat. She said nothing and only nodded slowly.

"Finally, this armorer figures out his mistake and comes looking for me. He must have looked at the paperwork, saw my signature, questioned my driver, and then figured I still had it. He snuck right into my Quonset hut and found it. Teach me to keep my door locked. Anyway, when I come in, he's standing there with it in his hand. That's a lot of balls. I offered to turn it back in, even to give him and his lieutenant a way out. You know, just slip it back into the arms room. He says, no problem, and goes away."

"He not take care of it for you?"

"A few days go by and I don't hear or see him. I assume everything is okay. I finally bump into him in his company area. When I ask if everything is good to go, you know what this punk says to me? He says, 'Sir, I can't find it.'"

"He lose this thing?"

"So he said. Immediately, I say that we have to see the old man. To let him know what happened. This little shit reminds me that it's my signature on the arms room log."

"You are major. Soldier cannot talk like that to you," she said quietly.

"I know, but I would like stay a major. Don't you see, he was trying to implicate me. I didn't really do anything wrong, but he was making it out to be something bigger. Even if I went to the commander it still doesn't look good for me. My name was on the log and I did have the box for days after we came in from the field. It just looks bad for the entire chain of command. We'd all be in trouble, including me. I am too close to making the next rank and retiring. I knew this kid was up to something, I just wasn't sure what his plan was. I needed to buy myself some time. When this kid suggests we report it lost the next time we were out in the field, I didn't like it, but hell, it was the only thing I could do at the moment."

"This solder, he beat the waitress?"

"The hooker, you mean? Yeah, he's the one." Streeter noticed Miss Kim's face harden for a split second and quickly caught himself. "I mean, yes, he beat up the waitress."

"You did not arrange that."

"Of course not. I just needed to figure out how to get him out of the way and get the box back. When I saw him head downrange early in the day before most soldiers were even out of bed, I just knew he was heading to TA-50 alley to try to sell it."

"No one there can buy that. Too much attention," Miss Kim agreed. "Police get involved if they found out it there."

"I guess you're right. I just had to figure out a way to separate him from the box. I followed him all evening until," Streeter paused. "Until he met the waitress."

Streeter stopped short of mentioning the bribe he paid the old Korean woman to take him to the small one-room apartment where Wickersham was enjoying himself. Wickersham, consumed by his own pleasure, never noticed the old woman silently slip in the door behind him and lift his backpack off the floor.

"I had nothing to do with him beating up the woman," Streeter continued. Streeter had waited in the hallway until he heard Wickersham's moaning and the woman's practiced screams come to a stop before sticking his head in the room to ask Wickersham the whereabouts of the black box. "I only wanted to scare him into believing the box was stolen. The fact that he assaulted the woman and was arrested seemed to be good luck at the time."

Streeter saw Miss Kim's body go rigid. He added, "What I mean is, I thought the solider would be out of the picture. I never wanted anyone to get hurt over this."

"You no slip it back then?"

"That bastard took the paperwork I needed to turn it in and by the time we finally handed that kid over to the local authorities it was too late. I guess I missed my window of opportunity. There was no way I could simply show up and say, 'hey everyone, look what I just found.' There was no easy way out. The whole thing just needed to go away."

"No one else knows?"

"No. This soldier's lieutenant will do anything right now to save his own skin. I had already told him to report it lost in the field and that's just what he did."

"Good," Miss Kim said. She placed her fingertips gently on the back of Streeter's neck. "I don't want anyone to get in trouble."

"No one else knows about it. I've kept everyone else safely from this mess. The commander, the staff, everyone. It's best that everyone thinks this was lost in the field."

"You see," Miss Kim smiled, "you good major, you take care of your colonel. You take care of everyone."

"You don't know what this box is, do you?"

"It no matter. What matters is I help you."

"You did find a way to destroy it, right?"

"Yes, Jeremy. It gone."

Streeter felt a sudden panic attack. "I need to make sure no one ever finds this thing. I mean, ever. It has to be destroyed, buried, incinerated, whatever. Gone forever. Do you understand?

You didn't try to, ah, I mean, you are absolutely sure this is gone for good."

Miss Kim pulled her face close to Streeter and whispered, "Jeremy, it gone. Trust me, no one ever find it again."

"*Kamsahamnida*, Miss Kim," Streeter sighed. "You are invaluable. But, I want you to know that I was really just trying to help. This mess was not my doing. I was just trying to clean everything up."

Miss Kim was staring blankly at him. Streeter struggled for the right words to make it clear. He desperately wanted her to understand.

"I know," she said. "I understand. It's okay, you worry too much. Why you not relax. Look, I've kept you too long. Myong Hae is in her room waiting to see you. You go back, see her, and relax for a while. Okay?"

Streeter looked at her for a moment. He saw the look of sympathy in her eyes and felt the warmth of her tight smile. With a light pat on her leg, Streeter stood and went through the door to the back.

■ ■ ■

Hours passed but Thomlin refused to move. He needed to understand what was happening. At last he heard Streeter's voice and it neared the door. Thomlin stepped behind the door and crouched behind a pile of trash. There was a rustle in the garbage and Thomlin said a quick prayer that he would not have to fight off an oncoming rat. The door finally swung open and Streeter stepped out with his back to Thomlin and continued to walk down the alley away from the bar. Thomlin had been holding his breath and finally exhaled. As Streeter turned beyond the opening of the alley toward the direction of Camp Kayes, Thomlin left his position and grabbed the door handle. The door wasn't locked. Thomlin quietly pulled the handle and stepped into the back of Kim's.

The back area wasn't much to look at. It was a fairly small space not much bigger than Thomlin's quarters, with a concrete floor and stacks of empty beer bottles. A larger cooler rested opposite of the door holding even more cases of beer. A large red plastic tub with a green garden hose was tucked in a far corner. Several doors were closed in front of him. He knew one of the doors led into the main bar while the others probably led into the bedrooms of some of the bargirls.

Just as Thomlin was again wondering which of the girls was frequently servicing Streeter, a door opened and one of them stepped out. She was dressed in a brightly colored silk bathrobe and still giggling from the conversation she was having with the other girls inside the room. When she almost ran into Thomlin her expression was one of complete shock. She gasped loud enough to stop the laughter coming from inside the room. Thomlin bowed his head slightly and greeted her in Korean. He wanted to appear harmless but the woman took a step back, still not recognizing him. Other girls now poked their heads out to see what was wrong. Immediately the other women started shouting loudly in Korean upon seeing the American. Miss Kim burst through the door from the main bar but stopped when she saw Thomlin. Miss Kim barked orders at her girls to go inside their rooms. She folded her arms and looked a little bemused. After a few seconds of awkward silence, she made a head gesture for Thomlin to follow her into the bar.

Miss Kim turned some of the lights on in the deserted establishment and stepped behind the bar. Without asking she poured two glasses of soju. She quickly downed her drink and slapped the glass on the countertop. She stared in silence until Thomlin followed suit.

"It's been a while, Greg. You no longer come here. You find new girlfriend?" she smiled but with a glare that was anything but friendly.

Thomlin ignored the remark.

"I've always liked this place."

Thomlin had been hurt by the conversation with Watts. Then, his bruised ego gave way to curiosity. Why would Streeter pick me to lead the investigation if he thought I would just cut corners, Thomlin thought. When Thomlin began to think of how involved Streeter had been, curiosity turned to suspicion.

"Why you here?" Miss Kim asked. She never stopped smiling while she poured herself another shot of soju.

Thomlin tried to read her. She did not seem angry that he had walked into her place of business, but her voice was sterner than simple curiosity.

"I want to know where the box is," Thomlin replied cutting right to the chase.

Miss Kim looked confused.

"What box?"

"Jeremy Streeter came in here with an electronic devise about this big." Thomlin used his hands to outline the measurements of the black box.

Miss Kim no longer looked confused. Her body position never altered and her facial expression never twitched but the look in her eye became harder. Thomlin was taking a stab in the dark, only suspecting that Miss Kim had something to do with the missing device. He could see he was having an effect and was encouraged to keep probing.

"He gave the thing to you and either you sold it, gave it to someone, or it's still here," he said. "Please tell an old friend where it is."

There was a pause before Miss Kim asked, "Why you care?"

"Streeter should not have given it to you. It wasn't his. It is very important that I get it back," Thomlin said choosing his words carefully. He needed her to understand everything he was saying without oversimplifying it so much that she did not feel the gravity of the situation. There was another long silence before Miss Kim replied.

"I have always liked you, Greg " she said gently. "You good man. I like all you soldiers. You come here for year, then you leave. Maybe you come back when you a captain. But you always go home."

Thomlin didn't understand what she was getting at. Miss Kim didn't say anything more.

"I need the box back," Thomlin said forcefully.

"I see you and your friends come here, drink lots, and go find women. You like butterfly, you know? They go from flower to flower. Why worry about Jeremy? Jeremy friend of mine. He come here, need help. I help him."

"Now you help me, right?" Thomlin mashed his teeth and tried to keep his cool.

"No. Sorry, " Miss Kim sighed. "I cannot help you this time."

"Do you still have it?" Thomlin demanded.

Miss Kim's expression turned as hard as the look in her eye. Thomlin could see the wrinkles across her face and thought for once she actually looked her age. Miss Kim leaned over to Thomlin to whisper in his ear.

"No. It is not here and I do not know where it goes. Jeremy come, he give it to me and I give it to someone else. I not know where it go."

Miss Kim leaned back and smiled to conceal the hard gaze she was giving Thomlin. Thomlin immediately knew by her posture that this was as much information as she was going to give up. He only needed to validate that Miss Kim had somehow served as the middleman for Streeter. He didn't know why Streeter had given her the black box, but it didn't matter. The fact that Streeter had it when he wasn't supposed to and had given it to Miss Kim was enough. Rules, important rules, had been broken.

Thomlin wondered who Miss Kim really was. Thomlin had a distant memory of a simple, harmless woman who ran the bar the battalion frequented, but the image faded now. Miss Kim was not afraid of him and Thomlin doubted if he was the first to challenge her. He knew this would be the last drink he had in this bar.

"Goodbye, Miss Kim," Thomlin said as he stood.

Miss Kim raised her shot glass and bowed her head slightly toward him, "*Ahnyong*, Greg."

Once he was through the main gate of Camp Kayes he passed the bus stop and continued walking the long stretch home. He enjoyed the cool night air and was left to his memories. As he neared the battalion area he thought about what would be in his final report.

■ ■ ■

Private Ko leaned back in his bunk and tried to sleep. The open bay of the barracks was black and quiet, except for the occasional creaking of the wooden roof. There were no more midnight visits from the older soldiers, but Ko's distaste for barracks life still saturated his every thought. Despite his bitterness he managed to break a slight smile concealed by the darkness. He had performed a small favor for his new friend across the DMZ. It was a small gesture that meant a great deal in the mind of the young soldier.

A few weeks before, after months of monotonous patrolling and routine guard duties, Ko and the other young soldiers were granted the privilege of leaving the compound for a day. Ko took advantage of the opportunity and took a quick ride south. He could feel the anticipation twirl in his stomach as he thumbed the slip of paper pulled from the infamous tree. Regardless of whether or not his superiors thought he was a good soldier, he would at least prove to himself that he could follow orders.

Soon Ko was sitting alone in a small coffee shop in Munsan watching the steady rain outside when an older Korean man approached. He greeted Ko with a simple head nod before pulling up a chair next to him to sip some tea. Ko was too nervous to look in the man's direction. Ko pictured the man's thin face and long gray hair, but did not look up into the man's eyes. He only stole glances at the water droplets sliding off the arm of the man's green windbreaker.

The older man did not speak to Ko except to announce his departure a few minutes after his cup was empty and walked out the door. Ko wasn't sure if the man was the person he was supposed to meet until he finally turned his head and noticed the small package left on the chair. He tried to suppress his grin as he quickly paid and left with the gift.

Later that night before going to bed Ko resisted the urge to unwrap the small package to look inside. He didn't care. What mattered was that he was performing a small act that would help his entire people in the end. He believed his country, his people, was torn in two due to the influence of foreigners. In school Ko had studied history and believed that the division of the peninsula was no different now than in previous times when other outside forces had come to lay their claim on his great land. He didn't care which government was in charge. Governments were all the same regardless of what they preached. As long as one government led by Koreans ruled the entire country then his people would be better off than they were then.

One evening Ko personally carried the package in the bottom of his rucksack while on a routine patrol on the south side of the DMZ. As the patrol stopped briefly to conduct surveillance Ko silently removed the package and left it near a tree. He covered the top with a layer of leaves. When the patrol finally moved back to the compound in the early morning hours, no one in the squad could see the expression of satisfaction on Ko's face.

One night later, Ko still could not help feeling good. He waited for sleep to overtake him as he thought about the day when others would not have to perform the mandatory military service that was required of him. Ko longed for the day when he could go back to his small town in the south. Perhaps someday he would tell his children or grandchildren the small task he had performed to help unify the country and rid the peninsula of the Americans. The thought made him smile again before he rolled over to finally close his eyes.

■ ■ ■

Thomlin looked at the clock and realized it was almost time to get ready for the morning reveille formation. He had been typing most of the night and was exhausted. He now had typed two separate reports and both sat on his desk in front of him. One report was several pages in length, longer than most Reports of Survey. He had tried to stick closely to the facts and the things he could actually prove if necessary. Still, the report contained details that he knew could lead to other investigations. If nothing else, it would certainly implicate several leaders in the battalion and probably encourage Lieutenant Colonel Gibson to reconsider some of his perceptions of people under his command. Thomlin also realized that this report could potentially make life very difficult for him as well. The other report was much shorter in length and did not contain many details, and it seemed to implicate the work of an unseen Korean whom no one had ever witnessed. The second report would make everyone, including Thomlin, sleep a little easier.

Thomlin left both reports on his desk and headed to the company area for morning physical training. After reveille, Sergeant First Class Wilson approached Thomlin.

"So, how's that Report of Survey?"

"I'm done," Thomlin replied.

"Are you going to do what you're expected and make your next rank or are you going to take the lonely path?"

Thomlin was stunned briefly at Wilson's knowledge but knew better than to ask how Wilson seemed to know everything before it happened. Thomlin wasn't even sure how to respond and could only say the first thing that came to his mind.

"Well, Sergeant, if all else fails I could just go AWOL and move to the Philippines. I hear they have multitalented women."

"Sir," Wilson stammered trying to recover, "Sir, you tell that lieutenant friend of yours up at the DMZ that I'm kicking his ass all the way up to the Mir space station the next time I see him."

The veins within Wilson's scalp began to bulge. He looked like he wanted to say more but was at a complete loss for words. He shook his head after a moment and muttered while storming away, "Goddamn lieutenants."

■ ■ ■

Thomlin jogged back to his room and stood over the two reports on his desk. He thought about the possible sequence of events in the near future until the phone broke his concentration.

Thomlin picked up the receiver and heard Michelle's voice, "Good morning," she said, "I hope I didn't wake you."

"No," Thomlin replied, "I've been up most of the night."

"So what's the verdict?" she asked.

Thomlin exhaled loudly, "Still haven't decided yet."

"Yes, you have," she said. "You decided a while ago. You just don't want to admit it."

"You're right," Thomlin laughed. "I'm not looking forward to the next few weeks."

"I think you'll be fine," she said reassuringly. "Who knows, maybe this is a new trend for you. Greg Thomlin, upholding truth and doing what's right…"

"Let's not get carried away. You still want me to come down to see you this weekend? That is, assuming I'm allowed to."

"I certainly hope so," she said. For the first time, Thomlin realized, there was something in her voice that made him actually believe she would be disappointed if he could not see her. He said goodbye and hung up the phone before staring at the two reports for a few seconds more. He grabbed the thicker of the two packets and headed to his company area. Watts was still not back from his morning run and Thomlin dropped the report on his commander's desk before joining his platoon in the barracks for a couple of minutes.

On his way out, Thomlin walked by his commander's office. Watts was already sitting in his oversized chair with a cup of coffee in one hand and the report in the other. He was scanning the details and flipping the pages.

"Greg, I'm not sure what to say about all this," he said without looking up from the report. "Can you prove this?"

"Sir, I think someone may want to go find Specialist Wickersham to get a follow-up statement. A copy of Padilla's revised statement is in the back as well as the copy of the arms room log. It tells an interesting story."

"Where do you think the black box is now?" Watts asked while finally looking Thomlin directly in the eye.

"Sir, I don't know. Who knows where it finally ended up? This is probably at a higher level now than what I should handle, but I think Major Streeter has to be questioned."

Watts leaned even farther back and folded his hands together over his desk. "You know, this is going to cause a major shit storm, don't you?"

"Yes, Sir. I suppose my days are numbered," Thomlin said dryly.

"Well, we'll just see about that," Watts said. "You won't stand alone on this one. I'm going to personally deliver this to the old man."

Thomlin smirked slightly and said, "Sir, if my presence here in the battalion is unwelcome, you could always transfer me down to Seoul. I hear there's a platoon leader position over at the Honor Guard."

Watts almost choked on his coffee, "Thomlin, no offense, but I don't think you stand a chance. However, Nelson is rotating back home next month and I'll need an executive officer. You up for the challenge? You'll have to extend your tour one more time, but I figure since you're chasing that American girl living down in Seoul, you might not mind."

Seeing that Thomlin's mouth hung open at the last bit of information, Watts added, "Don't worry, I have my sources. And before you ask me, you can have a pass this weekend. It might do you some good to get away from the battalion area over the weekend as the rest of the chain of command gets a hold of your report."

Thomlin smiled, "Thank you, Sir."

"Don't get soft on me, Greg," Watts said. "When you're my executive officer, I'm going to be even harder on you, so your shit better be tight, understood?"

Thomlin stood at attention and said with a gravity that surprised even himself, "Yes, Sir. I'll be looking forward to it."

Before Watts could say anything else, Thomlin did an abrupt about-face and headed back to his quarters to clean up. He smiled openly as he trotted over to his Quonset hut. For the first time in a long while, Thomlin really felt good. He was lost in his thoughts and was startled when a younger soldier snapped a salute and greeted him in a booming voice. Thomlin returned the salute and stared at the soldier for a brief moment, trying to recall where he had seen him before.

"Sir?" the soldier said to get the lieutenant's attention. "Sir, I wanted to thank you."

Thomlin peered at the soldier again trying to recall his name. Unable to put a name with a face, Thomlin finally responded, "I'm not sure I know what you're talking about."

"Sir, Padilla told me that you got a revised statement from him. I think that's a good thing, Sir. He told me everything that happened a while ago and swore me to secrecy. I thought he would be the one getting slammed for the lost black box."

Finally, Thomlin recalled where he had seen the soldier. When Thomlin had tracked down Padilla in the barracks, Padilla had been playing Nintendo with another soldier, the one now standing in front of him.

The awkward silence caused by Thomlin's lack of response almost forced the younger soldier to keep talking.

"Sir, I'm glad that some officers look out for soldiers. I'll remember that someday when I'm a lieutenant. My packet was approved by Colonel Gibson and it looks like I'll be going to OCS."

The junior soldier would soon be going to the Army's Officer Candidate School and eventually become an officer. Thomlin smiled and said, "Well, good for you. Best of luck."

"Sir, do you have any advice for when I end up a second lieutenant?"

"Yeah," Thomlin laughed. "Admit nothing. Deny everything. And as soon as accusations are made, make counter accusations."

Before the young soldier knew what to think, the lieutenant had turned and continued to run back to his barracks.

21

ONE-EYED BUFFALO

Major Brent Dougall stood over the body of the dead North Korean soldier. The dead soldier was naked except for what appeared to be a black G-string. He stood silently, lost in his own thoughts with his eyes fixed on a small black plastic bag next to the body.

Dougall had been traveling back toward the bridge over the Imjin after a routine visit at Joint Security Area near the Demilitarized Zone. His brigade headquarters diverted him and his driver toward an isolated area near the river to link up with his Korean counterparts and gather all possible information on an incident from the prior night.

While at the Joint Security Area, Dougall had heard the news of several North Korean infiltrators killed coming out of the Imjin River. This is Korea, he thought. The South Korean soldiers had done their job well. According to the information that filtered down from higher U.S. command, several North Korean infiltrators tried to slip into South Korea by swimming down the Imjin to a point not heavily monitored by ROK soldiers.

Unfortunately for the would-be spies, they came ashore too soon in the early morning hours and were immediately spotted by an ROK patrol. After a quick exchange of gunfire, three North Koreans were killed. One infiltrator eluded them for several hours before finally being shot crossing a nearby rice paddy. It was the body of this fourth North Korean that Dougall now stood over.

"Fucking terrorists," Specialist Martin Wakefern huffed as he joined Dougall. Wakefern spat a large wad of chewing tobacco near the body as he examined the scene. Wakefern was barely old enough to drink legally in the States and looked his age.

Dougall frowned. Since the September 11, 2001, terrorist attacks on the United States, all enemies were classified as terrorists. Dougall wanted to educate Wakefern but decided against it. Dougall's own experience years earlier provided firsthand knowledge of what the North was capable of. This is Korea, he thought again.

"Tell me again how this one was shot," Dougall asked Wakefern. Dougall stood a good five inches taller than Wakefern and had a habit of taking an almost paternal tone with younger soldiers. Dougall already heard the story once, but wanted to make sure of the details. Wakefern had picked up Korean with ease and was damn near fluent.

"Sir, the ROKs say they engaged the infiltrators as soon as they popped out of the water and this one managed to slip away from the others before they were shot. He makes it to this area, carjacks a one-eyed buffalo, and tries to make a getaway. The dumbass didn't realize that the one-eyed buffalo only goes about ten miles an hour, tops. The ROKs blew his ass right off the driver's seat."

A one-eyed buffalo was a uniquely Korean contraption used by most rice farmers. The front end of the vehicle resembled a small tractor with a diesel-powered engine resting on top of the front axle. Unlike an American tractor with a steering wheel and driver's seat mounted high above two oversized rear wheels, the Korean machine had two long, motorcycle-like handlebars extending from the front part of the tractor to the driver's seat, which rested on a wooden cart hitched to the front end. A single front headlight was positioned high on the frame, creating the eye of the machine. Dougall loved the vehicle. It was born out of necessity, built from scarcity and was completely functional.

The four North Koreans were engaged by the South Korean patrol just before dawn. It was almost summer, but not quite monsoon season. Early May was one of the few times of the year when the land balanced between the freezing cold of winter and the ungodly humidity of summer. It was simply bad luck for the North Koreans that their breaching site happened to be in front of a half-dozen men paid to keep them out. Capable only of walking speed, a one-eyed buffalo was the wrong choice as an escape vehicle by the only surviving member of the infiltration team.

"It's tough to imagine a small Korean dressed in a black thong riding a one-eyed buffalo while red tracer rounds scream overhead," Dougall said. Wakefern laughed. Dougall shook his head and focused on the dark waterproof bag beside the dead infiltrator. A couple of younger ROK soldiers emptied the contents onto an outstretched poncho, revealing a knife, small carbine, dry clothing, enough rations for about two days, a crude map, and a small encased device that immediately caught Dougall's attention.

"Sir, doesn't that look like one of our ANCDs?" Wakefern asked.

Dougall squatted next to the device and pulled it from its case. He opened the device and stared at the keypad. Closing the black box, he bounced the two-pound unit in his hand before setting it aside and examining the rest of the case.

"Sir, do you think these guys have learned how to make these things?" Wakefern asked.

Dougall found a small booklet tucked in a pouch within the case. Although it was written in Korean, he could see that it appeared to be the operating instructions, printed and not handwritten. Dougall flipped the black box over and ran his fingers across the back until he found the small, raised printing etched near the bottom. He peered at it closely and saw that the markings were in English. Dougall sighed out loud and answered Wakefern.

"This is definitely one of ours, and by the looks of it these guys have had it a while. At least long enough to study it, print directions, and distribute an owner's manual."

As protocol demanded, the ROKs would maintain all the captured equipment, log the information, and eventually copy the American commanders on any formal documented reports of the incident. Since Dougall would be unable to keep the black box, he walked back to the Humvee to find a notepad to record the serial number. He searched the backseat underneath the morning copy of *Stars and Stripes* with a headline about North Korea's nuclear program. Finally, Dougall returned with the pad and scribbled the serial number down.

"Specialist Wakefern," Dougall began thoughtfully. He rarely called Wakefern by his rank unless he had a task for the soldier to do. "I want you to go to Camp Kayes and try to track down this serial number."

"Sir?" Wakefern asked.

"Go to the 1-77th and try to track down some records from at least ten years ago and see if the unit lost a black box with this serial number," Dougall ordered softly as if he were giving the order to himself. He was lost in thought, no longer standing in the middle of a rice paddy, but somewhere long ago.

"Sir, are you shitting me?" Wakefern asked. "I mean, be real, Sir. No unit is going to have arms room records that go back that far."

Major Dougall snapped back to the present and calmly ordered in an icy tone, "No, Specialist Wakefern, I am definitely not shitting you. If the battalion doesn't have any records, then go to the brigade S-1 shop. If a Report of Survey was filed, then someone should have a copy somewhere, and that report will carry a serial number. I want to see if the numbers match."

Wakefern stood in disbelief for a moment with his mouth hanging half open. Finally, when he realized the major was completely serious, he spat another large wad of tobacco on the ground and shrugged his shoulders. Before he could vocalize a last ditch effort to avoid hours of hopelessly tracking down a decade-old piece of equipment, Dougall cut him off.

"Call it a hunch, Wakefern, but just humor me and check it out, okay?"

Wakefern sighed before grunting a reply. He spat one last time before cursing aloud, "Fucking terrorists."

■ ■ ■

Greg Thomlin's wife gently rocked him, waking him from a deep sleep. Thomlin forced his eyelids to open and shook the sleep off. The bedroom was bright enough to make out her silhouette. She sat on the edge of the bed with a silk bathrobe pulled tightly around her.

"What time is it?" he asked. "What's going on?"

"It's in the middle of the night. The phone rang so I got up to answer it. I swear, you're amazing. The phone must have rung for at least a minute. The only thing louder than the ringing was your snoring."

"Sorry, babe" he said. "Who's calling in the middle of the night?"

"Who knows. They hung up before I could answer it. It was an international number though."

"International?"

"The country code on the caller ID was Korea."

"Korea?" he asked. He sat up and looked closely at his wife. "Michelle, is there a problem with your parents? Now is probably not the time to remind you that I've suggested a hundred times that they move back here to the States."

"It wasn't their number. But, I did turn on the TV."

"And?"

"Kim Jong Il died. It's all over the news. Every channel is showing the same headline."

"Wow," Thomlin exhaled loudly. "Brain cancer finally got him, I guess."

"I think it was pancreatic cancer," Michelle laughed. "Looks like his son, Kim Jung Un, has officially taken control and decided to march a bunch of soldiers into the DMZ. Do you think that was someone from the Army calling you back?"

Thomlin laughed and laid back down on top of the covers.

"They would have to be out of stock of all available bodies to call me back now. I seriously doubt it was anyone from the Army."

"You're right," Michelle said as she laid on top of him. "It was probably some old girlfriend of yours tracking you down. Anyone shows up on our doorstep and I'm breaking out the baseball bat."

"That's not a very nice welcome."

"I meant I would use the bat on you."

Thomlin laughed loudly but stopped abruptly when he heard a crying noise from the other side of the house.

"Uh-oh," Michelle laughed. "You woke the baby, that means it's your turn to get her back down."

"That's not fair."

"C'mon, you don't need sleep, Ranger."

Thomlin grunted as he got up and put on a t-shirt. As he stepped out of the bedroom he briefly stopped to stare at an old picture framed on the hallway wall. He smiled as he looked at the photograph of himself posing with other lieutenants in some Korean valley with a forgotten name. He turned to say something to his wife but she was already fast asleep.

■ ■ ■

Several weeks passed and Dougall again found himself riding shotgun in a Humvee over the Imjin. The cool spring air was gone, replaced by the oncoming humidity that brought the summer rains. He could feel the trickle of sweat down his spine as the vehicle bounced over the wooden planks of the bridge. Dougall hardly noticed Linkin Park blaring through speakers hooked to Wakefern's iPod. Wakefern's spit cup rested on a week-old copy of *Stars and Stripes.* The cover story contained the latest developments in North Korea. Kim Jong Un, The Brilliant Comrade, threatened to turn Seoul into a sea of fire and dispatched a few hundred soldiers to take positions inside the DMZ to show his resolve.

Within minutes Dougall and Wakefern passed a long abandoned Camp Guardian and headed beyond Tent City. Dougall smiled as the vehicle turned down a dirt road toward the qualification ranges. It only took a few days for Wakefern's prediction to prove accurate. He was unable to locate any records of a lost black box within the logs for the 77th. Dougall was not entirely surprised but the news did not damper his mood. Perhaps, Dougall thought, it's been too long. And maybe, it doesn't matter now.

"You sure we should be out here, Sir?" Wakefern asked.

"What are you worried about?"

"Sir, don't you think the balloon is about to go up?"

"Wakefern, did I ever tell you the story about the lieutenant in the mechanized unit on Kayes that was convinced the North was going to invade? He had his unit on lockdown for most of the year, even at Christmas."

"Yes, Sir. You've mentioned that one a few dozen times."

"So, why are you worried about a war starting?"

"Sir, when you were here years ago, did the North Koreans move combat units into the DMZ like they did this past week?"

"Crazy shit always happens here. I can still remember exactly where I was when Kim Jong Il decided to ignore the armistice by ordering his men to dig fighting positions inside the boundaries of the DMZ."

"But, Sir, you have to admit there is a difference between a handful of fighting positions and an entire brigade of soldiers."

"Think of it as Kim Jong Un's coming out party. He's just trying to show his starving, brainwashed population that he has some balls. That's all."

"Sir, why did we come all this way up here again?"

"Just shut up and drive, okay?"

The vehicle rolled to a stop in the dirt parking lot of the firing range. Dozens of soldiers were lined up in the distance firing their grenade launchers into the hillside. Even with the vehicle engine running Dougall could hear the distinct metallic thump of the grenade launchers followed by the echoing boom of the detonation.

"Wait here," Dougall ordered Wakefern as he grabbed a small notebook from the visor.

Dougall noticed a squat figure in the foreground with his hands on his hips overseeing the firing line. Dougall strolled up to the officer in charge. He noticed a few gray hairs on the officer's scalp that slightly protruded from his cap and the crow's feet wrinkles near his squinting eyes. Finally, Dougall asked, "Tell me, why the hell they would put a major in charge of the firing line?"

"No one put me out here. I volunteered. I love this shit," said the officer in front of Dougall without turning around.

"I should've counted on that," Dougall laughed.

The shorter officer kept his attention on a couple of soldiers at the end of the firing line having a contest of who could shoot the most flare signals from their grenade launcher in under a minute. The overcast sky was lit with a dozen bright bulbs drifting slowly to the tree line. The burning flares sizzled like the sound of static and left a small trail of smoke behind them. Major Kevin Ward turned to face his old friend and extended his hand.

"It's good to see you. How's the military intelligence gig treating you? You miss being in the infantry?"

"No," Dougall replied, "the coffee is much better."

Ward chuckled and walked with Dougall off of the firing line.

"So what brings you all the way out here?"

"I was out this way a couple of weeks ago when the infiltrators were shot up."

"Oh, yeah?" Ward was unimpressed. "Typical stuff I guess."

"Yeah, pretty routine, although one of them was carrying a few weapons and a little black box."

Ward raised an eyebrow, "Really?"

"Unfortunately, I can't find any arms room logs that go back ten years so I can't match the serial number to anything."

Dougall pulled his notebook out and flipped to the page containing the serial number of the recovered black box. Neither one made a sound for a few seconds as they stared at the page. The only noise was the thumping of the grenade launchers and the cackling of the soldiers behind them.

"You still keep in touch with him?" Dougall asked.

"Thomlin? Yeah, I hear from him from time to time."

"I tried calling him a couple of weeks ago," Dougall said. "No one answered, but I could've had a bad number."

"Maybe I should drop him a line. I'll bet you a beer Thomlin probably has paperwork stashed away from ten years ago."

Again there was a long pause between them. Dougall noticed the sound of thunder rumbling close by.

"Yeah, it would be interesting to know," Dougall said quietly.

Dougall tore off the page and handed it to Ward. Ward folded it carefully and stuffed it in his shirt pocket.

"Do you hear that?" Ward asked.

"Thunder?"

"No, that sounds like artillery."

"I didn't know there was an artillery range close by."

"There isn't. You might want to get out here."

The muffled blasts in the distance now seemed closer. Ward stared at the sky for a moment.

"You don't think…" Ward trailed off.

"You better hope so. It will give you a reason to explain that," Dougall said pointing to the firing range.

"Ah, shit," Ward groaned.

The ridgeline looked like a tidal wave of smoke and flame. The dozens of hot flares had hit the dry brush within the tree line and instantly ignited. Pockets of fire quickly morphed into one large forest fire.

Dougall tried to contain himself but burst into laughter. Ward shook his head a few times before turning to Dougall.

"Please don't say it. I swear I'll knock your ass off the range. Just don't say it."

Dougall was hysterical with laughter. He was laughing so hard he couldn't hear the muffled booming growing louder. Finally, he couldn't help himself.

"This is Korea."